ON THE FRINGES

RANDI SAMUELSON-BROWN

WOLFPACK
PUBLISHING
— EST 2013 —

To my mother, Beverly Samuelson, first and foremost,
and
To all others who dared to be true to themselves,
especially when it wasn't "easy"

ON THE FRINGES

Go West young man, Horace Greeley's words on the paper extolled.

Well, hell, she thought. *At least the view will be different.*

At that moment it occurred to her; she'd picked up swearing somewhere along the line.

PART ONE
A CLAIRVOYANT

CHAPTER ONE
TWO RAILS OUT OF TOWN

OCTOBER 1895

By the time the train reached the wilds of Nebraska, Maude and her husband were barely on speaking terms. Plain and simple, their marriage wasn't working. Neither was he. Charley was known as a confidence man, but he sure as hell didn't inspire much confidence in her.

Their departure from Sioux City proved messy and loud. The landlady's husband hated Charley and, unable to pay the rent, they had to beat a hasty retreat to the train station in an undignified and haphazard manner. They took their clothing and one or two small items that might or might not have belonged to the room. Charley purchased the tickets while Maude stood at a distance keeping watch. But no one came chasing after them or paid them the slightest heed.

Flat out, no one gave a damn.

Which was how they liked it.

Tickets in hand, they boarded the train bound for

Wyoming. Scarcely had Maude settled into her seat before Charley was twitching and pulling out his watch, checking on the time.

"Wait right here," he said. "I forgot something."

Seeing her poised to argue, he gave Maude a *look*—the one that said she was treading on thin ice. She fingered the spot where her wedding ring should have been, lost to pawn a month ago. Vexed tears threatened, so she averted her face and pretended—with all her might—that something beyond the window was damned interesting. More interesting than anything he could come up with.

But he didn't care. That was part of the problem. Flat out, he *never* cared.

He bounded through the door out of the train without a backward glance. It went without saying he crossed the tracks where he shouldn't and dashed into the station, coattails flapping as he ran. Maybe this was his way of saying goodbye, leaving Maude in the lurch. The conductor's whistle sounded, sharp and insistent.

Of course, Charley had both tickets.

Doors to the compartments slammed shut one after another along the length of the train, but still no Charley. Her nerves jangled, but that was nothing new. Being caught onboard a train without a ticket, however, was no laughing matter. The locomotive built up steam, and Charley re-emerged from the ticket office, hurtling toward the train as it began pulling away.

A notable, thundering entrance, it captured everyone's attention, which suited him just fine. A showman to the last, he lived his life close to the wire.

They were already miles from home and now moving farther. On purpose and with intent. Make no mistake, they were headed into a lawless land—or so they hoped, but each for a different reason. Sioux City's abattoir stench was not the west Maude had pictured. For a strange second, the image of a slaughter-bound steer invaded her mind. Anything on a slow march toward death didn't strike her as fortuitous. Granted, the sky above seared strong blue, but the color gray had encircled the train and was more than simple spewing smoke. She'd seen a similar miasma once, right before a neighbor got mangled in one of the mills back home in Lowell.

It stood to reason that something might just fall over dead.

Which didn't bother her terribly much, all things considered. As long as whatever keeled over wasn't her; and for the moment she felt just fine, thank you.

Fate had delivered to her the second sight: a dubious family blessing skipping every generation or two. She should have read Charley as a man and a con better than she did, but there was nothing for it now. Hindsight proved so much more reliable, an inconvenient hazard in her line of work. At best, hers was a dubious trade where people hesitated at the door, eyes downcast with mumbled tales and sweaty coins. Yet Maude would weave them stories and warnings as best she could—but not always the ones they wanted to hear.

And the con sat straight across from her, wiping the sweat from his forehead and shrugging it off. "Aren't you going to ask me what I was doing?"

"You've told me to stay clear of your dealings." She flattened her voice out of spite.

"I got some money back from our tickets," he crowed with a lopsided grin, bragging as was his custom.

She didn't ask how he'd pulled that off, but it came as welcome news. They needed every last nickel they could hold on to. Still, Charley didn't usually sweat.

———

Painted barns and cultivated fields fell behind as the land opened wide. Unfettered vistas sprawled, fences misguided gestures in the endless expanse. Her pulse thrilled and quickened at the wildness. A freedom galloping and surging.

Charley fell asleep after the conductor checked their tickets for the first time, feverish from those erratic hours he kept. She eyed him slumped there, her opinion hardened and blood most certainly cooled. World worn at twenty-three, she'd found the last few months rough but illuminating in an unfortunate way.

The train thundered onward, swaying and clacking on endless ribbons of steel. Miles slipped by, behind them a distant and hazy history. One best left forgotten.

Charley's breath wheezed in and rattled out. In and out, laboring. He hadn't provided for her, not in any meaningful way. His promises never rang true, and his escapades most often involved skipping out on bills. When they left the mills of the east behind, no one was sorry to see them go beyond their families, and perhaps not even them. Her parents had warned her all along that he was nothing more than a bilk, but of course at the time, she didn't listen. She imagined herself in love.

Funny how experience had a way of changing things around.

Her parents' warnings, of course, proved well founded. In Sioux City the marriage faltered, and she landed upon the idea that he found her dull. He became hard to locate, never exactly where he said he would be. Right about the time his shirts started smelling of perfume. A cloying orange blossom scent that most certainly wasn't hers.

———

Beyond the train, gentle knolls gave way to the sandhills of western Nebraska—the space fearsome and unnerving. Miles and miles of undulating long grass bent and danced in the vast nothingness. The sky bore down, as thunderclouds roiled and loomed in the distance. It proved a vast, empty land that would breed cruel, empty men. Conductors came by after they pulled out of each and every blessed station, and all the time Charley was acting more and more off color. They had pulled out of Cozad when yet another conductor came by, asking to check their tickets. Charley handed them over.

"You were supposed to get off at that last stop." The conductor's voice carried.

Charley pulled himself into a posture approximating upright, coughed twice, and made a show of checking the tickets. "I paid for Cheyenne," he argued. Beads of sweat stood out on his forehead; black cinders lodged in the creases around his collar.

"Are you sick, mister?" The conductor spoke to Charley, but he squinted sharp eyes on Maude.

Obliged to act flustered, she offered her palms up, beseeching, as if Charley's ill health had somehow caused the mix-up.

The conductor lowered his voice. "He might have the typhus. It'd be best if you get off at North Platte, the next stop. He shouldn't be travelling like that."

The conductor moved off, continuing through the compartment checking the other passengers' documents one by one.

Charley ran his fingers through his sweaty hair. "That was close," he said, leaning back in the seat, eyes glittering and fever bright. Not even five minutes passed before he fell into a kind of trance, eyes half open, head rested against the window. When he finally shifted, an oil smudge marred the glass.

Everything about him got under her skin anymore.

Restless, Maude got up and made her way to the water bucket at the end of the carriage. People flashed her hostile glances, displeased at Charley's sickness and the fact that they should have already been off the train. But she had grown hardened to such disapproval. She met their eyes straight on though didn't blame them.

————

The train rolled on and on over miles of smooth, straight track as Charley's breath caught and rasped.

"We're getting off at North Platte," Maude told him.

"No, we aren't. We're going to Cheyenne." His eyes stayed closed.

Tired of him calling the shots, Maude tried reason in a voice held low. "Everyone knows we should have gotten off in Cozad. We'll get a hotel room, and you can rest."

He opened one eye, one eye only, and glared at her. "We don't have the money for new tickets." He handed over the slips. The destination stood out in bold typeface: *Cozad.*

She mulled the information over but couldn't figure out his trick.

Charley took the tickets back and rubbed them between his palms, smearing the ink and banking on the fact that no conductor of sound mind would want to touch them.

The wheels clacked on—a metal heartbeat that matched her own.

Charley's heart might stop outright on the way to Wyoming. His skin turned an ashen hue; his death appeared within the realm of possibility. Sure, life on her own would be hard. Then again, it had been no cakewalk with him, either.

"North Platte!" the conductor called.

Maude stood and grabbed her case down from the rack. "I'm getting off. You can do as you please."

He shot her a nasty sneer but didn't argue. Attempting to stand, he staggered and nearly swooned. Maude grabbed his battered valise, and, when the train stopped, they stepped out onto a platform alive with swirling dust eddies. The station stood perched atop a bald patch—a parched nothingness forsaken between the land and sky. Across the staging area, a rude two-story clapboard hotel hunkered down and endured, the name *Metropolis* written across its side in weathered and peeling paint. The name struck flat: an ill-conceived joke.

God, how the wind blew—but at least it dried Charley off some.

Heads down, they leaned into the gusts and struggled toward the hotel. By the time they reached the worn and decrepit porch, the wind had nearly knocked the breath clean out of them. A hanging *Hotel* sign swung, creaking and protesting above.

"We'll have to make do." Maude eyed the sagging balcony overhead, the rail gap toothed and none too sturdy.

Charley didn't answer, just thudded down on one of the rotting steps, holding his head in his hands. Maude dropped the cases alongside him, hoping to make a point.

But her point wasn't taken.

She pushed open the screen door, entering into what passed as a lobby. A sinewy man dressed in a faded work shirt shifted behind the scarred registration counter.

"A lick of paint might help." Maude's voice startling him, her criticism startling her.

"Doubt it." He took his time getting to his feet, sizing her up and clearly not liking what he saw.

A clock behind him showed seven minutes past three. "Got a room for tonight?"

Suspicious, his eyes were hard and not exactly friendly. "Are you a hussy?"

"Certainly not," Maude snapped. "Do I look like one?"

He swung his head in a half apology. "Had to throw one of them kind out last week. Things was getting out of hand."

So, it was obviously possible for her to descend even lower. God only knew what that might entail. "My husband's waiting outside with the luggage."

The clerk still straddled the fence. The clock ticked. She waited and wore him down.

"In that case, one dollar."

Doubtful, she scanned the room. "Anyone else staying? It's awful quiet."

He shrugged without offense, without hurry. "Come evening time, this place will be lively enough. If you want the room, you pay in advance."

Sliding four bits across the counter, Maude sensed the weight of the hotel's history press down, callous and cold.

The hotelman selected a key hanging from a hook behind him. "Room number four: up the stairs and to the left. It's away from the tracks."

Maude didn't thank him. She returned outside, letting the screen door slam behind her. Charley squinted in her direction, lurched to his feet, and grabbed the cases, stumbling.

She snatched hers away from him. "I'll carry my own. You look about ready to keel over."

The scraggy man held his post, only watching. Though Charley appeared none too promising, he gave the man a half salute, which seemed to clinch the matter. Perhaps the man's eyesight was none too good. Maybe it didn't pay for him to be too choosy. Either way, they had their room, and the hotelman hadn't tried to charge them more from fear of contagion.

CHAPTER TWO
THE ELEMENT OF SURPRISE

The view from room number four in North Platte might have been different, but the same problems followed. At least the room was roughly as clean, if one discounted the fly specks dotting the floor and sill. The window could use a washing, but the sash opened easily enough. Leaning out of the casement, Maude's reward was an unfettered view of the privies and spigot in the yard.

She pulled back inside, turned, and glared as Charley peeled off his coat, struggled with his boots, and wriggled from his suspenders. He dropped his trousers onto the floor before crawling into the swayback bed that sagged in the middle. He was nothing more than a huddled lump with his back toward her. Maude gave him the once-over, figuring the odds.

Reluctant, she still needed to know.

She sidled over and put her hand on his forehead without a trace of tenderness, the gesture approximate to pressing a steak in a pan, testing the heat.

"The conductor was right. You've got typhoid, the cholera, or a sickness akin to it."

"Bullshit," he mumbled without turning.

———

Outside, the bullying winds slammed rudely into her, tangling the skirt around her ankles, rustling the long grasses, bending down in waves. Fighting against the hindrance without much luck, she aimed herself toward the protruding pump.

All she needed was another shot to win a better future.

Sizing up the prairie unfurling beyond the outhouses, the vastness made her feel insignificant. It didn't bother her, although, by rights, it should have. She grasped that notion of smallness, an unspoken challenge that rode on the wind. The world was wide and wouldn't wait, especially not for those afraid to take their chances.

The handle pumped true as she primed, straining and stirring to the song of rising water. Tepid to the touch, it gushed forth from the depths, silvered and clear. As she shoved the pitcher beneath the fall, the wide prairie vista still mesmerized her: a place where the sky might swallow the land or vice versa, and all the while knowing that could never truly be.

One thing for certain. The wide-open spaces allowed for possibilities that the East never could. A person might simply wander off into the vast prairie swells and disappear—if the notion grabbed hold.

Some might take that desire as a sign of madness, but she wouldn't be the first nor the last.

Water splashed onto her boots, the sound bringing her back to the here and now. "Shoot!" Her voice consumed and blown away into the nothingness.

Pitcher brimming, the water sloshed over and was immediately sucked back into the parched ground.

Nothing more than a fading splotch in the late summer dry. One final scan of the horizon offered no answers at all, only challenges and chances that beckoned and called.

Games of chance were Charley's lark, never hers, or so it seemed on the surface.

Back upstairs, she returned to the room where he lay prone. She dragged the one battered chair to the window and sat down to wait. And told herself she wouldn't worry on his account. No, not this time.

———

Sure enough, people straggled toward the hotel as the sun's light waned and trains whistled on by. Scavengers emerged from the drawn-out dusk—converging upon a carcass or straggling toward the light. Solitary or in bands of twos and threes, they arrived: the hotel an unexpected beacon in that empty land. Loud voices and harsh laughter pierced the night and carried, razor sharp and only half concealed. Lying on her side, back towards her husband, she listened to the churning night, uncomfortable in the heavy air. Towards the middling hours of an unknown depth, the jangle of spurred boots and drunken mutterings poured back over the weathered porch. Horses, untied and mounted, clipped away as the ink blue of the night sky drained out and spilled over the land beyond.

———

Maude startled awake to find daylight streaming and Charley sitting up in the chair.

She stared at him for a long, hard moment. "Think you'll live?"

"Don't be so damned hysterical. What kind of place is this?"

"One that doesn't get started until late." She swung her legs out of bed and set her feet on the plank floor, considering. She lifted her gaze to him to make her point. "We have to pay in advance."

"To hell with that," he blustered, apparently feeling well enough to take a stand.

"The man downstairs was clear."

"I'm going for a wash." He made it sound like a picnic, grabbing a clean shirt and a change of underclothes. "If I see that man of yours, I'll have a word."

He came back twenty minutes later. "I've got a good feeling about this place."

"Did you pay for tonight?"

"Of course I did," he replied. "But stick to the room. You never know what's out there: maybe even prairie rattlers waiting to strike."

In other words, he was lying.

————

By evening, Charley verged on a near-full recovery. He was like that, always able to bounce back should the occasion arise. The possibility of dupes on the line had that peculiar effect on him and always had. Caught between a place of need and loathing, she held her tongue, more than halfway to disappointed that he had, indeed, survived.

Together they proceeded down to the dining room at seven o'clock, and Charley made the most of their entrance.

"Why, it's a regular restaurant, Maude!" His words, as much else, were purely for show.

One diner snorted. "I guess you could call it that."

Charley chose a table in close proximity. He leaned toward the man in confidence and in a lowered voice asked, "What do people do for entertainment 'round here —cards or anything?"

The man indicated Maude with a nod. "Cards usually. Things only get started once any women clear out."

Charley acted every inch a keen and eager participant, enthusiastic and nearly panting. No doubt plotting. He quickly ordered dinner for them both, taking no account of her preferences. "You've got fifteen minutes to eat. Don't dawdle and try to slow me down. This place is bound to get interesting, like the old boy says. *Once the women clear out.*"

Banished to the confines of their rented room, she watched the trains pass, longing to be aboard one of them and bound further west. Further away. As a consolation, she concentrated on the wide beyond, the blanket of stars and the three-quarter moon casting silver and gunmetal shadows over the landscape. The obscurity beckoned and beguiled. And, for one moment, she could process her impressions and secrete them inside where no one else could reach.

Charley came in when the hotel stopped rollicking.

"Any good?" Maude asked, not really wanting or requiring an answer.

"One hundred and fifty-seven dollars good," he replied, full of bluster.

A sharp knock came on the door, daylight already burning hot at nine o'clock in the morning.

They exchanged glances, both figuring it had to do with money. Charley answered. In the hallway stood the hotelman, but between his fingers he held a telegram. Charley snatched the envelope, tore it open, and devoured the words. They seldom received telegrams at all. This was odd. Especially since no one knew where they were. A threadbare smile played on Charley's mouth, half contrite as he shut the door. Right in the man's face.

"Well, Maude. This is it: the end of our line together. I've got a train to catch. I've got a better offer from a widow woman, and I'm going to make a new life for myself, and that life doesn't include you. In fact, you've already been replaced."

He waved the telegram around like a prize.

She didn't have to be told. She knew as sure as the sun rose in the east that it came from the other woman, the one whose perfume she had smelled on his shirts.

Still, the wind was knocked out of her. Her mouth cotton dry, she could only croak, "How'd she manage to find you here?"

He puffed out his chest, pulled up taller, and rocked back on his heels. In control and proud. "I wired her yesterday morning. I always told her I'd jump off somewhere along the line. The plan was for Cozad, but that stop got missed. You, however, were supposed to be in Cheyenne by now."

The truth hit hard.

The tickets had been intended for Cozad all along.

Something in the pit of her stomach curdled. His plan, his *trick*, had been to jump off the train leaving her without even a valid ticket to her name.

Charley shrugged and gave her a smirk—the one he reserved for suckers already fleeced. "So much for your fortune-telling abilities," he said with a laugh.

Gawping, she was being discarded with ten dollars

and thirty-seven cents to her name. He didn't even know she had that much.

As he gathered up his belongings, the silence must have gotten to him. A shred of conscience surfaced. "I'm not all that cruel, Maude. I'll give you fifty dollars while you figure out what you want to do. It's a fair sum—and it's not as if children are involved. God help me, but over these past few months, you've turned into a nag."

He flung a wad of bills onto the bed before latching his valise.

She all but pounced on that money, pride shattering into a hundred shards at her feet.

Case in hand, he paused in the doorway, frowning. "Aren't you going to cry or yell or say something?"

She hated how she stood there holding the money in a death grip. "Why are you doing this to me?"

He pushed his hat back on his head, considering, failing to recognize a rhetorical question. Squinting as he formed a response. "You're pretty enough with a certain cut about you. But you lack nerve. It turns boring as hell in time. I can do better, and I have. With plenty of money to prove it."

Heart enlarged to the point of choking, Maude stepped right on up to him, put her hands on his chest, and shoved. Hard. He staggered back into the hallway, and she slammed the door and turned the key in the lock with shaking hands and blood pounding in her ears and heart. She sensed hesitance on the other side of the door, but it didn't last. The moment broken by departing footsteps.

His failure to offer any semblance of a goodbye.

Silence fell dead and final in the room. Through the window she caught one last, watery glimpse of the cheat she had called her husband. A husband who all but skipped to the station and never once looked back.

The spring in his step was nothing short of treason and nothing short of unforgiveable. She never once thought she would be the one left behind.

CHAPTER THREE

SPIRITS—BOTTLED OR OTHERWISE

*S*he hadn't even seen it coming.

What kind of a clairvoyant was she, after all was said and done? Not much of one, it turned out. She didn't know whether to be mad, panic, or cry, so instead she almost froze. Cowering by the window and out of the line of sight, she watched people depart the hotel and her just standing there. Dazed. Trapped. And having no determined place to go at all.

The hard slap of realization. If she disappeared into the wide-open empty, no one would come searching.

Her view of Nebraska shifted...the vastness now holding an unseen danger. She couldn't see it, but she sure as hell could sense it.

In time, she dragged her body the three steps over to the bed, curled up onto it, and, eyes open, waited.

Those flat, daylight hours crept by as heavy as a curse, but they passed. Maude marked the sun's progress by how the light fell across the plank floor and travelled up the opposite wall. Sunlight splaying into that miserable room—which was all that stood between her and *out there*. She sought the creak of a floorboard, the brief

snatches of overheard conversation, or the simple shutting of a door. Anything that proved she wasn't alone in
that God-forsaken patch of sandy Nebraska ground.

An oppressive, ill-tempered breeze seeped into the
room as exhaustion crept upon her. Lulled into a heavy
numbness by the afternoon heat, eyes half -closed, she
drifted toward sleep. Too worn out to fight the swirling
currents and the fragments.

*The sharp cock of a gun's hammer and the reverberation of
a residual shot.*

Disoriented, she sprang from the bed, casting about
wildly, heart thudding.

That damn Nebraska hotel, and its fragments—a
glimpse of troubled history. A cowboy's brains had splattered over the wall, clotted pink and red gore.

No one had come running for him, either.

She sat on the edge of the bed, shaking. Driven to get
out of that infernal room. Spirits were calling, both in the
bottles and in the corners.

That's what she needed, by golly, a drink.

A drink to calm her nerves. Untrammeled freedom
stood right in front of her, coiled and ready to strike. Sixty
dollars and thirty-seven cents to her name seemed a
paltry amount. But it was better than nothing, and it was
all she had.

———

She descended the staircase with the sole aim of finding
liquor. Enough liquor to dull the edges and deaden the
pain. Enough liquor to forget the image of splattered
brains.

Of course, the attention of the deskman fell upon her,
and the odds were even that he had witnessed Charley's
exit. He looked at her and then looked at her some more,

chewing over a comment she didn't want to hear. But she wanted that drink bad enough to face it, so Maude squared her shoulders, fooling no one. Least of all herself.

"I'd say you're better off in the long run, although I expect it don't much feel that way now." His words dragged out in a drawl.

A flare of buried anger. "I was tired of him, too, for what it's worth."

He wagged his head like he hadn't heard right. Dismissing the notion. "Mebbe so, but you're the one who's stuck here. And, I hate to tell you, he skipped out on the bill."

The rising panic that wouldn't quash down. "How much?"

"One dollar for last night, and another for tonight. He paid for his drinks as he went along, so I guess that's something."

He thrust out a hand that wasn't entirely clean—dirt trapped in dark crescents beneath the fingernails. "Myron Harding."

A hell of a thing, nothing coherent came to mind. "Maude...just Maude for now..." A wild darting around at nothing in particular but most certainly avoiding the man's eyes. "Excuse me, but I have to step outside."

In the yard, sun blazing overhead, it was all she could do not to throw up or burst into tears. Forearm against the hotel's sunbaked wall and resting her head against it, she forced her breathing to slow. Hanging on to whatever shred of pride she had left, she forced herself to stop panicking and cast about for a plan of action, an idea to hold on to. It was either that or give up and crumple down into the dirt, a heap of misery.

A small voice surfaced in her mind and travelled down along her spine. This *freedom* staring her in the face was a notion she'd been entertaining for a while. The marriage had never been sound, not if she were to be honest about it.

And she wasn't destitute. The money would last her for a short time while she found her footing.

She didn't crumple. She stopped leaning.

Pulling herself up straight, she decided she would have to manage. Shredded pride was still pride, even if beaten down and trampled upon. And those remnants of pride demanded that she march straight back into that damned hotel and face her problems down.

So she did.

Her heels struck along the floor in the lobby as she approached the counter. The man, Myron, marked her.

"You've already figured out the gist of it. I don't have much money, that's for sure. But I do know this place changes into something more than a hotel after nightfall. What *is* this hotel exactly?"

Myron scratched his head, leaving tufts of brown hair sticking up, expression hardening. "What d'ya think? Your husband relieved a fair few men of their money last night. Is he some kind of card sharp? And what are you, now that we aren't pussyfooting around?"

An honest question, clear and sharp. And she had a choice. "I don't know."

"Which part?"

"Any of it. Whether Charley's a real card sharp or not, he runs games of chance. Shady ones. But I stayed clear of his doings. I'll apologize if I have to, but I'm the one who lost the most, all things considered."

The hotel keeper relaxed a mite, the ticking of the wall clock loud in that cavernous room. "Most of the mudsills can take care of themselves—although there might be hard feelings in this case."

Maude didn't flinch. "Doesn't sound like there's anything I can do to fix that. In the meantime, I'm hoping to drink enough liquor to forget my *husband* ever existed."

He stared down his nose at her like a man getting ready to draw. "You never said what *you* are, and women... well, women drinking unescorted are prohibited."

"Prohibited? That's kind of rich in a place like this. But if you want to know, I tell fortunes, and I'm good at it."

A twinge. There was no sense in dragging her second sight into it. Not when it had failed so spectacularly.

Myron's ears turned a tad pink. "Real fortunes, or are you a sham as well?"

"Real ones." For the most part it was true.

He pulled out a bottle of whiskey from underneath the counter with a couple of none-too-clean glasses. Pouring out two measures, he pushed one in Maude's direction using a fingertip, dirt still trapped beneath the nail.

A jumpy way washed over him. It didn't seem right to string him along. "I planned on going into the restaurant."

He wagged his head. "I'm serious. We don't serve lone women liquor in here."

"I'm not going to skip my bill. Besides, you're giving me whiskey right now. Isn't *that* against the rules?"

"You see me standing here, don't cha? You're not drinking alone, and I'm not saying you're going to skip out on the bill. Past history goes hard here. Women drinking only causes more trouble."

Hell's bells. She tossed the offered drink back, pretending like she drank all the time. Hoping to come across as hardened.

"You want to ask me—a question?" The words came out half spluttered.

He pretended to ignore her choking and poured out another round. The same as he would have done if she were a trouser-wearing man. "Don't think so."

"I'd say you're facing a matter of the heart. The answer

is yes, it will work out this time. Now, if this is a night-time poker setup, how high are the stakes?"

"*No...women...allowed*. Stakes can get high, and the games aren't particularly friendly, if you catch my drift. And how did you know I was thinking about a woman?"

"By the way you acted kind of jumpy. In a man that usually means one thing, and one thing only."

"*Hmmph*."

Conversation poised to dry up, but Myron didn't come across as concerned. Perhaps standing in abject silence drinking was commonplace.

Maude leaned against the counter, liquor coursing hot. "Thank you for the whiskey, unless you're charging."

A spark of humor. "No—I ain't charging. But I'm still trying to figure out what you're going to do."

A short caw of a laugh broke loose, tears pressing on right behind. "So am I. Food and more whiskey might help. Can't you make an exception in my case and let me be served in the dining room?"

A half shrug. "You ain't planning on getting stinking drunk, are you?"

Actually, she had been. "No, of course not."

He chewed that one over. "If you can tell fortunes, why didn't you know what your husband was going to pull?"

That was the five-dollar question. "He never would let me read his cards."

Myron scratched his jaw, doubtful.

Her pride flared. She wasn't an out-and-out trickster. "You know, that's another thing. I can't see into the future when it involves me."

The moment hung heavy. "A man killed himself in my room," she added, "and not too long ago, I'd say."

"More whiskey, then." Verging on impressed, Myron

poured again. "That story came about from those late-night goings-on you're so interested in."

Purple. A purple hue kept pressing down upon her. "He was unstable anyhow."

A raised eyebrow as he lifted his glass and met her eyes over the rim. "That's kind of one of them...foregone conclusions, ain't it?"

Shooting the whiskey back easier this time, the walls rippled in response. "Maybe I'll concentrate on the food. But thank you for the hospitality."

He drove the cork into the bottle with the heel of his hand and a nod of approval. And that was all there was to it.

———

The serving-woman's face fell when she saw Maude seated and awaiting service. Maude caught it, rightly figuring word had spread.

The woman approached Maude's table at an angle, tentative. "What would you care for this evening?"

"How about better luck?" The response sprang forth with a life of its own, but it sounded about right.

The woman's eyes searched the other tables. "Likely there's none of that here. Something to consider...in light of...recent events."

Maude forced a smile that came out near to a grimace. "Well. I'm stuck here for the time being."

It was another of "them foregone conclusions."

"You'll need to keep your strength up, and there's a nice roast tonight." The server's words offered sustenance beyond mere food.

But nothing would earn Maude a better outcome as it presently stood, and they both knew as much. How could it, when they were smack dab in the middle of a male territory and sorely outnumbered.

"Tell me. What happens in here after dinner?"

The woman weighed her words, surveying the few thin, hard men hunched over their plates. "A lot of things that shouldn't, and most of it involves gambling."

A few more men came in, withdrawn and on edge.

"Never stay here after eight at night myself, not if I can help it. Now, I'll go serve that roast up for you."

The woman went away and returned bearing a heaping dish, more food than one person could ever hope to manage.

"No one's talking much," Maude ventured, voice soft, as the plate was set before her.

"They never do. If you'll pardon my advice, when you've finished with your supper, head on back to your room and bolt the door. Whatever you do, stay well shot of the proceedings down here. There's nothing good that comes from any of it."

Maude didn't want to disappoint her, so she said nothing. She hoped the woman cleared out before long, having no intention of going up to her room.

She needed to earn money.

CHAPTER FOUR
FLIRTING FOR REVENGE

Spurs jangling from worn-down boot heels, men trailed in, singly or in hunting pairs—circling, wary raptors scanning the field for prey. A tall man in a long, dark coat entered like he owned the place, a range man by the cut of things. Maude's heart hitched, and she tilted her head just so, in a come-on that didn't come across as all that much. The cut of his figure and the strength of his jaw made the already warm evening that much warmer. Best of all, his eyes sparked when they lit upon her. She could have sworn he gave her the slightest of winks: a real man's man, bearing straight and strong. Several times his eyes rested upon her, and the flutter proved the attention wasn't unwelcome.

Of course, she feigned indifference.

Indifference, imitating heroines in those dime novels she used to read, and not all that long ago. And if Charles Montgomery could replace her, she could sure as hell replace him. One way or another.

Spun-out residue from earlier strife created a pull to the room, hard feelings lingered around the edges and in the corners. The darkness mostly gathered behind where the range-man presided, but that couldn't be right.

Steel-pointed, sharp glances shot in her direction, but, of course, she pretended not to notice them either.

Myron came in, his gait slow and unhurried. Conversations died out, but the men's expressions riled him up. On his way over to her table, he apparently thought better of it.

"Haven't you fellows ever seen a woman in this hotel before? She's a fortune teller and ain't a fancy lady, if that's what you're all hoping."

"Naw," one cuss bellowed. "I like a woman with more meat on her bones!" Unfriendly laughter burst out, aimed square in her direction.

The range man still marked her from across the room. "There's nothing wrong with how she looks." The way he said it came across as a near compliment.

There was no mistaking the eyeballing Myron gave her, yet she stayed rooted in place, determined to find a way to make money out of the evening. Evidently, the hotelman wasn't going to shame her in public, but he sure took his time clearing away empty glasses.

More harsh laughter, but the men settled down soon enough. Maude refused to meet Myron's eyes. No matter. He didn't tarry over long before he left the room.

The reek of cigars colored the air and landed in the pit of her stomach. Above the muted bellyaching, one voice carried as the general consensus: "Let's get started, seeing as how she ain't fixin' to leave anytime soon. Hey, Darren, you and I have a score to settle!"

So, his name was Darren. He gave her the eye as he changed tables, and she suppressed the obvious pleasure that she most certainly felt. He was physically much stronger than Charley had ever been, shoulders nice and wide.

Cards came out, the volume rose. Sidearms were set atop the tables, while others remained in holsters—all within striking reach and all ready for use. Chips clinked, and cards snapped and fluttered; the men regarded each other with caution and distrust as the activity pitched and rolled.

Unfriendly glances cast over unfriendly shoulders.

Eventually one reprobate piped up. "Well, what do you say there, fortune lady! Why don't you tell us who has the winning hand?"

She hadn't a clue about poker but had to come up with something fast. "Is that fair?"

Guffaws of derision.

She searched her memory. Nothing could be worse than four nines in a fortune, but they were regarded as a fine hand for poker. But if she hit upon something true, something valuable, they might give her a dollar or a chip. Reluctantly she got up and crossed the distance to the table.

They gave her nothing to go on, with their darting eyes and poker faces.

The hard case in the mended red shirt would win.

The men kept their cards face down upon the table, hands covering the backs. Snickering, the leader acted like he sure enough expected an answer.

The chips in the center of the table radiated as a fair sum of money, but the leader was an asshole. The range man remained in the corner, watching.

She had to make good.

The asshole's voice stayed mean. "Didn't you have a husband about a day or so ago?" His voice carried as intended, a cruel streak written across his face. He held his shoulders square.

"And here I thought you wanted me to tell you about the card game." A few laughs rippled, unpleasant. "I might not know a winning hand, but I do know death when I see it."

That caused them to pause.

There would be nothing for her to gain with that crowd. Maude turned on her heel and left. Stationed behind the front desk, Myron drummed his fingers on the counter.

"They're rough," Maude admitted, slowing down half a beat.

"I never told you any different. Now you see why things are the way they are."

There was no point in arguing the truth. "I'll talk to you in the morning."

"I'll be here. And, Maude, make sure to lock your door."

———

The blue-velvet night prairie unfurled; a chorus of horses pawed, nickered, and blew. Lonely whistles from passing trains split the humid evening into fragments while the locusts vibrated in the trees, their droning a constant thrum in the summer night.

If you lie down with dogs, you'll get up with fleas.

Her mother's voice came unbidden to mind. Those old, tired admonishments pierced the night as surely as the train whistle—unwelcome reminders of how events had turned.

The sounds of the men infiltrated her room, as harsh as North Platte's landscape, while she struggled with undressing. Her dress had grown uncomfortable, fabric clinging in awkward places—under her arms and the petticoat damp with sweat. Breaking free, she tossed the garments over the chair back: sleeves inside out and her uncaring. She thought of how Charley had promised her fancy dresses, and for a time they came, but already worn and always someone else's. Whenever money was tight, those dresses disappeared as mysteriously as they came. Charley always swore he'd replace them. After a time, there was no reason to believe they'd be replaced, but, in order to keep the peace, she'd held her tongue.

———

Rising voices and laughter made sleep damn near impossible. She would turn over, or plump the lumpy pillow, trying to find a cool place to rest her cheek. Any coolness would only last a few, fleeting moments, and she'd start all over again. After a while she stopped trying, resigned to lie there sweating holding on to the slim hope that exhaustion might set in, allowing sleep to come.

A floorboard in the hallway creaked, followed by the slightest of clicks.

Strange sounds, but not entirely out of place. Eyes opening in the blackness, she thought her mind must be playing tricks on account of the unpleasantness below. Yet the small hairs at the back of her neck rose. She sat up.

And heard...silence.

Nothing stirred in the hall. Chances were, it was nothing more than the building settling. Maude lay back down. A faint breeze stirred, the curtains billowing ever so slightly in the silver light.

The floorboards again. A careful, measured step. Boots, slow and deliberate. Stealthy.

Her doorknob rattled and turned.

Maude sat bolt upright, fixated on the locked door. Another rattle-click. Wide shoulders that shouldn't be there filled the doorway. The clap of the door shutting by a backward kick. A dark lunge and a hand clamped hard over her mouth. Her upper arm caught in a viselike grip. The smell of leather and whiskey smothering. The sound of ripping fabric as she was yanked from the bed. Fingers digging into her bones and her unable to utter a single sound, much less a scream.

This is what happened to solitary women.

Struggling, legs kicking out and slamming, but his hold never weakened. Fighting to twist away, her backside pressed against him, and his belt buckle dug into her hip. Feet skimming the floor, she knew what was coming next. One of his meaty hands thrust underneath her shift, crushing and probing. His grip loosened. She reached the floor still clinging to the forearm clamped so hard across her breasts that she couldn't breathe, air expelling in short, jagged rasps.

He spun her around to face him, shaking her so hard that her head snapped back, teeth clashing.

"Shhh," he hissed. "Settle down or you'll be sorry."

She was already sorry.

He knocked her onto the bed, hand clamping over her mouth. A heavy male body landing on hers, pinning her down heavy. With his free hand, he pulled out a knife. The steel glinted cold and sharp in the shadows.

"If you make a noise, I'll kill you. Now, are you going to play nice?"

Pressed underneath, knife tip under her jaw, she had no way to stop him. He eased the blade away as he fumbled with his pants. The door banged open, the knob smacking the wall. A sharp pain along her rib cage as a long rifle barrel pointed into the room. "You let go of her right now, and I mean it."

Myron.

"Mind your own business," the range man growled.

A warm liquid trickled down her ribs, making a blossoming stain. She screamed.

Both men startled—the rapist stared at the knife blade, the edge glistening dark from blood.

"Jesus! I didn't mean..."

Myron took a step into the room, the rifle pointed at the pair of them. "Step away from her, drop that damn knife, and get the hell out of here. This very minute or I'll shoot. Do you doubt me?"

Darren lifted himself off of her, knee digging into her side. He grunted his response, eyes shifting between Myron and the gun, back to her, returning and lingering on the gun. Sizing up the situation before easing his way out of the room.

He never did drop that knife.

Myron shut the door as Maude shoved away from the bed, clutching her side.

"Damn it all to hell," he swore, propping the rifle against the wall. "Let me take a look there."

Her hand came away wet and sticky. The stain across her chemise bloomed and spread; her knees buckled and threatened to give way.

Myron lit the dresser lamp and knelt at her side. Glancing at her for permission, he tugged at the bloodied garment, displaying a calm that came from practice. "Just a flesh wound," his voice soothed. "I'll be right back with some bandages. We'll get you patched up as good as new. Like nothing ever happened."

She tried to speak, but any words dried up. Myron didn't even notice.

———

Perched on the bed, and clenching her side to stanch the bleeding, her mind turned sluggish. Her heart knew the answer.

A man could simply *take* what he wanted, not that it made it right.

Closed doors, panels and mullions, contributed to a false sense of security when all was said and done. The jimmied lock proved no match for a man who wanted in. She stared at the door, blood coursing and heart beating in her ears. No matter how intently she stared at the door, she couldn't see through it for danger awaiting in the hallway beyond. Hand pressed against her side, she remained on edge and ready to spring. A man's approaching footsteps. Sharp inhale, breath held. The doorknob turned in an all but invisible movement in the dim light, but the sound came across plain enough.

She half bolted from the bed.

Myron stepped through, hands clutching the rolls of gauze. "What're you spookin' for?"

"I wasn't sure it was you."

"Darren's gone, Maude. He won't come back."

For a moment, her mouth hung open. "You can't be certain of that! Aren't you going to *do* anything?"

He turned a bit queer. "What do you mean? I'm going to bandage you up. What more do you want? You don't really need a doctor..."

"He tried to force himself on me!"

Myron eyed her as if she had gone crazy. "But I stopped him."

Of course, for him, the notion was that simple. Shamed, frightened tears burst out in a violent release.

Softening his voice, he took a few tentative steps toward her before laying his hand on her shoulder. "What did you expect would happen? The men will only say you were asking for it." He pulled out a bottle of whiskey from a back pocket, uncorked, and poured some onto a piece of cotton. "Here. Take a swig."

Grabbing the bottle by the neck, she took a big pull

that burned all the way down. She clutched the bottle's neck for dear life, never once easing up on her grip.

"OK, let me see and get this dressed," he said, six inches from her.

Averting her face, she lifted the cloth with her free hand, careful to keep her breast covered. The whiskey-soaked cotton pressed against the gash and stung like hell.

A hiss and a flinch; she took another swig.

"Steady...we're almost there." He placed the bandage and wrapped the cotton gauze around her ribs and beneath her chemise, clearly practiced in such administrations. With a gentle hand he lowered the undergarment back down, smoothing it into place.

"There. Now lie back and try to sleep. I'll stay downstairs at the desk tonight, keeping watch just in case. But, Maude, he won't be back."

He didn't wait for a response, for she had none to give. She proffered the whiskey bottle as he blew out the kerosene lamp.

Bottle in hand, he opened the door, a faint silhouette against the unlit hallway. "Maude? That's another thing. Drifters are out here, and there's no guarantee. It's always best to keep that in mind in your dealings."

And he closed the door with a click, locking it from the outside. Her key remained on the dresser, worthless.

A locked door did little good when someone was hell-bent on getting in.

CHAPTER FIVE
HARD TRUTHS
(AND THE SECOND TRAIN OUT OF TOWN)

The locusts droned on in the nearby cottonwoods, blanketed by the dark velvet night that had been torn and ruined.

Locusts, cautious by instinct, had enough damned sense to fall silent when danger appeared.

But not her, boy-howdy. She always blustered her way in, without the common sense of a bug.

Fingering the bandages underneath her shift, she felt too stunned to be grateful. The reality of what *almost* happened hadn't sunk all the way in. Numb and unnerved as she was, the wound provided all the proof needed. Violence had happened. Unarguable. Violence that would be considered *her fault*.

Propped up by a pillow and leaning against the wall, she no longer knew what was best. So, she kept the lamp lit and she...listened. Mercifully, the locusts droned on.

From the depths of the shattered night, time seeped out and lost all meaning. At some point she removed the bloodied garment, sensitive to the hitch and pull of the wound. Flinging the chemise at the basin, she let out a muffled sob—an elemental mixture of pain and despair.

Slumped upon the rim, half in and half out, it was all the accusation needed. She knew how to read the signs.

Ill at ease, she resumed sentry at the window, sentry for a man who might not return. The insects droned on, her straining to see into the heart of the shadows. The dark night covered the wide plains. One thing remained for certain: those plains weren't at all as empty as they once came across.

———

The mirror reflected the pale morning light and a young woman who had gone too far.

Welts had risen along her jawline and neck; the bruising didn't leave much to the imagination. Everyone would assume she got throttled during the course of a very rough night.

And that was only the half of it.

Dressing slapdash, she pulled on her worn travelling dress. She dragged the brush through her hair and pinned the locks up with trembling hands. Casting about, she gathered her clothes from the wall hook and dresser—all of them threadbare and mended. Her remaining possessions lay strewn about: a deck of cards, a battered volume of Shakespeare, and a small crystal ball that had never done her an ounce of good.

She turned toward the basin and halted. Blood evidence.

Snatching up the ruined chemise, she thrust it deep within her case and clicked the latch closed, emphatic. She was finished with North Platte, Nebraska, and that was all she had to go on.

As quiet and cautious as a thief, she slipped from the room, cringing along the stairway wall. Drifts of conversation threaded up from the people below—murmurings about "a disturbance," like events had all happened one town over. Or maybe her mind played tricks, but she wouldn't stop to find out.

Myron saw her, his eyes taking in the valise, but he never called out, and she didn't break her stride.

Caging her eyes, Maude refused contact with any of the nameless guests for fear of what she might find. The cold, hard fact remained. None of them had come to her aid. No one, other than Myron.

She turned her back on the Metropolis, but the unfurling expanse no longer promised sweet freedom. If anything, it held an undercurrent that unsettled.

The hardened, sunbaked dirt between the hotel and the depot still had to be crossed. The distance wasn't far, in truth, but it was enough. The weather-blistered station served as the gateway, and no-good idlers loitered about the platform or lounged alongside unattended baggage carts. A few stragglers of undetermined ilk paused in the shade of the station's overhang. Rabble had a tendency to congregate—they hung around stations in the East, and they hung around stations in the West. No matter.

Waiting for their next opportunity, they sized her up as prey.

Another drifter reclined near the station door, all taut and lean angles. One boot flat-footed against the siding; a tilted hat slouched down and hid eyes that missed very little. Claiming his patch, by the feel of things. Mouth dry, she hesitated on a bare dirt mound and knew she shouldn't have.

Of course, more than one set of eyes marked her, and they would sense fear.

Head lifted, she tightened her grip on the valise's handles and got on with it. She drew up level alongside the lounger. His one cold blue eye stared back from under the brim, wide awake. Watching. A half snarl masquerading as a smile.

Her knees trembled.

She lunged for the doorknob. The man laughed deep and mean.

The knob wouldn't turn, and the panicked jangling carried, clattering and desperate. The latch finally turned, and she burst into the empty waiting room. The ticket agent stirred at the commotion. She tried to pretend that nothing at all was wrong, that her heart wasn't pounding. *The station in broad daylight must be safe.* But she refused to look back at the men in the yard, afraid they might stalk her through the glass.

She approached the ticket counter, the sound of her bootheels tapping, far too dainty to ever survive in a place such as this.

Two things were for certain, and two things only. She wasn't staying, and she didn't have enough money for a mistake.

"Had enough, have you?" The gray-haired ticket agent's eyes were magnified and sharp behind his spectacles. He took in the bruises a split second too late.

"Something next to it," Maude replied, clutching her purse hard and feigning indifference. "What time's the first train out?"

"The ten-o-five heading east to Omaha. You'd change there if you're traveling further. Going home?"

Her breath hitched. *She could simply return home.*

"No. Heading west."

A slight twitch at the side of his mouth. "In that case, all west-bound trains pass through Cheyenne."

"What about Denver?"

Resigned, the ticket agent busied himself shuffling bits of paper that came across as official but likely meant nothing. Stalling. "Travelling by yourself, you could just as soon go one way as the other. But the next west-bound train stops at 3:20 in the afternoon. If you're set on Denver, you'll have to change in Cheyenne."

"I'm sure I can manage."

The agent shrugged, stoic. "Which class?"

"Third." The clock on the wall showed 8:10 in the morning.

"Twenty-eight dollars and fifty cents. Everyone's headed to Colorado these days. Gold, you know. The land of opportunity some say, but I don't buy it."

Maude loosened her purse strings and counted out the fare.

Taking his own sweet time, the agent wrote the ticket and recorded it in his ledger. When he handed her the slip, their hands touched in the exchange. "Not a lot of women seem to like it here."

"It's kind of rough."

His eyes lingered again on the welts, a slow nod that captured the situation. He knew full well that it was rough, as did everyone else in that forsaken part of the country. She was the one who'd come late to that conclusion. One night too late for the realization to do her any good, any good at all.

"You're going to stay in here to wait?"

A surreptitious glance over her shoulder. The loungers were all still there, pretty much as she left them. "I need to settle my bill at the hotel."

"I can get Earl to accompany you through that lot, if you choose..."

"No need," she replied, turning on her heel and striking back out toward the dirt mound.

No one had to know that her heart still pounded wild, but it did.

———

Inside the Metropolis, a suited man settled his bill. She hung back and waited her turn. A bob in her direction after pocketing his change: his eyes flickered, and the color rose in his cheeks and blotched about his neck.

Stepping up to the scarred counter, she set the valise at her feet, very precise. "I'm leaving today." Her voice came out too young and small, like it belonged to someone else.

Swallowing hard as Myron's face distorted and shimmered. "I should say thank you. For everything," she offered.

He scratched his head, running through possible responses in that slow way of his. "No sense in cryin' over any of it. I figured you'd take your leave, especially under the circumstances."

She struggled. "Already bought my ticket. If you want to tell me 'I told you so,' well, I deserve it."

Fearful at going forward, and fearful at turning back. Truth seldom yielded.

He just scratched his shoulder and shook his head.

"I'd best settle up the account," she concluded at length.

Opening the stained ledger, his movements slow, he rubbed his knuckles over patchy gray beard stubble. Pondering the page like it held the answers to some great mystery.

"Thought you might have taken the notion to skip out on your bill earlier. Don't feel right about charging you for last night, no matter whose fault it was. Let's say you owe two dollars: one for the meals and one dollar for the second night only when your hus—" The word got cutoff midway, and he never went back to fix it.

"I won't make the same mistake again." Trembling fingers fussed with the knotted strings. Those same fingers pulled out the silver dollars and set them on the counter.

"There's others to be made, I reckon," he said, pretending not to notice anything amiss as he gathered up the money. "We both learned a few lessons last night, especially how rules are there for a reason. Maybe that's a notion we'd both best consider. I'll not be turned by a pretty face again."

"You sure about that?" She barked a half-strangled laugh, echoing and out of place.

Color rose in his cheeks. "As sure as I can be." He stiffened, then softened back down. "Well, I wish you the best."

Afraid to even attempt a smile, she turned and left.

And, like Charley, she never once glanced back. Although she halfway wanted to. The singular reason why she didn't look over her should had to do with Myron watching her. If she saw kindness or concern on his face, she would fall apart and shatter.

CHAPTER SIX
DEEPER WEST

The shiftless had vanished—gone elsewhere and doing God-only-knew-what.

Stripped of pretense, she sat straight backed in the station's waiting room that echoed, trying her best not to jump out of her skin. Ordinary people went about their business, people who meant her no harm. She'd intercepted a fair few appraisals from women whose eyes never quite met her own.

Well. She could live with their disapproval. It was usually sympathy that got her in the end, and they apparently had none to spare.

Strong, harsh light flowed through the station windows; dust motes sparkled in the slanting sun. Rigid, Maude never once eased her hold on that one-way ticket, and she entertained a few unwelcomed doubts. What if Colorado was a bust? Well. She'd find out first hand.

At four minutes to three, holding her possession in a death grip, she edged out onto the platform. The train's whistle cleaved the prairie in two. The engine, at first a faint black spot, came boring from the east—ground vibrating, faint yet swelling. The juddering travelled from her boot soles and fastened around her heart. Locked coupling rods brought the wheels to a standstill. And it was now, or never.

Maude boarded in third class just like her ticket said. Just like she had paid for. Thickets of passengers sat scattered throughout the compartment, their eyes taking her in and spitting her back out—and all without a word exchanged.

Bothered and holding her wound, she half hefted, half flung her case onto the waiting brass rack above the seat single handed. It clanged off and ricocheted back.

Again, the darting assessments followed.

She chose the closest man. "Do you mind?"

He gave her the full once-over, disapproving and hard. He might even have been one of the poker-playing men, but he took her case and stowed it above without effort. Without favor.

"Thank you," she said, consonants emphasized to drive her point home.

She didn't owe explanations; but any she might have offered dried up in that brief moment. The train pulled out of the station; the railyards of North Platte fell away, and the undulating dry hills slipped on by. The train, gaining speed, swayed and rocked its way through the Nebraska plains, the rhythm a metallic heartbeat that matched her own.

She was on her own, on her own, own, own, own.

———

Switching trains in Cheyenne, there was one vacant seat in the third-class compartment in the train bound for Denver. It faced a dungaree-wearing man sporting a tobacco-streaked mustache and beard. She caught the telltale whiff of a hard night's drinking. Sure as hell, he noticed her sniffing and locked eyes with her.

She'd had enough of men and stared him down, smell or no smell.

"Think you might help?" She nodded at her valise.

He didn't act inclined to move. At length, he unfolded himself and relieved her of her burden. "This ain't the East, you know," he corrected, hoisting her case onto the rack above.

She claimed the vacant seat. "Never said it was. If my ribs weren't hurt, I'd manage for myself."

Pointedly staring out the window to avoid further conversation, she didn't take notice of the scenery but studied his reflection in the glass instead. Sure enough, he eyed her, appraising. Their gazes almost collided, but she darted away. When the train rolled out of the station, she dropped the act.

For his part, he never pretended he wasn't staring. Straight up, he'd been caught, but he could have cared less. "You've got me puzzled," he remarked.

A sensible woman would have left it alone. "Why's that?"

"Habit. Trying to figure you out. You married?"

Too old for her, but that didn't always slow men down. "That's none of your business."

The man stuck his thumbs through his belt loops, unoffended. "True. But you're acting hunted, not to mention those marks on your neck. Looks like you've fair been strangled. Kind of touchy, too."

"It's been a rough couple of days," she replied.

"Amen to that."

He stretched his legs out, taking up over half of the floor. She drew her feet back and under her skirt. He might not be bothered, but she was. Still, he might know something of value. "You from Colorado?" she asked.

"On occasion. You wearin' your best dress?"

"No," Maude lied.

His eyes sparked. "Uh-huh. Me, I'm a miner these days, but I can't place you. You don't exactly strike me as the 'fancy' type, nor a Sunday school teacher either."

"Good. Wouldn't care to be either of those." Maude shifted in her seat, turning toward the lengthening shadows of the night.

He snorted, amused. "Prickly. I kinda like that. You might want to consider that Colorado ain't exactly a place for a woman on her own."

Her response was a long-eyed stare.

Fond of the sound of his own voice, his words dragged out in that Western drawl. "Sure. Have it your own way."

She intended on it. She just needed to figure it out first.

———

She drifted off and awoke to the dungaree-wearing miner, again or still, staring at her.

"Been watching me sleep long?" A sharp-edged question, but she'd let her guard down.

"Didn't mean anything by it. Maybe I was watching over you like one of them guardian angels." He chuckled as he pulled out a pocket watch. "I almost lost this feller in a hand. Ten twenty-eight."

She had to seize the chance, or let it go. "What can you tell me about mining?"

He blinked, then guffawed. "Stay away from it! Every Tom, Dick, and Harry is out here for the same damn reason. Anyhow, it's kind of a queer line of conversation for a woman, I'd say."

"Maybe. How do you know where to dig?"

He chuckled, pained. "The bosses tell us. If a prospector's on his own, he'd follow his instinct. You're kind of scrawny to drill and muck."

Maude cocked her head, eyes narrowed. Firm and superior. "It's a business question. I'm going to sense out gold deposits, not work in a mine."

"Boy-howdy, that's a new one. How's that supposed to work?" His eyes sparked, but he didn't exactly laugh.

"Not sure yet. That's why I'm asking."

He regarded her kind of close. "It's a stretch."

She smarted at the criticism but wasn't flush with options. "Maybe, but I'm going to give it a try." Her words came out meaningless and small.

He stuck his hands in his trouser pockets, smile half-cocked. "Hope you don't mind the snow and the cold."

CHAPTER SEVEN
PARAMOURS FOR HIRE
THE MIKADO BROTHEL

CRIPPLE CREEK, LATE OCTOBER 1895

Everett still liked to grapple her well enough, or so it seemed.

"I figured you'd have come down before now." Julia tossed the remark over her shoulder, after they'd finished with the first business. He sure wasn't measuring up to her expectations, not to mention that she hadn't seen him for five weeks.

Sitting on her bed in the afternoon hours while the house remained quiet, clad in his long johns and drinking whiskey straight from the bottle, he eyed her. She eyed him back, preferring her men a bit rough around the edges, but at times he pushed the limit too far. Leaning against the brass head frame and sprawled out upon her clean sheets, those long johns none too clean. Still, she couldn't have stomached one of those scrawny suits that the Mikado pandered to. Everett was her fellow—but a preoccupied one who didn't have the sense to be grateful. And he wasn't paying her for the trick. If anything, it was more the other way around.

Nevertheless, it was a piss-poor madam who couldn't afford brawn for display. And that brawn had a price tag attached. But the need extended deeper than that. Every woman wanted a man to call her own, but at times the truth loomed too damned obvious to ignore. Ev wasn't towing the line with the enthusiasm she bankrolled. Something had to be done.

"I've told you how it is. The mine's about gone bust, and I'm left racing around Denver trying to figure out how to salvage what I can from the fire. The situation's damn near poised to fall down around my head. If I wanted a woman to nag me, I sure as hell don't need to come down to Cripple Creek. I've got a wife at home for that."

Julia considered the alley from the vantage of her second-story window. Dressed in nothing more than corset and pantaloons, she didn't care if someone saw her. Her figure still passed, and her undone hair remained thick. From a distance, she might come across as twenty-five years old, instead of the truth. The Mikado was a whorehouse, after all. There was no harm in flaunting the goods; in fact, there was the decided benefit known as *free advertising*.

She didn't like talking about his wife, didn't like being reminded of her existence at all. She swung back around. "You got a remedy up your sleeve?"

"What—the mine or the nagging?" He took another swig.

"Either." Julia replied, tiring of the banter. Not to mention that Everett knew full well any mention of his wife caused her hackles to rise.

Of course, he believed he had one over on her. "Damned if I know. You haven't heard anything of interest, have you?"

She offered a dry, bitter laugh. "Oh, I hear interesting things all the time. Most men say their wives don't understand them. Others say their wives won't do what they want. Once the bedroom door is closed, you understand. Which is it for you?"

He gave her an annoyed, level stare. "None of your damned business. I thought you were on my side. Maybe I was mistaken."

"What are you driving at?" A veiled threat. Charming. She never forgot a threat and filed it away for future use.

"If a new vein or mine doesn't turn up right quick, the investors' dividends are going to dry up mighty fast. When that happens, all bets are off."

Everett took yet another swig, and her heart expanded a notch or two. *Her man* having no prospects other than those she offered would suit her fine. "How about I'll kiss away your cares, making everything all better. Is that what you want to hear?"

He emitted a rude snort. "A fat lot of good that would do. The board at the consortium has forgotten that they were the ones who forced the mine into overproduction. Convenient, isn't it? I wanted to drill exploratory shafts for new veins, but no. They didn't want to take the time or make the investment. They think the gold won't ever run out."

She knew one of those titans. A man who had rather *specialized* tastes.

"Is that so." She didn't pose it as a question but rather a statement. He acted as if *her* money would never run out either. If she were younger, their relationship might have been a different story. She could deny the details all she wanted, but she was older than him by at least five years. Maybe more.

To counteract that galling conclusion, she sashayed over to the bed in as suggestive a manner as she could. Snatching the bottle from him, she ran the tip of her tongue around the rim before taking a big swig. Without spluttering. She took pride in the fact she could drink like a man and hold her liquor with the best of them. If she chose to do so. On occasion, when a night played out slow, it helped to pass the time.

Despite her lurid performance, his mind was stuck elsewhere, and he didn't even skip a beat. "...not an endless supply. The deeper in, the harder conditions get, and that vein is petering out. If they don't want to pony up for exploration, we've hit the end of the line for the Scavenger, I tell you."

Words, words, words.

She drifted away, back over to the window, cradling the whiskey bottle against her breasts. She would bide her time. Everett continued to drone on about the mine and its dead-horse prospects, but she listened beyond his voice to the sounds of the house. Her money came from out there, not in her bedroom. Not attending to an ingrate who owed her far more than he guessed.

"...without a producing mine, I don't have a job. Without a job, I can't pay my mortgage. Not to mention that I'll be a laughingstock in Denver and in Cripple Creek."

She didn't bother to turn toward him but kept her attention trained outside. She had given him one hundred dollars in gold the last time he blew into town and shared her bed. To tide him over so that precious wife of his didn't end up on the street herself. "You forgot about Victor. You'll probably be a laughingstock there, too."

"Nice of you to point that out."

"It's the least I could do." Riled, she made sure her smile came out nasty. After all, there was no value in having fangs if the owner was afraid to show them.

CHAPTER EIGHT
WIDE-OPEN TOWN

LATE OCTOBER 1895

The landscape's sheer blastedness caught Maude off guard. Hacked-off stumps were all that remained of trees, dotted and scattered about. Discarded mining entrails spilled down the mountain-sides, those same slopes crisscrossed by roads meant for hauling. The ground vibrated underfoot while industry echoed—a strange symphony, almost musical. But maybe that was pushing things a bit too far.

Rooted on the platform and eyes still scanning the hills, a man tipped his hat in passing—about to offer a pleasantry until he took in the bruising on her neck and thought better of it.

Shaking off the insult, she bumped alongside the other passengers, down the incline toward the center of Cripple Creek's business district. Jangling music of another kind leaked out from saloon stacked upon saloon, the occasional grocer or dry goods horning in for good measure. Respectable and upright.

But she wasn't fooled.

Her palms itched. She recognized the undercurrent and flat out didn't give a damn.

None of this was old money, for damn sure and a good thing. Unsettled, unashamed, and with a decided swagger, the gaudy false fronts loomed. Men's strides exuded optimism, even if their boots spoke of hard labor. Fortunes were there for the making. Or the taking. It didn't much matter how any of it came about, as long as it came.

Cripple Creek shouted *MONEY!* Newly minted and not quite square.

Heading downhill for the simple reason that it was easier than climbing, she landed on Myers Avenue, an off-kilter place if ever there was one.

The street was a slapped-together affair, smelling of green lumber and slops. More saloons, gaming hells, and dance halls, all sprouted in various states and disorders. Hawkers called from shell games set up in the rutted street. "Step right up and take your chances..."

She'd *already* taken her chances, and there was no turning back. The come-on familiar, and old as Moses. Only the uninitiated bet their stakes on such shoddy gambling games. Of course, they were rigged.

Prostitutes lounged in windows and doorways, soliciting and none too refined. The accompanying trades burst forth without apology, without restraint. It was her kind of town—a town where rules were thin and easy to ignore.

For a Wednesday afternoon, Myers Avenue stood wide open and ready for business. The dissolute women lolling about gave her the twice-over. Drunk or sober, eyes stone hard and calculating, Maude knew enough to keep a tight grip on her belongings.

"What are you gawping at?" a drunken harridan

bellowed, accosting a punter leaving a hovel. He did a double take and skedaddled.

Barefoot and far gone, the woman swayed in the center of the road. Wagons and horses avoided her, cutting it close. Too close. Dressed in a dingy white Mother Hubbard, the bawd was half hunched over, her hair a tangled mess that hadn't seen a comb in ages.

For no obvious reason, she crumpled to her knees. Ranting. "No, no, no..." Clawing at the road and flinging handfuls of muck into the air that rained back down upon her, making everything considerably worse.

Maude didn't need any portents to predict what would happen there.

A well-dressed dolly paused beside her and in a soft voice said, "You might be in the wrong part of town."

Maude weighed her options. "Oh, I don't know about that. I just need to get set up."

The pretty dolly's eyes flickered with the wrong idea.

"I tell fortunes," Maude added, almost quick enough, "and I just arrived."

Interest followed, as it usually did. "I sure could use a good fortune. Will you read mine?"

Her clothes displayed a fashionable fine cut, but they had seen better days. No matter, they were still a hell of a lot better than Maude's. "If you like. But it'd be awkward out here in the open." The wind pressed down and whispered of cold remoteness, scuttling a can, clanging and careening along the ruts.

Predictably, a crowd formed near the bawd ranting in the middle of the road. Two whores came up on either side and pulled her to her feet. "Shut the fuck up, Peg. Go sleep it off! You're going to git run over..."

Peg rewarded one of the well-meaning sylphs with a right hook that barely missed her chin, followed by a second swing toward the other that flew wide.

The dolly pointedly ignored the commotion. "There's a decent enough café across the street, unless you prefer strong spirits."

Maude regarded her new companion. "Make it tea or coffee, and you have yourself a deal. My name's Maude. If you could help me get my bearings as far as Cripple Creek is concerned, we could consider it an exchange."

The girl tilted her head, jaunty and bold. "They call me Long Lizzie, and I'm a great one for helping newcomers get their...*bearings*."

The only response to that was to laugh.

They headed toward a shoestring enterprise intended for a rough clientele. Once they were inside and seated next to the window, the sky darkened. Cold gusts sent people scurrying, pulling at their collars. Rain broke loose and transformed into a veil of snow in nothing flat.

"It's no more than an early flurry," Lizzie remarked. Eyes lingering lightly on Maude's neck, but she didn't ask. "You watch, and it'll all be over as soon as it started."

Maude fussed at her wrinkled skirt, but the damage had set in. "I'll take your word for it. As it stands, I need to find decent lodgings and to get myself in a position to learn about ores and minerals."

"Like gold?" The girl's tone conveyed the foregone conclusion.

"Like gold."

The dolly scoffed. "A bastard gave me an ore sample the other day as a tip, and I was too drunk to argue."

A zing of electricity travelled down Maude's spine.

A woman in a splattered apron delivered a pot of tea and two mismatched cups. Lizzie's purse came out in a flash—either displaying a generous nature or guessing how things stood with Maude.

She raised her cup in a mock toast. "Welcome to

Cripple Creek, where everything is up for grabs. Just make sure no one grabs you, unless you're up for it."

The spark in the girl's eyes dimmed. "You know, the mountains beyond are called the Sangre de Cristos—Christ's blood, they say it means. Well, I wonder what Christ would think about this creation here. There's always bleeding going on, in one way or another." Self-conscious, she made the effort to gather herself. "Oh, never mind me, and never mind all of that. The Morning Glory Boardinghouse advertises rooms for fifteen dollars a month, which is a fair bet, as far as those things go."

Maude's head snapped back. The fancy-girl pretended not to notice and gave her a moment to calm.

In a softened voice, she offered an explanation. "Living comes expensive here because a whole lot of money comes out of the ground. You can take advantage of it yourself. We all do." A bitter half laugh. "Watch out for the men once they're drinking, no matter where you are. A skirt is a skirt, and it doesn't matter who's wearing it when they're half in the tank." Resigned, the girl turned her attention out to the street, her profile fine and pleasing.

Maude tapped on the table and forced a levity into her voice that she didn't exactly feel. "Now, a deal's a deal, and I'll read your fortune for you. Put your hand in mine, palm up."

The contact of flesh provoked an unease that webbed through Maude, and she couldn't fake a professional smile. There was no mistaking the patterns on the dolly's palm—too many crossed lines for comfort, and some of those creases ran deep and treacherous.

She met the dolly's eyes. "Be cautious and careful in your dealings. There's a man who promises more than he intends. While professing affection toward you, the truth, his truth, is another matter. He's a committed family man who will never leave. Ever. And stay away from laudanum and morphine, whatever you do."

"I don't take the dope," the dolly claimed.

It was a hell of a way to start off in town. Maude hated giving hard fortunes and usually lied to avoid them.

It was difficult to say why she didn't—this time.

CHAPTER NINE
POVERTY GULCH

T rue to the dolly's prediction, the weather lifted as quickly as it descended. The sun emerged from behind the clouds, dazzling shafts splaying down and across the freshened mountainsides. Traces of the storm reduced down to small puddles in the dips and dints of the boardwalks. A new metallic tang rose from the dirt, a scent brought to life by the rain.

Heedless, smelters belched incessant smoke into the sky.

"You can see the ore if you want. But it's at the house, and you know what *kind* of place that is, don't you?"

Maude jutted out her chin, considering that she was poised to cross a line she probably shouldn't. "Well...mind if I wait outside?"

"No. But don't go spreading this around. Tips are split with the house, and for obvious reasons, I didn't bring this one up."

The two women walked the rest of the way without further conversation, Maude gawping and the dolly jaded.

They stopped in front of a two-story clapboard structure, and Lizzie gestured, half-grand. "This is the Mikado, the second-best sporting house in Cripple! Now you wait here, and I'll be right back."

Maybe third or fourth, a voice corrected in Maude's head. A twinge of shame followed. The rest of the bagnios didn't come across as all that fancy either.

Lizzie reemerged as nonchalant as the crisp breeze. True to her word, she held out a rock the size of a fist. "Good job I didn't fling it out the window after all."

A few tiny gold flecks glinting from a deep black streak, it sure didn't come across like much. But, then again, Maude had never seen raw gold before.

"Did the...man...say anything about it?"

Lizzie's voice held plenty of contempt, but it wasn't clear where it was aimed. "Bragged as long as anyone would listen about how the mine will make a fortune."

The rock smelled of common rust. "But perhaps not you. How do you get valuations?"

The dolly took her for a greenhorn, and rightfully so. "Assay offices. And I have other ways to get money— never you mind about me."

Maybe the mine would make a fortune, but the lump remained a mean-spirited tip. Maude wet her dry lips, thinking. "I saw one of those coming in. Should we see what they have to say?"

Lizzie waved the suggestion away. "*You* can. It's not a Tuesday morning."

Maude blinked.

Long Lizzie's voice turned a shade toward the bitter. "City ordinances. Tuesday morning we're allowed out on the town. That way, decent women know to stay indoors or take their chances."

It wasn't the time to bristle over grievances that had nothing to do with her. "I see. I can take it over if you like."

"Suit yourself." The dolly could have cared less. "Want to leave your bag here so you don't have to lug it around?"

Maude's grasp on the handles instinctively tightened. "It'll be fine."

The girl's eyes flashed, dark and canny. "As you choose."

In response Maude offered a stiff smile, just to show there were no hard feelings on the matter.

———

Three heart-pounding uphill blocks later, her gash throbbed. Hard going in the altitude; she discovered that even simple breathing came difficult. The steep hills would force a body to either strengthen or succumb, one way or another. Wagons rattled by, and people thronged the streets; the *activity* of the town surged with life and industry. She sensed possibility—*very* strong possibility in the rawness of her new surroundings.

Taking the hill at a slower pace, Maude paused to catch her breath outside the office. She pulled her dress collar up as far as she could and marched into the assayers'— a gritty, dirty place. Without ceremony, she plunked the rock down on the counter and dropped her bag at her feet.

"What do you call that?" the man on the other side asked, eyebrows raised.

"Ore," Maude replied. "Is it any good?"

He grew bug eyed at the notion. "Not like that, it's not."

She pulled up short. "How so?"

He cocked his head, took on an exasperated expression. Like she ought to have known better. "Mineral content is determined after firing—which would be a fairly expensive undertaking for something so small and average looking. I take it you're new in town." He nodded at her case.

She batted her eyelashes a couple of extra times to keep him sweet. "I arrived this afternoon. How do you know whether to accept the ore or not?"

Gobsmacked, he spluttered. "You didn't take this for money, did you?"

She had him on the hook, and her voice fell to a low purr. "I shouldn't say, but...that's close to the truth." If she had a dime for every time a woman claimed they were "asking for a friend," she wouldn't have traveled third class and could have paid for her own damn tea.

Manners struggled and kicked in, and the assayer picked up the ore and studied it again. "It's telluride. The dark vein is promising. California's where they have most of the nuggets, but I suppose you already knew that. Here we have ore along with the occasional nugget and gold wire. But only use real money unless you know what you've got *and* have a scale to weigh the gold dust. No one, and I do mean *no one,* trades with unrefined rocks."

Of course. *Had Lizzie been sober...well*. For her part, Maude hadn't known that Cripple Creek didn't have much in the way of nuggets. That proved valuable information right there.

The hours were running short before night took hold, and she didn't have time to beat around the mulberry bush much longer. "How do you know when *telluride* is promising?"

He ruffled his hair, but she could tell he found her pretty. "Dark veins, quartz, experience. Finding the veins is the hard part of mining, of course. Your guess is as good as any. Nearby working mines are strong indicators that the ground is producing. As far as your sample goes, where it came from in the seam would be important. If it was away from the vein, it means one thing—favorable in this case. If the sample was taken from dead center, that's another proposition altogether. If that's the case here, on the face of it, no one would get too excited."

"Meaning worthless," Maude murmured in way of an apology, toying with the ore before pocketing it. She offered a distracted smile as she headed for the door.

"Hey! What's your name?"

"Maude," she replied with the hint of a flirt.

"I'm Sam Evans."

While his name held little importance, there was no reason to advertise. Allure was a commodity, too, one she might just have to use further. She closed the office door behind her without a second thought. The fact remained that, while she was finding her footing, her stomach rumbled, hungry.

She needed to grab hold of some of that loose prosperity lying around.

CHAPTER TEN

LINGERING GHOSTS WITH WARNINGS TO TELL

Maude held onto Lizzie's ore sample, noting there were rocks and dirt aplenty in that scrappy town. For comparison, she picked up a rock of similar size lying at the edge of the street, sensing and weighing. Lizzie's rock struck her as vibrant, while the other struck her as nothing much. She cast it aside. The rock thudded back into the muck of obscurity.

Not enough to go on, but she was learning.

Her return was downhill. Gravity pulled, and she fell into a swinging gait more pronounced than customary. Aiming toward the Mikado.

"Well, hello there!" A wide-shouldered brute entertaining the wrong idea tipped his hat, stepping right up to her and grabbing her by the arm. He had, of course, emerged from one of the myriad of saloons.

"I'm not on the town." She backed up a step, grip tighter on the ore. Stomach clenching.

He grinned. "Oh? How about I buy you a drink, and we could talk about it?"

It wasn't the altitude that caused her heart to thud this

time around. She glared at the sleeve where his fingers clasped, damned if anything of that sort would happen again. She held up the rock, ready to bash his temple in if needed.

He might have failed to notice valuable ore, but he weighed the outcome and concluded he'd best let her go. "My mistake," he grumbled, though he didn't sound sorry in the least. Only peeved.

————

The sun declined behind the peaks to the west, and she had precious little time to waste. Unsteady and reeling, when the Mikado came into view, she paused. The prospect of going straight up to a brothel door left a whole lot to be desired.

She couldn't see any other way.

Cringing, she searched around, up and down the street, like that would make any difference. In the end, she sidled up to the porch and twisted the bell.

Footsteps approached, and the door swung open wide. "It's the fortune-teller," Lizzie called out over her shoulder.

Maude shot a rude, curious glance into the interior when the dolly's attention was turned. An ordinary entryway the same as any other.

A woman emerged from the shadows. "Is that a fact. Searching for a room?"

Her hair dyed an impossible shade caught between red and orange, wearing a ripe red silk brocade, the woman flashed what sure appeared to be real jewels, spangling in the waning light. Her bearing came across as hard, decisive, and shrewd. She eyeballed Maude and her valise up and down, without bothering to hide the fact one jot.

"In a proper boardinghouse," Maude stuttered, trying to gather her wits. "A man just accosted me in the street."

The hard woman laughed. "You're in the part of town for it; what'd you expect?"

"She's not like that," Lizzie countered.

Maude felt that old dull sting of judgment and being found wanting.

The woman smirked. "Well, in case you didn't know, men are good for money."

"Not always," Maude replied, the words escaping.

A nasty cackle from the madam.

Lizzie jumped in. "She tells fortunes. She told me mine..."

The electric flash preceding a request. The madam glinted. "It just so happens I've lost an emerald ring. Don't suppose you'd be able to help with that type of thing, would you?"

A challenge. In normal circumstances, Maude kind of liked that. Lost property had never been one of her strong points, but she wasn't awash in opportunities. "The air's a bit thin here. But, yes, maybe I can."

She steadied herself, placing her hand on the door-frame, pretending it was for support.

Wondering what she was about to get herself into.

A flash of a woman's bedroom, vivid in her mind. "Up the stairs and toward the back of the house is a room painted blue. There's a bed and a couch atop a rug that curls alongside the wall. The ring fell down in there." She saw more than that, of clothing coming off and tangled bodies wrestling. The vision of a pale, white rump jiggling up and down.

Maude kept a straight face.

The madam's eyes flickered at the description; she retreated into the deep interior without saying another word.

Maude waited for the woman to pass out of hearing. "This ore might be of value," she whispered, holding the rock out, "but it costs to fire. And, drunk or sober, stick to cash no matter what happens. No doubt you already figured that out."

"Yeah, I'll not let that bastard near me the next time, if I can help it..." A quiet laugh that never quite reached Lizzie's eyes.

The madam returned, brandishing the ring as a prize.

"I'll be damned; it was exactly where you said it'd be." Another once-over. "My name is Julia Robinson, and I'm in charge here. And you sure look like you could use some money."

Stunned, Maude had no ready response. But the madam didn't require one. "You're welcome to...return. To tell fortunes here, of course. We operate on the late side, as you might have gathered. Come between the hours of one and five in the afternoon if you're of the mind. Provided the surroundings don't bother you overly much."

An offer that could disappear in a flash. "I arrived today and have to get settled first. But I thank you for the offer with all sincerity."

Of course, she wouldn't. *Not unless she had no other choice.*

Julia Robinson seemed able to read her expression and guess her thoughts. She smirked as she returned to the interior, skirts swishing. "Well, either way you've landed in a hell of a place. Good for you."

The dolly started going all bothered but restrained herself until the madam passed out of earshot. "I didn't expect the fortune you gave me to be *real*."

They were a strange lot out in Colorado. "Of course it was real. Why wouldn't it be?"

Eyes averted, the girl didn't answer but brushed past.

"I'll take you over to the Morning Glory before things get going in here."

Halfway down the walk, Maude fell into step. A few different choices and a few less options, and she might find herself exactly in Lizzie's shoes.

Each had bitten off more than they could chew, one way or another.

"You *can* change your fortune you know."

Lizzie never broke her stride. "Maybe you got it wrong."

Impatient, Maude held out her hand. The girl hesitated, but finally gave in. "I'd say your past is plain. Loss has accompanied you from the onset. I'd say you attracted the attentions of a man you shouldn't have. Probably a slip of a girl. Which part have I got wrong?"

Maude noted that Lizzie just stared down at her boots. Or the ground. It didn't much matter either way. "You can't know all of that by just a bunch of lines," the girl claimed.

Maude didn't release her hand but gave it a quick squeeze and an almost friendly shake. "Clairvoyance plays into the fortunes, too. But the warnings are there. *Change how you do things.*"

The dolly's eyes held enough fear to consider the warning. For the moment. But that fear wouldn't last long. It never did.

"I've got to get back. Men don't lay themselves, and Julia'll have my hide."

The madam already had the girl's hide, but Lizzie just didn't know it yet.

The girl pointed to a rude clapboard structure—the boardinghouse—in plain sight atop one of the numerous rises. Without saying anything further, the girl sauntered away with a swagger in her step, a come-on to anyone who watched and wanted. Time ran against them all, but for that single, brief moment, the dolly shone bright, close to glorious.

And Maude's purse held nine dollars and forty-six cents. Which was nowhere near enough. Not when the housing rate came at fifteen dollars a month.

———

Sure enough, a paper vacancy sign hung in the window, edges curled and discolored from the strong mountain sun. Maude set her case down and knocked. Answered by a woman in a faded dress, salt-and-pepper hair pinned back severe and tight. Like the madam, the woman gave her the once-over.

"I'm here about a room. My name is Maude...Sinclair. I arrived in Cripple Creek this afternoon."

"Well, Maude...*Sinclair*, we're an honest house, despite what goes on one street over. I aim to keep it that way."

"I'm honest, if that's what you're asking."

The woman moved aside, prompting a foot-wide glimpse into the interior. "Never said you weren't. On account of our proximity, it's the same speech given to all single women who inquire...not that there's that many of them."

Nothing fancy, it came across as an honest house that offered a refuge she desperately needed. Clean enough, and at any rate the premises *felt* fine.

"Don't just stand there out on the stoop," the landlady said, interrupting her gathering. "We don't hold much on ceremony here."

Maude stepped inside, trying to peer into the corners without being plain.

If the woman noticed, she didn't care. "The boarders are men in the main, but there's one wife, and I've had a lady schoolteacher in the past. The men, for the most part, are fine, and I won't tolerate anything off-color."

"Has there been trouble?" Maude's voice came out a bit strangled.

The woman cocked her head. "No. At least not yet. It's obvious you've run into some along the way."

Maude covered the bruising with her hand. "I got a scare—that's all. Nothing that I can't handle."

The landlady wasn't convinced. "Uh-huh. If you say so." A pause. "Now, there're a few house rules, but the most important is that everyone who lives here works. No loungers tolerated. I charge fifteen dollars a month or five dollars a week for room only. Other places may be cheaper, but this house is clean and respectable. Board's available at fifty cents per day if wanted."

Maude pressed a thin hand to her stomach, stifling a rumble. "I don't have a position yet but aim to find something tomorrow."

"Understood. And I try to make sure my boarders keep honest."

That caught her. "How do you mean?"

"After raising four boys, I've developed an *instinct*. Usually, the malarkey kicks off with late payments and stories that don't add up. Liquor tends to be at the bottom of it. Want to see the room, or have you gone off the idea?"

Maude wilted, fatigued. "No—let me see it. Please."

"What kind of work do you do?" The woman waited.

"I read fortunes."

"Ain't that dandy," she replied, setting off down a tight, dark hallway. "My name is Eunice Weston, unless you figured out that much already."

Maude followed the landlady, drained. "It doesn't work that way," she mumbled, but the landlady didn't care.

At the end of the hallway, Eunice opened the door.

Nothing more than a vacant room, it was a small space boasting wide-plank flooring with gaps. "Do mice ever come in?" Maude asked.

"I haven't found any droppings."

Plain white-papered walls, a narrow single bed, three hooks for her clothing, and a washstand. Nothing fancy. Overlooking the road, a solitary window was dressed with worn lace curtains that nevertheless appeared recently laundered. Maude kept hold of the doorknob out of habit. Sensing. "What happened to the woman who lived in here before?"

Eunice stiffened, the telltale eyes darting. "Consumption—but she didn't die here, if that's what you are asking."

Maude grasped a definite imprint of a long-haired woman wearing a pale nightgown in the corner, staring out beyond the window. An undeniable sense of longing.

"But she did die in the end," Maude murmured, fingering the curtains.

The landlady scrutinized her, close. "Lou Ellen? I liked that girl, for what it was worth. What do you think?"

Maude figured she could tolerate a lingering ghost. "I'll pay by the week and see how I get situated."

"Payment is up front, but I can wait until you go get your things."

Maude shrugged at the battered valise. "That's it."

Setting the case down and against the wall, she unwound the purse strings from her wrist and forced herself not to fumble with the coins because that would give it all away.

Five silver dollars handed over.

Something in her expression must have registered with the landlady. "You'll be fine. New places take time and getting used to. That's all."

"I'm hoping to advise on mining matters."

That caught the landlady. "Well, some mines and crushers hire women to sort through the ore scraps. It's hard on the back, but it's a place to start. The pay is seventy-five cents a day from what I've heard."

That certainly didn't sound like easy money from where Maude was standing, so she offered an apologetic smile.

And she was sharp enough not to act worried. Something would turn up. It had to.

CHAPTER ELEVEN
NONE OF IT COULD BE CONSIDERED GOOD

LATE OCTOBER 1895

W*ell, well, well. That was one hell of a thing.*
Julia'd be damned if that fortune-teller wasn't what she claimed. Good-looking too, in a thin sort of way. Obviously needed money: her clothes told that story loud and clear. It would only be a matter of time until she came knocking on the door. *To tell fortunes, of course.* She stuck her tongue in her cheek. Everyone had to start somewhere.

The housekeeper stuck her head into the office without knocking. "There's a man at the back door asking for you."

Julia glanced over, sharp, irritated. "Who is it?"

The woman shrugged. "Some no-account. Says he's got an important message to give you."

Whatever the story, Julia doubted it would be important to her way of thinking. So she took her time and got up slowly from behind her desk, taking pleasure in how her silk skirt swished, nice and oh so expensive. Nothing rustled quite the same as thick, quality silk. The beaded border displayed a fashionable weight that spoke of money. Plenty of money.

Anyhow, it remained good practice to keep unknown callers a-waiting. Just to make sure they knew who was in charge, and it wasn't *them*.

Casting a critical eye over the furnishings, she wasn't quite satisfied and wondered for the twentieth time what the Homestead House had that she didn't. The recent updates had cost damn near enough. No matter what anyone thought, money didn't just roll in through the door and hit the bottom line. There were a whole lot of expenses involved in running a whorehouse.

She crossed the dining room and burst through the swinging door into the kitchen. Whatever Gretchen had cooking smelled good. No one could say she didn't feed her girls well. A man in a battered jacket hovered just inside the back door, twisting his equally battered hat in his hands.

"Yes?" The likes of him couldn't afford the Mikado, and she was fair-on certain she'd never seen him before.

"Ida, down in Poverty Gulch, sent me."

Another man trying to broker a deal in a business of which he knew nothing. "I'm not interested."

A slow head wag marking the wrong idea. "Nothing like that. She's sick, maybe even dying. Says she used to work for you up in Leadville."

"Is that a fact. What does she want?"

He swallowed, Adam's apple bobbing and jaw setting. "She wants *you* to *go see her*."

Julia narrowed her eyes. "How many other houses have you tried first?"

He managed to come across as offended, which was rich. "She asked for *you*. Now are you going to see her or not, because I've got better things to do than just standing here jawing. She's sick, I tell you."

Sick, diseased, or far gone on drugs or alcohol was how most of them ended up. Bothered, Julia sure as hell wasn't going to show it. Out of principle and self-preservation, she didn't go rubbing elbows down in the Gulch. Nothing good could come from any such associations.

Still, a niggling inside started up in the region of where her conscience ought to be. "Fine, although I have better things to do than go traipsing after used-up whores who once worked for me. Wait here—I'll get my coat."

Gretchen raised her eyebrows at the exchange.

"Don't go spreading this around, whatever you do," Julia warned as she brushed by the housekeeper, dead serious on the matter.

Surprised she was even contemplating going, she thought about it. Maybe she was attempting to cheat her own possible fate. If that was the case, it was nobody's business but her own.

———

The jake, whomever or whatever he claimed, hadn't much in the way of manners, keeping himself a step or two ahead of her. Clearly not wanting to be seen in her company, he couldn't figure out a way to avoid it. For that matter, his attitude rubbed her the wrong way, too, and she wasn't all that certain she wanted to be seen in *his* company. Sure as hell, he headed toward the Gulch, the part of Myers that gave Julia the willies. Low, rude cribs were stacked together like so much kindling, barely big enough to swing a cat. Likely to blow over if a strong wind rose up. Fires weren't uncommon, and no wonder.

Hell. She wouldn't end up there. She had too much money and common sense for that.

However, events could turn, and that was what got her. Even the best businesswomen grew sloppy or tired.

Other times, sentimentality was what got them in the end. Rearing its ugly head when matters of the heart were concerned. Usually centering around some *man* who did his damnedest to bleed them dry.

Men like Ev.

She sure as hell wasn't going to be making that mistake on account of him, no matter how his thoughts might turn.

The jake stopped in front of one of those low cribs, the name *Ida* painted rough on a plank above the door. He tipped his hat sarcastic-like and made himself scarce.

The madam lined the tips of her polished boots together, contrasting against the rough-cut, weathered boardwalk. More like planks strewn about for good measure, she thought, displeased. She lifted her head, took a deep breath, and knocked.

"It's Julia Robinson."

An indistinct voice squawked out a response, the door unlocked. Pushing through, she crossed the threshold of that sorry squat, shutting the door behind her although she didn't want to. Three feet away at best, Julia didn't need to move any closer to see that the woman in the bed was in a bad way. Sick beyond the standard ravages that caught up with them all. Flushed cheeks and eyes fever bright.

"You asked to see me?" She kept her hand on the door-knob in case things turned nasty.

The soul in the bed struggled to sit up and failed. "It's me—Ivy. Don't you remember, Julia?"

No recollection at all. "I've been in the business a long enough time, darlin'. Who'd you say you were?"

"Ivy Lovejoy...changed the name to Ida down here." A cough and a rattle.

Julia's stomach turned cold. "I remember."

"I don't want to get pitched out in the paupers' field."
The woman's voice wheezed.

Back in the day, the girl called Ivy had nicked another
whore's dress or some such nonsense. Whatever the issue,
the dispute had caused a load of trouble at the time, *if* she
recalled correctly. And she felt pretty sure that she did.
Such matters, she supposed, could be discounted in the
circumstances.

"Can't blame you there. It's kind of cold in here. You
got any coal?"

Ivy shook her head, shamed.

"I'll send a boy down with provisions, including soup.
That should help."

The offer didn't exactly register much. "You'll take
care of the headstone? I got money. In the box in the
corner, over there."

"Come now! No one said you're going to die." But
there was a fair chance that was precisely what would
happen.

"I said it." Ivy lay back on the bed, breath raspy. "Take
the money as long as you get me buried decent."

An unwelcome responsibility, but there, for an unbeknownst reason, Julia refused to shirk. "If it comes to that,
you've got my word."

One thing for certain, she didn't want to stay in that hovel
a minute longer than necessary. Kneeling on the dirty crib
floor, expensive skirt probably going to hell, Julia rummaged
through rags and bits and bobs before she latched upon an
envelope—*Grave* written in pencil, large and scrawling.

Inside were six silver dollars and a bunch of smaller
coins. Whatever transpired, the marker would be a
wooden one. "You want me to count it out for you?"

"No," the woman gasped. "Take it with you. Before the
vultures descend."

Putting the lid back on the box and folding the envelope over, Julia stuck it in her coat pocket and struggled to her feet.

"Rest up and marshal your strength. How old are you, anyhow?"

"Thirty-two."

More like forty, Julia thought, but didn't they all lie about *that*.

"Who's to say you haven't years left in you yet. Do you want me to send a doctor down?" Dying alone was a hell of a way to go, and, without a doubt, Ivy listed on the brink.

"No. They're all bastards."

Julia backhanded the dust and dirt from her skirt, not exactly overjoyed by any of it. There was nothing a doctor could do, other than charge her the going rate. Maybe extra, on account of the location. "I'll send that boy with the provisions. He'll be down within the hour. You have my word."

She figured she'd send a bottle of whiskey as well. Some of the lesser quality. Doubtful that Ivy would even notice the difference, and the liquor might make her passing that much easier.

CHAPTER TWELVE

SHADY MONEY SPENDS
THE SAME

NOVEMBER 1895

D esperation was a strange thing, and no laughing matter. Women could sort ore, but it would be a damn cold day when she signed up for that lark. Still, there were lessons she might pick up in the mining district. And, for that, she sought out Eunice. "I know we're surrounded by mines and more mines in Cripple Creek, but could you point me which way I might go?"

Of course, the landlady concluded that Maude was seeking paid work and pointed northwest. "A mile or so in that direction are a few larger concerns. They're as good a place to try as any. Keep uphill, and you should run into something."

So Maude labored up the road, heart thudding from the altitude's thin air. A thunder-like sound droned in the distance, a swelling din that reverberated along with each passing step. More than once she had to stand to the side of the road as loaded ore wagons thundered down toward the depots, throwing up dust as they careened. Her boots and skirt hem were coated. Goggle-eyed stares followed when the drivers cottoned on to the fact that she was an unescorted woman. An extra flick of the cracking whips in attempts to attract her attention.

Steady-on, git-on, whoa...it made no odds to Maude, who had no interest in haulage. She wanted to know about veins.

A quarter mile further up the jagged road, the crusher mill building came into view—a giant structure towering over the chutes and belts, and at least three stories high.

bam thud bam thud BAM!

Reverberation horrendous and deafening. Ore clattered down shutes, a tumbling torrent of rock—the vibrations traveled through her thin-soled boots, settling into her chest, her organs shuddering. She stood there for a few moments, staring at the steel sheet walls—the name Brodie Mill painted on one hulk in large, white letters.

A returning wagon headed uphill stopped for her. "Need help?" the dusty driver shouted, doffing his cap.

She shook her head and pointed. "Loud!"

"Most go deaf!" he shouted back, cracked his whip, and headed slowly up the hill.

The crusher mill was impressive, dangerous, and deafening.

She had another option and a better game to play.

———

When she returned to town, in the harsh light of day and stone-cold sober, the "row" sure didn't come across as any too fine or fancy. In fact, it viewed as downright shoddy, constructed of warped boards and lack of paint and flat out not giving a damn. Maude picked her way through the dregs as the street shook off the previous night. Given her new surroundings, it wouldn't have been natural if misgivings hadn't surfaced, but hunger had a way of dealing with those. Three days in and unable to find paying work other than of the back-breaking kind, she had literally no better place to turn. Well, other than one line of work she wasn't ready to pursue. Stomach rumbling, she made a decision and set upon a course.

Straight up to the Mikado's door she marched, aware of crossing an invisible line that marked the point of going too far.

"Can I help you, sugar?" A flaming red-haired coquette draped herself against the doorframe in a lewd, suggestive manner. Dressed in a type of kimono wrap and bare-footed, she gave the impression she had scarce rolled out of bed. And if she'd been in bed, she sure hadn't been sleeping. And making no secret of the fact, she flaunted it.

If she wanted to shock, she had succeeded.

Maude hesitated on the stoop, flushing despite herself. "Miss Robinson said I could come tell fortunes in the afternoon."

The dolly pulled herself up straight and knocked it off. "You the one who told Lizzie's fortune?"

That caught her. "Yes...I did."

"She said your fortunes weren't parlor games but are for real. That right?"

"They're real. Well, as close as I can get them and based upon what I see." A pang of knowing that wasn't always the case; she stuffed the notion right back down.

"Who's at the door, Florence?" The madam's voice cut through the depths of the house.

"It's the fortune-teller lady," the redhead hollered back, brash and bold as she gave Maude a wink.

"Don't leave her just standing there, let her in."

Maude crossed the threshold. *Good lord almighty*. She stood square inside a brothel, and it sure seemed rich. Laced with an unfamiliar, cloying scent, an overripe blend of spilled liquor, cigars, perfume and the "night before." The fragrance struck immediately, raw and liquor soaked.

The furnishings nevertheless came across as impressive, substantial, and well-polished—the walls papered and the carpeting thick underfoot. In fact, she'd never entered a place so finely presented. But it was the overripe smell that would stick with her—the smell and the fleeting impressions of turmoil and few choices. The deeper sense of being where she oughtn't.

The madam emerged into the hallway and gestured, proud and self-satisfied. "Welcome inside, Fortune-Teller."

Her response poised to tumble out, Maude's attention snagged on a painting. A naked woman reaching for a low-hanging apple. Stomach well fed, breasts full, and shiny hair crowned bountiful, her curls restrained with blue ribbon. Just like that vision of Columbia in *American Progress*. Well, without her clothes. Those breasts could have used binding, too.

Of course, the madam caught her. "Like what you see?"

The spark of a deeper challenge.

"I've seen better renditions of skies," Maude tendered.

The woman hawked. "That's rich, and I'll be damned. Look at a lot of paintings, do you?"

Driving away Columbia's image, never mind the sky, Maude pulled herself together and changed the course of the conversation. "I'm hoping to take you up on your offer," she said.

The sharp glint of steel. "Which one?" the madam asked.

CHAPTER THIRTEEN
RUMORS OF OPPORTUNITY

D ark splotches crossed her vision, intruding. For an odd moment, she thought she might faint. "Fortune telling," she spluttered. "You said I could..."

"Oh. *That*. Can't blame a soul for trying." Julia's smirk came across as second nature. Maybe even first.

The madam eyed the full length of her, up and down. "I would say that by the way you hold yourself, you've always had a man's support. Ain't that so?"

An uncontrollable flush rose, hot and spreading. But, for the life of her, having a husband was not a cause for shame. If anything, it was the other way around.

"Until Nebraska," Maude answered, not sure she should divulge even that much.

The madam *tsk*ed. "Never did like that state."

Maude's pride flared. "It's not like I didn't get money out of the deal."

"Glad to hear it." Something lingered in the madam's underlying calculation that Maude couldn't quite reach.

Anxious to change the conversation, Maude searched

around the room—only to have her gaze snag on that damned painting again.

"The Garden of Eden, don't you think? The Mikado ought to be a damn sight better than wherever you hang your drawers. That painting there? Well. It came from another bagnio that flopped over, belly up. No chance of that happening here. As a matter of fact, I've recently had the house redecorated. The wallpapering all came from France."

A jumble of maneuverings and shady dealings, the hanging silence meant that Maude had to come up with something. "That's a long way to send for wallpaper."

The spark of amusement at her expense. "Money shows, every time," the madam proclaimed.

The half-clad dolly made no move to leave the room or the conversation but instead twirled a lock of hair around her finger. "You *sure* that wallpaper came from France, Julia?"

"I just said so, didn't I?" the madam snapped.

Red-headed Florence rolled her eyes when the madam's back was turned.

"You can set up through the partition at the dining table. Florence will let the girls know we have a fortune-teller on the premises for their entertainment. Won't you, Florence? And, while you're at it, why don't you go ahead and get dressed."

Unnerved, Maude sat down. Her own dress was growing looser by the day.

The madam continued to scrutinize her. "You know, I'm not letting you set up in here out of the goodness of my heart. For right now, and to keep the books balanced, let's say you owe me one."

One what, Maude didn't know.

And it wasn't exactly the time to quibble as one of the

boarders slipped into the awaiting chair, blue eyes wide with an elusive longing. Maude didn't need to read the lines or consult the cards. Whatever the dolly wanted would be difficult, if not impossible, to find. Especially in a whorehouse where dreams got ground underfoot.

Sometime later, three girls done for, Maude couldn't leave the Mikado fast enough. The dollars in her pocket would go a ways toward solving her problems. The fortunes she'd doled out...well. Perhaps not so much.

———

Fragmented rumors on any number of topics drifted around the peaks and carried on the autumn wind. Cripple Creek was nothing if not fueled by half-truths of booming production and boundless possibilities. But gold production swaggering often rang hollow when held against the threat of labor strikes, reports of double-dealings, and contagion outbreaks. By the time the bruising on her neck had faded, Maude still struggled to find her footing. About that time, disjointed accounts of another fortune-telling woman found her. Of course, Maude followed the vague, whispered tendrils to the upslope side of Bennett Avenue, the hint of winter snow pressing down in a cold undercurrent.

Sure enough, at the intersection of Bennett and Fourth Street, a wooden placard advertised one *Madam de Silva —Clairvoyant*. A painted arrow aimed up and around the corner.

The spelling struck her as wrong, but Maude traced along regardless. In twenty paces she stood in front of the *Fortune Emporium*, gold and black stenciled letters spanning a large plate glass window, bold and jaunty. Prosperous from all outward indications, and her stomach warmed with a rare hope taking root. Here, perhaps, was somewhere she might belong. One half step forward, an all-seeing blue eye caught her in its stare. The *Eye of Providence,* to the best of her knowledge. Odd and suspended from chains. The message could be taken as a type of warning, or perhaps it meant the Masons were involved.

Inhaling, she hesitated. Either way, the door had a fine brass knob, well carved and substantial. And, whatever the particulars of the establishment, no one was visible inside.

Hand on the knob. When no warning came, she pushed on through. A bell rigged to the door cascaded, cheerful and light. First impressions—rough-hewn, it didn't look like much, but a stove was lit and casting heat. Once a mercantile or shop of sorts, but there was no harm in that. A high counter dominated, covered with newspapers strewn about in no particular order, and the corners begging for a good sweeping. Whatever the case, it didn't strike her as profitable.

More telling than the lackadaisical housekeeping was the pronounced lack of wallpapering that the Colorado people held in such high regard. Heavy, sun-faded velvet drapes hung off to the side, and the clapboard walls could have benefitted from a lick of paint. A couple of mottled mirrors hung on naked joists, reflecting slapdash shelving that displayed disparate curiosities. Fading prints of cake-soap beauties dotted the walls, and a single table waited in the center of an uneven floor.

No doubt where the fortunes were proffered.

Ready to dismiss the operation out of hand, until a chill brushed across her shoulders—a cold, dead breath. A low, man's laugh resonated behind, traveling from the base of her spine up between her shoulder blades. She turned, slow and deliberate, locking on an old skull grinning from a makeshift shelf. Empty eye sockets nowhere near as dead as they ought to be.

Oh yes, she could feel him, fine hairs rising.

"*I* am Madame de Silva," a voice boomed behind her.

CHAPTER FOURTEEN
MADAME DE SILVA'S FORTUNE EMPORIUM

Maude stifled a scream, spun back around, and stopped, heart stock-still.

Before her stood a woman of uncertain age, framed by the doorway, kohl-rimmed eyes and a knotted purple headscarf tied to one side.

"What kind of magic do you do in here?" The question came out closer to a gasp.

The outlandish woman blinked, then belted out a raucous laugh. "You mean Charley? Don't let him put you off; a punter couldn't pay for his reading, so we traded. He got his reading, and I got that skull. There's no magic involved. Or, if there is, I sure don't know about it."

The woman waved off any ill impression with the flick of her wrist. "Of course, I didn't *know* the punter couldn't pay until it was too late. Now people pay *before* their fortune is told, and Charley there, well, he makes sure everyone minds their manners."

Charley. That was one hell of a coincidence.

"Can I touch it..." Her words popped out of their own accord. Uncertain about handling such a *personal* thing, yet a rare heat coursed through her fingers and hands.

"Suit yourself."

She sidled her way over to the cranium and lifted it as gently as she could, careful to cradle the jaw. What she got was an electric current jolting through her arms. She shuddered.

"How's your business been since he's been around?"

A cagey manner stole over the woman. "I don't have many complaints. Why?"

"A notion, nothing more." She set it back down, gingerly.

"What difficulty can I help you with?" The gypsy reverted to a practiced pitch, her accent pure American.

A half smile tugged. "Employment. Could you use another seer?"

"I don't know. Are you French?"

Did she sound, or look, French? "No, I'm from Massachusetts. My name's Maude."

The woman's features relaxed a mite. "Good. The French are bad business altogether. What brings you out here? Fortunes back East get too boring?"

A laugh escaped. "Something like that. I figured to give it a whirl out here. What do you say?"

"Fine. If Charley there hasn't got you too spooked— you've gone kinda pale. So, you figured you'd come all the way out from Massachusetts to make your fortune. Just like everyone else around here."

Maude shrugged. "You might say that. I'm hoping to advise on mining prospects. Everyone's talking about the strikes here. Cripple Creek seemed a good proposition all the way 'round."

Madame de Silva took the seat on the customer side of the small table. A scruffy card deck waited, stacked and in the center. Smudged roses and violets on the backs, well worn. The woman tapped them twice with her index finger. "Go on. Read."

"Those are ladies' playing cards."

The fake gypsy tossed off the criticism. "What of it? They work the same."

That much held true. Maude took the empty chair at the table, shuffled the cards, and splayed them face down in a fan shape. "Pick one and put it down on the table, face up."

The woman drew a card and set it down with a snap. The five of clubs. *Alliances being made.*

Maude dealt out four cards, face up on the table and in a straight line. The four of clubs, the two of diamonds, the four of diamonds, and the four of hearts.

Lies and betrayal, a business partnership resulting in a financial upswing, and a change of location.

The woman stared at the cards without the slightest glimmer.

Maude met the woman's eyes. "No offense, but it doesn't appear you have the ability at all."

The woman leaned forward and slapped the table. "Outstanding. But you *can* read, and I know three of a kind is a fine hand in poker. What's your angle?"

"As I said. Mining consultations. Otherwise, I guess run-of-the-mill fortunes until the right opportunity comes along. How's the money here?"

"One dollar, without a clue. I tend to work on what you might call...an opportunistic basis, meaning I don't go any lower than one dollar unless there's no other way. Are you serious about sensing ore deposits, or is that just a notion you're bandying about 'cause you like the sound?"

"Well, I don't exactly know yet. I haven't figured it all out."

The gypsy frowned. "Well, watch your step. People in these parts do not take kindly to being strung along, and especially not about prospecting. That whole Mount Pisgah hoax left a bad taste in a lot of mouths."

"Hoax?"

The woman waved her hands in a vague manner, but her eyes were sharp. "Salted exploration holes and a bunch of greenhorns flashing more money than sense. People have wised up a fair bit since then. That said, greenhorns are still greenhorns and assume the gold's going to reveal itself like magic."

"I'm not a fake."

The woman's expression turned wolfish as she made for the door. "We'll see. You wait right here. I'm going to go get someone."

And she bounded outside, leaving Maude alone with the skull.

———

Madame de Silva returned with a dirty-shirted, heavy-booted fellow in tow. Of course, he presented the image of a miner or prospector. But whatever his profession, he didn't appear all that willing or interested.

The most unexpected thing. Maude's first thought was that she should have taken more time doing her hair.

"She's the real deal, I'm telling you," the gypsy declared, but for whose exact benefit was hard to say.

"How long is all this going to take, Rose?" The man wiped his sweaty forehead with his shirtsleeve, eyes widening when Maude finally registered.

Flushing in return, Maude tried to concentrate her energy into securing a paying position. She motioned for the man to take a seat. "Not long at all," she replied, low and aiming toward the melodious.

He sat down, sheepish.

"Shall I read your palm? That goes a bit faster." She held out her hand in as alluring a manner as she could manage. *Out of habit,* she told herself. "Do you have a question you want to ask, or am I simply reading?"

Confused and uncertain, his clear eyes sought out Madame de Silva, who folded her arms across her chest. "Just read so we can see how good you are—or aren't."

"Place your hand in mine, palm up...unless you'd rather use the cards." She wet her lips.

"Palms should be fine," the gypsy interjected. "I've already seen you do the cards."

He wiped his hands on his pant legs before setting one hand in hers. The contact sparked. Rough and calloused by hard work; his fingernails were dirty and ragged. But money stood out in those lines, and she had to hit upon something true.

"Deceit," she pronounced, words flying out by their own impetus. "In the past you dealt with deception. A woman, by the looks of it. And death. There's also death in your past, and a change of heart in your future."

He expelled his breath, irritated. Like she was an out-and-out fraud.

She hadn't intended on a shit-hole fortune. Maude let go of his hand, breaking the bond. Rubbing her palms against her skirt, sensations careening and conflicted.

Neither the gypsy's nor the man's expressions changed. Oblivious to the turmoil welling inside her. The panic setting in upon studying lines when the message just wasn't there.

An image swooped into her mind, fear swirling. "Indians."

That notion hadn't come from her at all.

Sure as shooting, the skull had planted that image in her mind, and channeling him might prove a dangerous thing. But she had nothing else to go by. He supplied another image. Scared gray eyes held wide, and arms flailing. Work-worn clothing. "A man wearing blue overalls was struck down in the raid before..." The impression of a small, dry gully. "...water ran out."

He blinked. *Good.*

"Money will come through your own labor. But whether that comes from mining or another source, I couldn't say. Seems a different trade to me, but related."

Eyes haunted and wild, he got up fast. Stared down at her, bothered. "What's the change of heart in the future?"

"It's unclear, but I'd say a change of location is part of it. Maybe even a new love interest."

He rubbed his jaw, finally dismissing the comment out of hand. "I've no intention of leaving here."

She shrugged. Time would tell. A girl sure would have to scratch beneath the surface to get him to flirt. In hindsight, she should have found an honest man earning honest money instead of a con always willing to flatter.

He pulled a silver dollar from his pocket and held it out for her. Reluctant to take money from him, she knew the reason why. But pride be damned, and need won out. She held out her hand, clutching the coin when it rested in her palm, wrapping the shawl tighter across her chest.

Conflicting emotions swirled, and distrust won out in the end.

He shoved his hat down on his head, and his big, sturdy work boots clomped him back outside and into the street. He glanced back at her; interest sparked. With flattered approval, Maude watched his wide shoulders and narrow hips through the delineating window...measured his confident, unhurried, graceful gait.

But he didn't turn again.

The masquerading gypsy crowed. "Ha! That was a test: he's a blacksmith. I predict we're going to make money here." She rubbed her hands together in pure glee. "Now, how do you do that?"

Maude snapped back at the notion. The skull laughed at her expense, but the woman couldn't hear it.

"Ummm...it just comes to me." She blinked. "That's probably some Indian's head you've got there."

The woman shrugged it off. "Sure about that, 'cause I'm not. Maybe he was an old shavetail without enough common sense to survive."

"You don't believe that..."

"Well, he don't eat much," the gypsy snapped.

"You're inviting trouble keeping him in here like that. I'd guess he doesn't approve."

Madame de Silva guffawed, a rude sound originating from down around her toes. "A superstitious clairvoyant. You've got to toughen up, girl! That old noggin can't do anything to you."

But hunger could, so Maude let the matter drop.

CHAPTER FIFTEEN

WHAT'S IN A NAME?

Cards, tea leaves, life lines, or vague impressions —gold wasn't lying in the streets, and that was a real shame.

Each day, Maude settled in at the business end of the fortune-telling table and waited for customers to come.

They didn't.

Neither did the blacksmith come calling.

All she got was plenty of long-necking through the window, which didn't count for much because it didn't pay. Belvideres made a habit of giving her the once-over and each other the nudge. Working more than one punter at a time through the glass seldom turned out in her favor, yet she grew desperate enough to try. So she wet her lips and beckoned them to enter. Inevitably, their eyes grew wide, and general jostling followed: a show of punching arms and loud horseplay. Right before they burst into coarse laughter and sprinted away.

"Mudsills," the gypsy would grouse. Like that declaration might make Maude feel any better.

One of those custom-stricken afternoons, the most interesting thing the clairvoyant could find was to focus on the mystery of Rose, which wasn't her real name anyhow.

"What name should I use for you?"

The gypsy didn't even bother to pause from her reading. "Rose."

"It's more the *de Silva* part I'm asking about. Your sign down the street needs to be fixed. I'm pretty sure that *Madam* has an *e* on the end. Besides, *Madame* de Silva sounds so...fancy. You made it up now, didn't you?"

That got her. The gypsy came out from behind the counter, not exactly friendly on the matter. "I *use* de Silva as a last name, which is as good as any and better than most. So, now that we've ventured into this territory, it's your turn to come clean."

Maude exhaled. "Fine. Let's settle on Sinclair. Maude *Sinclair*." She smiled to show there were no hard feelings, at least not on her part. "Doesn't that name just sound of money?"

"We'll see." The woman leaned her backside against the counter, ankles crossed, and arms folded in judgement. "Back in Massachusetts, how'd you ply your trade? I'll bet you wasn't set up in a storefront, huh?"

"No."

"Well, then?"

Uncertain about the advisability of telling the full truth, Maude pointed down the middle path. "It was all kept quiet. Kitchen table stuff for the most part, but the neighbors knew." And talked. And suspected. It had been a lonely existence in more ways than one, come to think of it.

Nevertheless, a gleam of triumph lit Rose's pale eyes. "Uh-huh. Then this is an *improvement* over your last situation, wouldn't you say? So, you earned your money by delivering fortunes at your kitchen table. What else?"

Maude rubbed the nape of her neck. "Does it matter?"

"I'd say it is of interest." Rose didn't move and waited her out.

Maude shrugged. "Fine. I worked at the mill for a while, too. Fortune-telling was a sideline I inherited from my grandmother. She had the second sight as well, but she handed the readings over to me." Another twinge. "How many customers come through here in a day?"

Rose unfolded a bit. "Oh, hard to say. But let's move this table next to the window to make it more...alluring. Can you do that type of thing—predict numbers, I mean?"

"No. Absolutely not!" That was one quick way to get run out of town. "I was asking, in a roundabout way, how the rent gets paid."

Rose tossed her head, earrings flashing defiance. "This here is what they call an *ongoing* concern. For seven months now, I've managed to scrape the rent together more or less each month, and more or less on time. There's no cause for worry on that count. Besides, I got a deal on the lease on account of some information."

The somewhat hollow words rattled about the room, threat implied. The skull hummed low.

Having nothing to gain by being difficult or getting involved in matters where she shouldn't, Maude tried to smooth things over. "How'd you start out in this line of business, anyways?"

Rose lifted one hand upwards to an invisible balcony and placed the other on her breast. "Travelling... performer." Rose de Silva projected over-enunciated and drawn-out words, wringing each syllable for its last drop of blood.

Maude smiled.

Rose took an elaborate and low bow, certainly worthy of a curtain call. "I ended up in Cripple when gold was first discovered—*really* discovered."

That notion twanged a chord only Maude could hear.

A pause. She tried again, the hoax hanging in warning. "Not many customers have been coming in, and half of nothing is still nothing."

"You bet your sweet backside. You gone cold on me now?"

Maude waved away the suggestion. "No, but it would be nice if respectable clients came in. That's all."

Rose shrugged that off. "Respectable comes in different stripes. What passes as the 'quality' out here ain't always so fine. Fortunes are made; they do come slinking in through that door when they're worried it's all about to slide down the chute."

Indeed, the prospect of Cripple Creek still beckoned beyond the window glass, but gold was proving far more elusive than expected. "All fortunes will read the same— for the quality or otherwise. Take that blacksmith's fortune for instance. It turned out well enough."

A gleam lit up Rose: a gleam that said she knew Maude was fishing. "That a fact?"

An inward flinch. Maybe she *had* botched that bit about his future. "Seemed to."

A quick diversion away from tender topics. Maude continued. "You know, word of mouth usually brings in business, but people have to come in to get all that started. Women used to come to my door in Sioux City, but there came a time when I couldn't keep promising their children would get well or their husbands would drop dead..."

"Yeah," Rose chortled. "I can see how that might become a problem, all right. Too bad Clayton ain't the kind to go shooting his mouth off. He used to be a miner before he wised up. I was hoping to get someone else in here, someone with interesting business prospects, if you catch my drift. But no. For once no one was hanging about down at the forge, shooting the breeze. It was either grab him or a punter out of a saloon, and drunks are just too damn gullible."

His name was Clayton. "So, what's he like?"

"Clayton? Solid and stable. Boring as hell when it comes right down to it, but I guess he thought you were pretty."

And that, as far as Rose was concerned, ended the conversation. Maybe for Maude, it was just the beginning.

She wondered what he'd be like to kiss, and her mind stuck on the notion, although it shouldn't have. But niggling beneath propriety, another practicality surfaced. A hefty portion of her interest stemmed from need. That blacksmith would provide for a wife—and provide with honest, hard-earned money.

That would sure be a change, a voice inside her taunted. But such respectability seldom came for the likes of her.

———

If the days were thin and drawn out, the nights got to her worst of all.

The dark hours left a fair amount of time for considerations that seldom helped matters along. Try as she might not to dwell on the past, it crept in along the edges. The gnawing in the pit of her stomach signaled more than mere hunger. More than once, in the feeble light of the kerosene lamp, she flexed her fingers and held them out against the light. All she had to do was turn over her palms and search out the warnings.

But superstition pressed down.

Instead, she contemplated each grievance as a link in the chain of events that comprised her marriage. A better man, and her situation might have been different—but that knowledge didn't exactly pay out.

The comparison between "Skiptown" and the blacksmith kept cropping up, and she kept letting it on in. She had no right to venture down that path. Hard done by no matter the measure, the truth remained.

She was far too young to be without a man, and she didn't want to be alone.

In fact, she didn't want to be shoved along the fringes, but she was. People in her line of work always were, and that was just the way of it. She'd do her damndest to survive.

CHAPTER SIXTEEN
PROBLEMATIC FORTUNES

The mountain morning hung frigid, her breath a visible cloud. Waiting outside the Emporium's locked door for all the world to see, she pretended a fascination with the mountains she didn't feel—a half-contrived regard over the tattered-lace snow. Rocks pockmarking beneath slate storm clouds looming above in the western sky. Shafts of light pierced through at intervals; ever-changing rays played down on gullies, ravines, and outcroppings. In turn, the light would recede, the gray stealing back, flattening distinctions. The cold seeped into her bones and through the thin soles of her boots. As she stifled shivers, passers-by eyed her over their mufflers and scarves, curious and disapproving in turns.

If they stared too long, she met them full on. She had nothing to be ashamed of, as far as they knew. Nothing... unless they were clairvoyant as well, and that boiled down to plain unlikely.

She hugged her arms about her to ward off the chill, not even having the price for a cup of coffee. Again the blacksmith came to mind, him and his unexpected dollar tip. There was money in those lines. Honest money. But he hadn't come calling. Just another flash in the pan that wouldn't amount to anything at all.

Rose's purple scarf came into view at long last. A well-dressed woman stared at the clairvoyant a trifle too long for comfort.

Maude locked eyes, refusing to back down.

A wry smile and calculated approval from Rose as she reached within striking distance. "A stomach for notoriety! I do like that in a person." Her voice carried, loud enough for the street to hear. The well-dressed woman turned and stalked away.

"You're late." Maude emphasized the word *late*.

"Says you." Rose unlocked the door, all nice and jaunty.

Following in on her heels, Maude hovered near the unlit stove for no other reason than habit. "I have better things to do than lollygag outside in the cold waiting for your arrival."

Still chirping, Rose wagged a triumphant finger. "You sure about that? Anyhow, that's not how things came across from a distance. But you were staring the world dead on. It made a distinct...impression. Which, of course, got me to thinking." Rose launched a slow circle around Maude. "You're young and pretty, with a brash way about you. You could stand outside and drum up business every day."

Maude stiffened. "Like they do down on Myers Avenue."

That same mocking spark from Rose. "Not the most flattering comparison, I suppose, but it's close enough for horseshoes. And what do you know about Myers?"

A half shrug she sure hoped came across as casual. "I told a few fortunes down there when I first arrived."

That stopped the gypsy dead. "You did?"

"Needed the money," Maude challenged, without much give.

Head cocked, Rose frowned. "Anything else besides?"

"Of course not." The jangle of the madam's offer ricocheted in her mind. "Just fortunes, and even that's nothing to go bragging about. But it kept a roof over my head all the same."

Rose crossed her arms like that somehow settled things. "Well. Everyone kicks about loose when they first arrive, I suppose. But you've got to watch out for yourself and stay away from the underbelly—you know that, don't you?"

Maude waved the implication away. "And well you know that we aren't seen as exactly straightforward."

"That I do." She eyed Maude hard. "But I also know to stay on this side of the divide. Hope you understand that distinction as well."

Maude pretended to ignore the barb and drifted over to the fortune table. Back turned toward the gypsy, she picked up the deck of cards and gave them a good thump before absent-mindedly chopping. Over and over again.

———

Muck-flinging wheels proved a hazard of thawing roads, and the mountain weather in Cripple Creek whipsawed back and forth. When the temperature lifted above freezing, the dirt roads warmed and became a morass of slop. Foot traffic ebbed and flowed along with the mines' changing shifts, miners mucking through the peaks and troughs without a second thought. It was the women and businessmen who picked their footing through the ruts, dainty and cautious. Not that it always mattered—for accidents could, and did, happen. Pratfalls were better than landing hapless in the mire face first. Through it all

—the changing of the shifts, the business meetings, and the shopping—Maude stayed rooted in place on the boardwalk. Touting in front of the Emporium's door, unless she'd already snagged a customer.

"Read your fortune for a dollar!" she all but sang the typical come-on.

Dodging the ugly blend of mud and horse shit, she pulled the gray shawl tighter and made last-ditch efforts to avoid flying filth.

———

It was a gray day stuck in the depths of December. Unbeknownst to Maude, a mudsill eyed her up and down from an alley vantage. Decision made, he sprang across the street, bounded straight up, and leered into her face. "Do anything else?"

She recoiled into the safety of the fortune parlor's door. "What do you mean?"

"Two dollars if you'll take me back to your place and get down on your knees." Removing his hat with a flourish, he held it over his heart in parody.

Her customary luring smile faltered and dropped. "You're mistaken."

"Well," he drawled, grinning and confident, "I'd treat you real soft, and your dress is kind of shabby. What do you say?"

To her credit, Rose burst outside in a flash. Hands on hips and leaning in for a fight. "This codswallop giving you problems?"

Eyes narrowed and with an unkind smirk, he looked about ready to take Rose on. She took another step toward him.

"Oh, go to hell." He spat, aiming at Rose's boot. He missed, jammed on his hat, and skedaddled before she could react further. The evidence of the skirmish remained on the plank, revolting.

"Well, ain't that just dandy. A Rocky Mountain canary," Rose groused. "And to think the women on Myers would see nothing amiss in that exchange at all. Well, other than the hacking."

Maude glanced at the phlegm, both sickened and insulted. "How's that?"

"A braying jackass. Good Lord, there's a lot you don't know!" She paused. "Them on Myers don't exactly get to say *no*, you know."

With that, Rose went back inside to the warmth and her newspapers.

Hoping the fluster didn't show, Maude called out again. "Fortunes read for a dollar, now don't be shy!"

It took a while to draw in a punter, leaving plenty of time to think between the pauses. Lines were getting blurred, and she needed to toughen up. *That's all,* she told herself, but was it really?

———

The Emporium's lack of customers drove Maude straight back to the Mikado, trailing for crumbs. No matter Rose's opinion on the subject. And, while she wasn't exactly welcomed with open arms, at least she was allowed in.

The madam acted off-color and heated, ready to spring. "If I was you, I'd cut to the chase and take up residence here," she jeered. "You'd solve all your problems in one fell swoop—a roof over your head, two meals a day, and money to spend. Besides, I'm down a girl. Tempted?"

Not that again, although her heart dropped to the vicinity of her stomach. "I've taken a position reading cards at Madame de Silva's Fortune Emporium."

The madam smirked, unkind. "So, you're going to

prolong the agony, then. Good old Rose. Chances are she hasn't had a man in her bed for years. How well do you know her, sugar?"

Maude braced herself. The *sugar* endearment got to her, no matter how sarcastically offered—an ache she swallowed down. "She seems honest enough." They both heard the hitch. "Don't you like her?"

Julia tapped her fingers, rings glinting and her acting superior. "How I feel about Rose de Silva is none of your concern. Her business can't be going all that well, for here you stand."

But the madam was annoyed at events beyond her mere presence. "I've got a riddle for you," Julia began, testy. "What do you do when someone is lying to your face and you can't prove it? Or if that same person refuses advice, how do you convince them it is in their best goddamned interest to listen to common goddamned reason?"

The currents were uncertain and charged. "I don't try to convince people of anything," Maude said. "I just tell them what I see. The rest is up to them."

The madam hissed and tossed her head. "I'll tell you one thing, Fortune-Teller. Sometimes people don't want to be told what is clear as day, and their jackassedness gets pretty damned irritating."

Mercifully, the cook stuck her head through the kitchen door into the dining room. "The ice man is here and wants you to settle the account."

The madam spun on her heel. "I've got a bone to pick," Julia pronounced, jabbing her finger into the air, emerald ring glistening.

Half a minute later, her voice resonated from the kitchen, words unintelligible but tone distinct and cutting.

Three fortunes down.

Another downtrodden destiny of misplaced hopes; Maude wrapped up the threads of a hard life and a dark future into a misshapen bundle. Another habitué lurked, and the profile sure matched Lizzie's. The first girl was only halfway to standing when Lizzie swept in from the parlor, angry and flaring.

The girl took in Lizzie's expression and made herself scarce.

"I told my jake about your predictions. How you said he had a wife, and how he wouldn't keep his word." A hard splinter of a voice, intended to wound. "He didn't even bother to dispute it. He said I got notions above my place."

Lizzie sat down on the chair sideways, ready to strike or leave. Whichever notion grabbed her first. "He won't be back." Her voice flattened, although she held her chin high.

Maude detected a quiver.

"Don't take it too much to heart. Nothing he says is worth much anyhow. I guess that's what we're all expected to do. Take a man's word. Well. Every girl wants a different last name, I guess."

Lizzie leaned forward, eyes flashing and color high. "Happy?"

"No. Why would I be?" Sadness lingered, heavy. "You know you can talk to me. For free."

"And who do you talk to, Maude?" Lizzie sprang up without requiring an answer. "You really don't want to get too involved in this place. It might be catching."

And with that, the girl flounced out just as the madam steered back in, silk and ruffles rustling, heels clicking, emphatic. "Time to clear out unless you've decided to take me up on *my* offer. Hooking's bound to pay better than that pile of coins."

True, the money Maude earned wasn't much to boast about. Gathering up the pieces of silver and dropping them in her purse, she remained bothered by Lizzie. "Would you care for a reading before I go—for free, of course?"

The madam's expression was one of pure calculation. "Not right now, Fortune-Teller. Let's wait for the day I need one."

Maude gathered up the cards, marking that weird prickle. The madam would have need of a fortune. It would only be a matter of time and regrettable circumstance.

PART TWO
GOLD CAMP LIFE

CHAPTER SEVENTEEN
MERCENARY HEARTS

JANUARY 1896

Maude didn't give a damn about Auld Lang Syne.

The year 1895 lay dead and buried, and the New Year loomed inauspicious by any signs she knew how to read. The weather moved in as a shroud of snow, the Fortune Emporium felt cold, and the stove wasn't throwing heat like it should. Her breath, a white vapor hanging in front of her, proved she was still alive, but the splayed-out cards on the table were nothing more than a game of ordinary solitaire. Indifferent, she flipped over the playing cards one by one, fingerless gloves unravelling around the edges. Winning or losing made no difference at all. Not when money wasn't involved.

Five feet away and two shawls deep, Rose perused outdated newspapers and hummed a flat old half tune. Every so often she marked Maude's location but offered no comment.

The clairvoyant turned over a card—the king of hearts. "I ran into that blacksmith of yours the other day."

A grunt and a half shrug followed, not as disinterested as came across on the surface.

"Barely broke his stride to give me the time of day." Maude snapped down another card.

A sharper look from Rose this time. "Normally he's got manners. What brought that up?"

"This card, that's all."

She ought to leave well enough alone. Oh, there was more to it than an abrupt encounter, but a shy, apologetic smile that, unfortunately, hit her square. Men like him would never go for the likes of her. "Wasn't exactly rude, and I'm still married. There's no avoiding that one. But he doesn't know that part, does he?"

He'd also crossed the street to avoid her. That part stung, no matter how she portrayed it.

Rose was eyeing her too close for comfort and weighing her words. "I kind of figured he'd come a-calling, but...too straitlaced, I guess."

Which, of course, left Maude twirling.

A tap on the front window snapped her out of disappointment. Lizzie hovered outside the door—face unpainted, clothes plain, proper and, most surprisingly, unremarkable. Not to mention, it wasn't a Tuesday morning.

She tapped again. Maude beckoned her inside.

The dolly shot a cautious glance over at Rose as she pushed through the door and made a beeline for Maude. "There's trouble at the house. Violet ran off, and Julia's in a foul temper. She sent me for you, fines or no fines."

That was all Rose needed to hear for the disapproval to flow. "How do you two know each other?"

Of course, the gypsy already knew that answer.

A stab of unspoken accusation hit Maude, a caution far more important than Rose's moralizing. "I didn't do a reading on that girl, so what does Julia want *me* for? I can't change what's already happened."

Rose continued a hostile stance, elbows locked and palms flat against the counter. All the while staring the dolly down. Making damned certain she knew her place wasn't in the Emporium. "Well? I asked how you two know each other."

"The Mikado," Maude replied.

A bitter laugh from Rose summed it all up.

For her part, Lizzie could have cared less, not bothering to even look over at Rose. "I don't know what Julia's thinking. Now, are you coming or not?"

Serving at the underworld's beck and call couldn't be considered good by any stretch. Then again, there were no customers that morning either.

Lizzie remained in the center of the plank floor, waiting.

Maude went for her coat.

Rose horned in, voice edged on the rough. "Seems you lot are all getting mighty chummy. I'll remind you that we have a business to run here as well."

The dolly pointedly took in the contents of the Emporium and spat them back out with a toss of her head. She exited straight out the door, leaving it wide open for the cold air to come rushing in.

"Shut the damn door!" Rose hollered.

The girl flipped her off before stalking away.

"Did you see that?" Rose spluttered.

Maude grappled with her coat, struggling to pull it on. "I'll hurry." She rushed out to follow the girl, catching up to within a half a step behind her.

"There's a stop I want to make first." Lizzie's voice caught on the wind, tough and unyielding.

The girl wasn't as kind as the first day they met—no

denying it. There came across a pronounced hardness of bearing that even her heavy coat couldn't hide.

––––––––––

Snow caught in the ruts and gathered in drifts along the ass-end of Myers Avenue. The dolly made for the rear door of a flea-bitten saloon of no particular quality, other than low. When her knock remained unanswered, she outright pounded. "Come on, Mary, open up in there!"

Maude stuck her hands deep inside her pockets, fingers worrying the shredded lining. "Why can't we go through the front?"

Lizzie scowled at her. "Good lord, Maude. Women can't just go marching into saloons unless your name is Rose de Silva. This one serves women out the back." Another hard wallop, and the door cracked open.

"We're here for whiskey, if you think you can manage," Lizzie groused, none too refined.

"What, the Mikado run dry?" The woman gave no indication she would open the door any wider.

"Look, there's been trouble, and it's too damn cold to stand out here arguing. Are you going to serve us or not?"

The woman's interest travelled over to Maude. "I reckon."

Lizzie pushed on in, and the proprietress didn't offer up much resistance. Still, the dislike flowed strong and nasty between the two. Like two cats circling, hissing and spitting. Nevertheless, there the three of them stood. Confined in the space of a rigged-up sink room.

The dolly cracked first. "Violet's gone. Does that make you feel better?"

"No reason it should." The woman grabbed a brown bottle from a shelf and held it up for approval.

Lizzie's features eased ever so slightly, jerking her head so the woman would pour.

In nothing flat, two measures waited before them. The woman still glared at Lizzie, wary and put out. "Gone how?"

"No one's saying." She slapped the silver down on the rickety table propped against the wall. The woman handed the first glass to Maude with hard intent. A slight hesitation before she let the girl grab hers.

Lizzie snatched the drink and tossed it back in one go. She thrust out the empty glass. "Another."

Maude held on to hers, annoyed. Two bits could have purchased a decent breakfast. The saloon-woman poured out the second measure and gathered up the coins, pocketing them as she eyed the bottle level. "Do I need to draw a mark on that?"

"No, and it's not like I won't be back, or you don't know where to find me."

The woman stared down her nose. "Don't make me chase you for it."

With a slight acknowledgement in Maude's direction, the woman returned into the main part of the saloon. Male voices were rumbling and swelling, bellowing for service.

"Shit," Lizzie swore under her breath, waiting until the woman was out of range before offering anything of the slightest value. "Violet used to come here when she could. She had a plowboy who acted sweet on her." Bothered shadows lingered around her eyes. "Found anyone yourself?"

"Haven't had time for looking," Maude lied.

Lizzie poured herself a third shot and held up the bottle in an invitation. Maude declined, growing impatient.

"Don't you worry," the girl grumbled. "Under normal circumstances, I don't drink in the morning."

"If you say so," Maude replied.

Refusing to be chastened, the dolly brightened. "Listen to this. A punter's taken a shine to me. We'll see if he turns out. Says his wife doesn't understand him, but it might be so."

Doubtful that anything ever turned out well in their world, Maude held back on any encouragement. Besides, that would only delay their departure from the sink room. "If Julia thinks I'll find the girl the same as I found her ring, it won't happen."

The dolly shrugged. "Whatever you do, charge her the going rate."

That was plumb impossible. Annoyed, Maude sampled the whiskey against her better instincts. Admittedly, it warmed nice going down. "I owe Julia a reading, so there's not much collecting to do."

"Are you sure of that? Whatever the case, Julia *always* manages to collect. That's how she runs her business. Nothing is for free with her. Ever."

Morning poised to career downhill, Maude wanted it over and done. "Finish up. We'd best be going."

Lizzie fidgeted with her purse, cast down and faltering. "You didn't see me dying this year, did you?"

The harsh whisper of inevitability.

"Nothing that certain..." Maude answered, now taking her time. "But the warning still stands. *Change* how you do things. Drinking in the morning isn't anything to boast about, and neither is the rest of it. If you don't change, the possibility of death is right there, staring over your shoulder. Want me to take another look?"

The dolly tucked her hands beneath the table.

"No need. Life at the Mikado ain't what it's cracked up

to be, no matter what Julia says. These days, she don't much believe it herself."

The twanging chord of truth only Maude could hear. "Then I'll tell you again. Stay away from the drink and the drugs for the chance at something better."

"And I told you, I don't take the dope." The same old tired lie, and Lizzie colored. "You'd drink, too, if you led the life I lead."

Need won out, and Lizzie's hand darted out from underneath the table to grab her glass and down it. She eyed Maude's, abandoned on the table.

"No need to let good liquor go to waste," she claimed, snatching up the other glass as well and offering a mock toast.

Maude held her tongue at the defiance.

Lizzie was boldened by the whiskey. "And don't bring up this stop, whatever you do. If Julia asks what kept us, explain you were in the middle of a fortune that couldn't be rushed. *We came just as soon as we could.*"

"And if our breath smells like whiskey?"

"Well, if you don't kiss her, she'll never know," Lizzie snarled.

CHAPTER EIGHTEEN
SHE STOOPS TO CONQUER

"Have a drink on the house. Today's sure a hell of a banger."

Her hand already halfway toward the booze, Julia's jewels sparkled, and her skirt and petticoats rustled along, as expensive as ever. The offered drink wasn't exactly a polite request or an invitation. It was a command, and Maude treated it as such.

"I'm taking you up on that fortune you offered the other day. Perhaps you've already seen that written in the stars, or whatever it is that you do. Today I want to know what the hell's coming next. No use pussyfooting around."

She set the two glasses of liquor down on the table, rings flashing and clean fingernails shaped into ovals. A slight tremble telegraphed unsteady nerves.

Maude pulled out a deck of cards from her purse, noting her own jagged and not-quite-clean nails in comparison. "I can do that, but I've got to warn you. People in this town don't seem to take to straight fortunes much."

The madam could have cared less.

"Don't you usually read palms?" The question came out as sharp and cutting as a blade.

"Cards reveal more with situations. Of course, the choice is yours."

Lizzie lingered in the parlor, eavesdropping. The madam's irritation flared. "This is a *private* consultation, which means you are not welcome. Now, get out."

The girl flashed a nasty look at the madam before moving away, an expression Maude did her best to ignore.

"This here is a *situation*. So, read me the cards." The madam shot one final dagger-glare into the girl's retreating backside.

Maude fanned out the cards, flashing the undersides before flipping them back over. Just another trick she'd learned along the way, but that didn't put her in league with the card sharps and gamblers. In her mind, at least.

"Gather the cards and shuffle. Cut them into piles when you're ready."

Quashing any fancy pretenses with a couple of abrupt chops, Julia held her gaze dead level. But she didn't hand the cards over, nor did she place them in piles. She sat, holding them. Protective. "What are the chances of getting leftovers from someone else's fortune?"

An interesting question that showed an unexpected level of insight. "Never heard of such doings, but anything is possible. If you're worried, rub the cards on your skirt and give them a thump. That should knock anything remaining clear out."

The madam gave them an emphatic whack.

The ripple of surprise before she had the chance to mask it. "Cut the deck into however many piles you want," Maude murmured.

Five piles. The trait of a complex person.

Gathering the stacks back together, Maude fanned them out again. "Now, choose whichever card you like."

Julia selected one after a fair bit of deliberation...and clasped it to her chest. Once again, the madam showed no inclination to release the hostage card.

"I'll need to see that," Maude prompted, thinking how the madam proved far more interesting than the cards could ever do.

Julia hesitated long and hard before thrusting out what she guarded, stiff armed.

The five of hearts. No wonder. Confirmation that Julia herself had played no small part in the unfolding drama.

Maude thought about it, then thought about it a bit more. "There's a fair amount of jealousy and ill will from people around you, a portion of which originates from inside this very house." There seemed no sense in not hitting the nail square on the head.

To her credit, the woman didn't flinch. "Tell me something I don't know."

Maude dealt out a facedown, nine-card spread. "Each set of three represents the past, the present and the future."

The madam stared at the backs of the cards, trying to bend the fortune to her will.

Another first.

Maude waited, allowing the tension to build.

She flipped over the first set.

The jack of diamonds, the joker, and the ace of spades.

Impressions gathered and competed, forcing Maude to sit with them for a moment. "You've got an odd spread of intrigue, with an upturn at the end. A person who arouses discontent is jealous, and that jealousy could lead to misfortune. Others will be affected by subsequent events. The joker shows new developments and the taking of a risk. The ace of spades represents conflict, obsession, and death."

Julia drained her glass. "I take it Lizzie filled you in?"

"Only that a girl named Violet is gone, but no particulars. Do *you* want to tell me what happened?"

Large glittering rings, the jewels hard and cold as the madam flexed her fingers, dismissive. "She left, that's all. Now I want to know how things are going to fall out."

Reputations would indeed be falling. She nodded at the emerald ring. "You know I can't find her like your ring that first day, don't you?"

Julia smirked. "If you could, I'd use that talent for something more important than finding an absconding whore."

Maude turned over the next set of cards: *the eight of diamonds, the seven of clubs, and the five of spades.* "As for the present: a change in a business situation is on the horizon, and a warning of approaching trouble is there. A man close to you is up against greater forces that he can't control, but *you* hold some sway in the particulars."

"Some sway" was an understatement.

Julia suppressed a feline smile. "Keep reading."

Maude turned over the last set of cards. "The *king of spades* shows a dark-haired man who's authoritative. The *queen of diamonds* shows a fair-haired woman who's a gossip. Finally, the *ace of diamonds* signals a change in fortune. Money, by the feel of it."

But there were secrets in those cards and the order in which they were dealt. Maude set out three more cards, trying to marshal the forces gathering.

The two of clubs, the three and the nine of hearts.

Maude took a sip of the whiskey, stalling. "Disappointments come from opposition and emotions. Finally, things get better after the initial difficulty passes. Does that mean anything to you?"

The madam stared at the cards with hungry eyes. "Maybe."

She hated when punters played cagey. "There's also a

definite warning in the cards. Something to do about sickness."

Julia's head snapped back, an obvious secret beyond Maude's reach. A secret that the madam guarded tight and close.

"More to the point," Maude said, "I can feel the deception coming." An edgy feeling cloaked over her. "No one is trying to blackmail you, are they, Julia?"

The madam lifted her head, her eyes widening before she belted out what could only be called a whore's laugh. "Only emotionally, darlin', only emotionally." Another low chuckle. To make matters even worse, she *winked* at Maude.

Maude resorted to a sham tactic that usually worked just fine, sitting back and pretending to be drained from the effort.

The madam shook her head. "You had me going there a couple of times."

It was now or never. Maude leaned forward to offer an intimacy of sort. "Can I ask you a question, a confidence kept between the two of us?"

"Think we're on terms now, do you?" Breathing a shade on the shallow side, the madam reclined back in her chair, her disinterest false.

"I have a business proposition for you."

Julia scoffed. "You've already turned down what I'm interested in."

"You must hear a fair amount of mining talk in here."

"What of it?"

Poised to sink right down into the muck alongside the rest of them, Maude didn't pull back. "I need to know what's being said. In exchange, I'll help you by watching for warnings and reading signs."

Hands upon the armrests, Julia sat like a queen upon her throne. "Who said I need help? Today is a bolt out of the blue. As far as rumors circulating, most of the mining talk is bluff and bluster. Nothing more."

Maude tried again, purring persuasive. "But, on occasion, those fragments might hold a particular value, a fragment of truth. Maybe I could string together the signs in a more...beneficial way. For the both of us."

"And here I figured you were all sweetness and light. My business is based on discretion. Relaying information poses considerable risk to the house's reputation, and therefore my bottom line."

Maude offered a close-lipped smile and a calculation. "The odd comment dropped in passing shouldn't cause much harm. Why, I've heard such talk fills the saloons! What if I give you my word that no one would trace anything back to you here?"

The madam sat appraising, both Maude and her words. "I, for one, don't know what your word is worth. *Have* you been able to find gold?"

"Not yet."

Julia tossed her head, accustomed to such maneuverings.

Maude waited her out.

The madam flicked her fingers. "As a gesture of goodwill, I'll tell you no one's gone shooting their mouth off about the next big strike. If anything, it's been the reverse."

"The reverse?"

Julia turned beady. "A large mine *might* be failing. Hardly the type of thing men boast about, but there you have it."

An edge or a toehold, onto something that mattered. Maude offered her hand. "Do we have an understanding?"

The madam spat in her palm to seal the agreement.

Maude spat in return; the friction of the flesh and saliva left no doubt on the matter.

"I'd say that calls for another drink, Fortune-Teller. You might as well start calling me Julia. Since this is a 'show me yours and I'll show you mine' meeting, I have a question. What's your plan if you don't land a winner? Obviously, things haven't gone without a hitch, for here you sit."

The ticking of the clock got a bit louder, and Maude's heart thudded a bit harder. "There's no other plan. This has to work...but the coming together is a bit harder than expected."

The madam choked back a bitter laugh. "And here we are, two women sitting in a whorehouse and making our own choices. It don't always feel so good, does it?"

It certainly didn't. Not when phrased like that.

———

"Well?"

Rose's tone cut as sharp as a broken bottle. Occupied shuffling through a drawer, she consulted the scrap of paper in her hand, satisfied. "If that's your version of 'I-won't-be-long,' you're like a fair number of men I've known."

"A girl they called Violet is gone."

Rose waved that tidbit off. "So? Good for her, I'd say. Now, out with it. How did you get mixed up with the likes of *them*?"

"I met Lizzie my first day, and she helped me find a boardinghouse. I've read fortunes a couple of times at the Mikado like I've told you. Anyhow, this time, Julia wanted a reading for herself. That's a first."

Unimpressed and disapproving. "Now you can tell me to mind my own business, but hear me out," Rose said. "If you fly with the crows, you'll get shot with the crows. It's from the proverbs of hard knocks. Heard it before?"

"You made that up." Maude would have laughed but thought better of it.

"Maybe. But if the sporting kind hangs around here, decent women won't come in. You know for a fact that I wasn't great on fortunes before you turned up. And I'm not even going to make you crawl for it. Julia has her patch, and I have mine. She'll notice your...potential...in more ways than one. Chances are you're being played and don't even know it."

"I'm not as naïve as everyone seems to think," Maude snapped.

Rose snapped back, "Prove it, then."

"I've already turned her down. Pride doesn't pay the bills, you know." Fingering her worn skirt, she knew she got that part right.

"It's not only your reputation on the line but mine as well. And about her fancy man: I hear his business is about belly-up, not to mention he's been frequenting other establishments, if you catch my drift."

"Is he? How'd you hear that? Oh, never mind." Maude waved the notion away, but inside she cursed. "Her romance is none of my concern."

Rose considered her, expression hard. "It bloody well better be. Besides, you haven't sensed any ore. Don't forget that one very fundamental detail, as you go getting high and mighty along the wrong side. You still live on this side of the divide, and if you're going to work here, you stay on this side. I suggest you remember that detail."

"And if this doesn't pay?" Maude gestured at the contents of the Emporium, defiant and glaring.

"Then you'll know where to go, won't you?"

And so she might. But only as a very last resort.

CHAPTER NINETEEN
FALLEN WOMEN DON'T ALWAYS STAY DOWN

FEBRUARY 1896

The small of the evening should have been dead, or at least winding down to a literal crawl. God knows they'd seen it all more than once. Yet Julia heard a man's voice, low and rumbling. Individual words indistinct, the tone got her hackles up and nerves twitching. That voice was warming up to someone.

And sure as hell, it sounded like Ev.

A girl's voice lifted and answered. A muffled, hushed-up laugh that had no legitimate business purpose by her definition.

Crouching against the wall Julia held her fire—torn between stopping whatever kicked off or letting it all unfold.

Another low rumble. Another laughing response leaking out from the boot room. No one had a reason for being back in there, not when there were perfectly good bedrooms upstairs.

Not to mention there weren't any paid all-nighters that evening. That meant one thing, and one thing only.

Coiled and ready to strike, Julia grabbed that old knob and flung the door open, hard. "Well, what do we have going on in here?"

Sure enough, she caught them. Not exactly in the act, but *her* man was on the verge of kissing Florence, and on the mouth, too.

Julia had a very good idea exactly where that mouth had been.

Ev eyed her with what could only be interpreted as disgust. Still, he dropped his arm.

That disgust got to her. Deep down, there was more to it than the fact that he'd gotten caught red-handed.

"Upstairs, now!" she hissed at the hussy, who ducked for the door but not fast enough. Julia grabbed her by the arm, wrenching and hoping it hurt. "You don't want to cross me, girl. He's *mine*."

She released her clawed grip.

A flinch and a dodge in that confined space, although nowhere near as meek as Julia wanted. Still, the girl had enough sense to flee.

Everett, on the other hand, folded his arms across his chest and tried to stare her down.

A fight ensued. No doubt everyone in the house heard the ruckus because she didn't bother keeping her voice down. Didn't feel like it, in fact.

Of course, Julia prevailed. Still, something would have to be done about Ev and his wandering eye. If he didn't watch out, she just might blacken it.

Stomach for it or not, she needed to draw the line.

———

The mortician emerged from the back rooms. Images of stacked corpses rose in Julia's imagination, most unwelcome. Heaven only knew what he did to them in those same back rooms. Poor, helpless sods. Just another necessary evil in a world full of them.

Julia Robinson didn't enjoy dealing with dead bodies or the people who tended to them.

Wearing an apron, he leered at her with a hint of the grave. "Ah, good afternoon, Mrs. Robinson. I trust all is well?"

She smothered her irritation and plastered on yet another deadened smile. "Never better, Mr. Blake—unless it was summer, of course. I've come to settle the account on that girl, Ivy. You've got her safely stowed away, I presume."

"Of course. Just waiting for the ground to thaw."

He leaned against the edge of a display table, hands stuck under his armpits and his back resting against a coffin. Like his position was the most natural thing in the world.

She pulled out a wad of bills. "There's twenty dollars —the agreed amount for a marker and a decent enough coffin."

"Care for a receipt?" He folded the money over in his hand, nice and neat.

"There's no need." She turned to leave.

"No one else has gotten sick or come down with... illness...have they?"

Hand on the doorknob, she stopped, door ajar and letting colder air into the already cold room. She half turned toward him, standing in profile. "How would I know?"

He acted dead serious on the matter. "Because you would notice another one of your...kind...struck low. That's how."

Julia shut the door against the outside world and turned to face him full-on. "I told you, she wasn't one of my girls."

"I heard you the first time." He tapped the folded bills against his hand. "But this is a matter of public health. I wouldn't be doing my...duty...if I didn't alert the proper authorities should contagion emerge."

He was one shifty son of a bitch.

Julia's grip on her purse got a tad tighter. "Ivy inhabited one of the *cribs* and has never once set foot inside the Mikado. The reason why I'm handling her arrangements is that I'm keeping my word to her. Nothing more."

The mortician didn't seem inclined to back down. "You know, people aren't necessarily going to believe you in this instance. Besides, there's been talk about one of your girls as of late. Didn't you lose one recently?"

"Lose one? She wasn't a cow to be lost. *She left town.* Satisfied?"

The undertaker shook his head, stubborn and lit with the steadfast sense of advantage. "Not really. Who's to say she's not lying dead and discarded, identical to the one you had brought in? The influenza seldom strikes merely once."

She took a step closer, finger jabbing the air. "Violet has years left. The girl you've got lying dead back there was near the end of her career."

"Sickness doesn't care about careers."

Having the house get slapped with a quarantine order was the last thing she needed. The *very* last thing was to catch any spreading sickness herself.

"There is no sickness at the Mikado. Good day."

She stepped outside and shut the door behind her. Firm.

Ivy plied from the cribs, and Julia's house was clean. Nothing was spreading that she knew of, other than the usual gossip. That damn undertaker had her spooked, no two ways about it.

The manner in which he tapped those folded bills

made his intentions all too clear. She hadn't heard the last of the matter. Sure as shooting, he'd be coming back to the well, and she didn't have an easy way to fend him off.

Bastard.

———

On that unpleasant note, her mind stayed uneasy all the way back to the house. But first things first: she'd have to phone down to Denver to see if a spare girl needed a circuit.

Decent in appearance and un-burned.

Not fond of owing favors, that's what it would all come down to. She'd owe a Denver madam one hell of a favor, or she'd have to pay. That about summed it up in a nutshell. And those damn Denver flesh-traders knew what they were handling. Maybe an actual cash payment came cheaper in the long run.

Everett still ogled Red Florence; she'd caught him at it once or twice since the fight. Another fresh girl would provide that much more temptation. She'd have to make sure the battle lines were drawn, and that the girl understood. Whoever she was.

Yes, that's what she would do. She'd make sure the girl *understood*.

One problem resolved. The morgue issue wasn't so easily swept aside. But one thing stuck as certain: if she were lying on her deathbed, no one would do a damn thing to help her.

They'd all die, one way or another. That girl Ida was dead. Or Ivy. Whatever the hell she called herself, it didn't matter to anyone anymore, and that was the pity of it. Ida would still end up in the paupers' field, but she'd have a marker with a version of her name upon it.

But who would rescue *her* from an unmarked grave when the time came?

Her savior sure as hell wouldn't be one Everett Stevenson. He'd likely sell her jewelry if the opportunity came around. And that conviction chafed her pretty good.

The Mikado coming into view, Julia paused, running over the exterior with a fresh consideration and a wariness that hadn't been there before. Just another cathouse. It sure didn't stand up to the daylight as much to boast about. But did any of them? Leadville, Cripple Creek, Denver…a different name, and a different town. The game rolled out the same no matter where located.

Until it played out. When it fell over, dead.

Ev sprawled in the front room, draped over one of the divans and smoking a cigar.

"Comfortable?" Julia hoped he heard the sarcasm in her voice and took it for what it was. Midday monotony fell common in the whorehouse, and it wore against her.

Sure as hell, Ev wasn't doing anything to make the atmosphere any better. "Depends on your definition," her prize grumbled. "I'm stuck here waiting for an opportunity to appear."

"A whorehouse opportunity? You've been told to keep your hands off the wares."

"Here we go again…"

Spoiling for a fight now, figuring she'd be forgotten in a pauper's grave, it sure chapped her hide being the only one pulling. And, for the moment, Julia wanted him out of her sight. "Why don't I give you fifty dollars and you go play a couple of hands?"

Everett sat up and put his feet on the floor. "If you do, I'd say you're a peach!"

A peach with fifty dollars. Eyes narrowing, she stepped into her office. Taking care to block his view of the safe's combination.

It always did her heart good to open the safe. A few piles of money, ounces of gold in bags, and her little black book. That little black book might prove worth the rest of the contents combined if ever needed. Madams relied upon discretion. Until the point came when they didn't.

Twirling the dial, she full-on noticed him trying to see past her, trying to discover the contents and what she had.

Well, he could just drop dead.

After counting out fifty dollars, she shut the safe's door with a reassuring clink and spun the wheel.

A fraction of a second later, Ev was rushing up the stairs and taking them two at a time.

He was back before anyone had the chance to say "jimmy crack corn;" jacket on, hair combed and pomaded, smelling of cologne, Ev jogged down the stairs raring to go. These days, he sure as hell didn't bother to spruce up for her benefit.

Folding the bills over and holding them out with half a mind to make him beg.

But she didn't.

"I'll be back tonight," he said, pecking her on the cheek as if that would fool her. Still, it was a step in the right direction. Half of her wanted to believe as he bounded across the porch and down the steps into freedom beyond.

Truth was, she never knew where the money she gave him walked off to. One thing for certain, it'd be near enough gone when he returned. Of course, he would blame it on a couple of losing hands.

There was more than one way to lose at poker, but that knowledge didn't make her feel any better.

Julia listed about. When certain he wouldn't return for something forgotten, she lifted her skirts to steal up the stairs, footfall as light as possible. At the top she paused, straining to catch the slightest note out of place. Eavesdropping on nothing more than the murmurings of lethargic whores in the early afternoon hours.

She slipped into her bedroom, closing the door behind her ever so gently. Inhaling Everett's own musk of smoke, whiskey, and alcohol-based sweat.

Tired of getting the raw end of the deal.

His clothes lay scattered, pants and a shirt draped over a chair. Picking up the cast-off shirt, Julia inhaled the scent of the gambling table, mourning what had once been a sure-fired bet.

Snapping that notion in two, she flung the shirt down into a heap in the corner. And she picked up his pants. Without a second's hesitation, she thrust her hand in and rifled through the pockets.

CHAPTER TWENTY
SCATTERINGS OF COLOR
AND RICHES TO BE HAD

APRIL 1896

"I have a bad feeling," the woman announced in no uncertain terms as she stepped through the door. The spring snow cascaded down heavy and wet, catching in her hair and clothes.

"In that case, you've come to the right place." Jesting aside, Rose's lack of a familiar greeting combined with a once-over cinched it.

Maude took the hint.

She gestured across the table. "Take a seat, Miss..."

"*Mrs.*," the woman said, brushing herself off. Her emphasis made it sound like the most important distinction in the world. "*Mrs.* Arthur Harper. You can call me Millicent."

She unfastened the man's coat she wore and took a seat. Her blouse might have been threadbare but was starched near to saluting. Millicent, or *Mrs.* Harper, dabbed the melt from her face. The snowflakes trapped in her hair clarified and dripped.

"Of course. Millicent," Maude murmured as she

stretched out her hand. "Cross my palm with silver, and your future will open wide before me."

Cold fingers fumbled as the woman shook small coins from her purse—nickels and dimes. One by one, she laid them out with a studied concentration. Sixty-five cents.

"Fortunes cost a dollar," Maude prompted, voice lowered.

The woman scowled and, if anything, got louder. "What you're holding is what I've got."

Rose cleared her throat, but the woman pretended not to notice.

Maude closed her fist and gave the coins a jingle. There seemed little point in quibbling about rates when no other customers were in sight.

"Well, since we are quiet at the moment, and if you'll *tell* folks if you're satisfied with your fortune, we can make an exception in this case. How can I help you?"

The woman didn't waver. "I want to know if I should sell my husband's claim or not."

The small hairs on the back of Maude's neck tingled. There it was. Her opportunity.

She had to be careful. Incredibly careful. "Put your hand in mine, palm up so I can see."

What she saw was a tangled mess.

A deep breath to steady herself. She couldn't afford to get this fortune wrong. Eyes closed, Maude pressed down on the woman's palm using both thumbs, concentrating on the blood coursing through the veins beneath the woman's skin. Strong blood, strong heart.

None of which was enough to go on.

Maude released the woman's hand and struggled. "Make a tight fist and bang it once on the table, *hard*."

Mrs. Harper walloped the tabletop at full force.

"Now, open your hand," Maude commanded.

The lines were deeper, more distinct. A jumbled tangle, and still a complicated chain of loose events.

The woman exhaled in a hiss. "You're going to make up some cock 'n bull story, ain't you?"

Forces were gathering and pressing in. "No," Maude replied, uneasy. "I don't give crooked readings."

But nothing displayed into any pattern that made good sense. And desperation could rearrange scruples at times.

Charley, show me something for her.

But the skull refused to be drawn in.

Maude sat up taller and gathered a false confidence that would have to work. "Let's try these. Shuffle the cards as long as you want, then hand them back to me."

One shuffle and two decisive chops. *Mrs.* Millicent Harper thrust out the deck without ceremony.

Maude flipped the top card over. The four of clubs landed face up on the table.

A flickering wisp of insight that faded almost as soon as it came. *Trouble in the past and the ability to deceive.*

Regardless, it was nothing she wanted to open with.

"A pronounced change is going to affect your circumstances."

A nerve in the missus's cheek twitched. "A good change, or a bad one?"

Rose hung onto the fortune as well, lips pressed together in a tight, thin line. A toss of the head that told Maude to get on with it.

Easy enough from where she stood.

Maude pointed a long index finger at the card with no real idea which way the change would go. "This is the indicator. As it's placed, it acts as a cautionary card. I'd say the meaning is to avoid blind acceptance of what others tell you—even those you trust."

Mrs. Harper snorted. "That's nothing more than common sense."

Maude's stomach tightened. She dealt out three cards above that one. She turned them over, one by one.

The nine of hearts, four of spades, and the ace of hearts surfaced. Low morals would feature, playing a significant part. But the woman's hands were red and rough from work. It didn't make sense.

"Taken together, the spread adds up to a complicated chain of events. Deception is in those cards; the interpretation, as it's laid out, reads uncertain." Maude pushed back from the table. "That's as much as I can do."

The woman's eyes narrowed. "But that is not enough to go on! I still don't know whether to sell or not...I work at the National in the laundry there. I wouldn't mind telling them what they could do with it..."

Tapping on the table to draw a new focus into the room, Maude tried to still the currents swirling. "More background might help. There's precious little to base an impression on. But as to whether or not you should sell, deep down your mind is already made up and set upon a course. I think we both know that much."

Exhaling, the woman's voice emerged flat and bitter. "My husband's a drunk, you see." She searched Maude's face.

A twist in her stomach. No, Maude hadn't seen.

"That means a lot falls to me. He's had this claim for a while and hasn't done jack squat because he hasn't the gumption. He takes up day shifts at other mines. *When* he can manage."

The flash of a consideration half hidden.

Mrs. Harper leaned forward. "A sharper came by when Arthur was out. Maybe I shouldn't have let him in, but he offered one hundred dollars for the deed." She sat back with a justified nod.

"Tell me about him."

The woman shifted in her seat, deciding whether to withhold a particular. "I ain't never seen him before, but he looked like money. The way he said he 'knew' about Arthur usually means the drinking. I only came here today because I wanted to hear how things would turn out. But you haven't told me that at all."

Clutching at straws, Maude still decided upon caution. "If you're asking me if you're going to become rich, I don't see that in the lines. None of which means you can't sell the claim. Doesn't a hundred dollars seem inexpensive? For a mine, I mean."

The woman huffed. "I don't know about you, but that's a fair amount of money where we're concerned."

Tight and constricted across the shoulders and chest, Maude tried again. "I'm not saying that it isn't, but what if it's more valuable than that? Do you have any of that ore? It would help if I could feel it."

"Yeah," she half laughed, shifting sideways in her chair. "I've got sacks full of rocks and not much else. But I don't know that I feel like lugging them across town for no particular reason."

"It wouldn't be for *no reason*. That's how I sense ore, by touch."

"And then what? You tell me they might be good, but you need another dollar?"

Rose piped up at that. "You're the one that came in here for help, and Maude there's trying to give it to you. What's the problem—you grown partial to them rocks?"

The woman scrunched up her nose. "No. It just don't seem sensible to go scattering samples around."

"That's not what I'm suggesting," Maude replied, measured and calm. "If they *feel* promising, we could take them to an assay. That way you'd know exactly what you have."

The woman waved away the suggestion. "All I wanted to know was if this would work out. I want a glimpse into the *future*. Aren't you supposed to give warnings or such? All I want to know is if you see events going to the bad." The woman's eyes burned.

Maude held her voice steady. "I can't tell. All I'm confident of, is that whatever is about to kick off is a strange sequence of events."

The woman's manner remained hackled. "By and large, Arthur hits jackpot ground."

"And?" Maude prompted.

The woman did a double take.

"Maude's recently arrived from Massachusetts," Rose deadpanned. "She don't know what 'jackpot' means out here."

"I know firings cost five dollars," Maude snapped.

"Well, I ain't got it," the woman shot back. "Not to mention, I never planned on using an assay in the first place."

Maude drifted into a corner as feelings ran high all around. "There's nothing more I can do for you, without a sample."

The woman got up, pausing at the door. "I can bring samples, but I'm not agreeing to any assay. Just another waste of good money as far as I'm concerned."

She shut the door like it ended matters, the overhead bell jangling in her wake.

———

"That was rare," Rose groused, "even beyond the fact that you didn't get paid the going rate."

"What was I supposed to do, turn her down? What do you think she has against assays?"

"The cost." Rose gave a half shrug.

"It isn't as if I like going into hock, either. How much money have you got?"

Rose straightened up, indignant. "How much money have *I* got? Not enough to be paying for other people's assays, if that's what you're alluding to."

"Who is she, other than *Mrs*. Arthur Harper?"

"How should I know? She's not exactly the clientele we're going after, but I've heard tell about her husband."

Maude's palms were itching fierce—a surefire sign of money on the horizon. "Money, Rose. In case the samples are good. It's the only way to tell, beyond a doubt, whether I can sense ore or not. I've had just the one other shot at it, and the telluride was too small to fire."

Rose fetched the strongbox, coins rasping as she thunked it down on the counter. Making a show of it, she removed one silver dollar and tallied the remaining coins.

"Telluride, huh? Three dollars and seventy cents. That's it. And you want to blow it on a stranger's assay. I don't like it. Not one bit."

"Like I said," Maude tried again, voice coming out tight, and a bit harder than planned. "We'll only need to borrow if the ore feels promising. But that's not even enough to get it fired."

Rose strode up to the window, tapping the glass in an absent way while she calculated. "We've got to bring in more punters—the paying kind. And who's to say that she'll even repay us?"

"If the ore's good, there's got to be money to be made." Maude joined her at the window, surveying the kingdom of the rutted street beyond. Snow caught kept on falling. "How long will this go on?" Maude asked, searching the sky.

"As long as it wants to. Springtime in the Rockies." Rose folded her arms across her chest. "Nothing is ever straightforward in mining. You should know that by now."

"Well, what about her husband? Is his character considered good?"

Rose tossed her head. "For a drunkard? Sure. He's outstanding."

CHAPTER TWENTY-ONE
NOTHING MORE THAN SACKS OF ROCK

The following day, Mrs. Millicent Harper returned lugging a sack of ore, expression resigned and put out at the effort.

"You asked." She dropped it onto the wooden floor—a tumble of striking rocks, a barely discernable deep metallic ping. But the *ping* was most definitely there.

"Let's see what you've got." Maude crouched down, fighting with the twine tied too tight. Coarse and pricking sharp where fibers stuck out, she picked at the damn knot until it loosened. Then she plunged her hand in the sack and pulled out the first rock she felt. Lifting it for consideration and studying it from all angles. She sensed...nothing.

"No..." Discarding it on the floor, she tried another.

And a third. Nothing. Mrs. Millicent Harper shuffled.

About to give up, Maude stuck her hand in one final time and felt around.

"This," she exclaimed, holding up the source. "This one's got a spark."

Rose came over to stand by the ore samples, peering

down at them. "Well, if the first three don't feel good, that prospect hole must not be all that great."

Mrs. Harper shrugged and blinked a couple of times. "Maybe I got the bags mixed up. The bottom busts out at times, and it's hard to say. I can't leave them lying around on the floor, so I chuck them in along with the others. They're all samples from the claim. No rhyme or reason. Just rocks."

"Well," Rose drawled, "wouldn't they all be coming from the same place?"

A shifty glace. "I reckon they would."

Maude tapped the one with the spark. "Well. To the assay we shall go."

"And, like I said. I don't have the money for that. Look, I'm thinking to sell the claim and hope for the best. One hundred dollars makes all the difference."

Seeing as how Maude wanted proof of her abilities, one way or the other, that notion didn't suit at all. She pressed ahead. "Listen, if we front you the money for the assay, will you pay us back? You could pay us out of the selling price."

"I don't know. That would leave me only ninety-five dollars."

"In the worst case," Maude countered. "If the results come back good, you'll have documentation and can ask a far greater price."

A new, sharper gleam. "Phrased that way, I suppose so..."

Rose eyed her. "Sounds like a five-dollar gamble to me. 'Course, there's nothing to say you can't sell it on sharper anyhow. It's always been a 'buyer beware' business, and who's to say what's further in."

Mrs. Harper rubbed her chin, eyes calculating. "You're right. I'll pay you. Once I have some money."

"Yeah," Rose grumbled. "And whatever you do, don't

tell anyone anything about this arrangement. I sure as hell don't want word to get out that we're fronting people money."

The woman's shrewd smile wasn't at all pleasing. Nor was it intended to be. "And who would I tell?"

"I don't know," Rose snapped. "And that's part of the problem."

"It will all work out," Maude ventured, not particularly caring about the tussle. "Before long, we'll have our answer. And that's all we need."

———

Dapper Sam Evans bristled behind the assay's wooden counter, poking the scarred worktop with an emphatic finger. The recipient of the gesture stood positioned across from him, equally hostile.

Heated words flung about in rapid succession.

Just inside the door the women hesitated, lugging the burlap sack between them. They let it thud onto the floor for effect, stopping the argument. For the briefest of seconds. The two men, distracted momentarily by their arrival, locked into each other again.

"This gentleman doesn't agree with his contents," Sam announced, as if the two women didn't have eyes in their heads or a brain between them. Trying to draw in sympathy.

"That's because there's something wrong with the way you did it," the man snapped. "I *know* the content is higher. I've been around long enough to know a thing or two when I feel it. Here!" He thrust a rock into Maude's hand. "Notice the weight?"

That same radiating spark and disquieting tingle.

Sam's voice rose exasperated, his posture taut like a bare-knuckle boxer's. "As I've told you, it's the content..."

The man snatched the rock out of Maude's hand to wave it in front of Sam's face. Close enough to smash in his nose, the thought clearly in mind. "And this ore signals *gold*. You'd know that if you're any kind of assayer at all!"

A vein in Sam's temple throbbed, but he didn't reply, nor did he step back.

One final, nasty sneer, and the customer stomped out, taking his ore and slamming the door behind him.

"Go to hell," Sam muttered under his breath.

Maude untied *Mrs.* Harper's sack and grabbed a rock. It didn't feel the same, but there were similarities.

Sam started up without apology. "...don't realize that everything's not gold... It's human nature but sure as hell gets on my nerves. If anything was going on, it would fall along the lines of inflating the results, not giving out the honest truth. My reputation's in my name..."

He'd been caught red-handed, that much felt certain. Yet Maude offered a troubled smile, hoping to come across like she cared. "What *is* he accusing you of, exactly?"

"Nothing that would stand up in a court of law, that's for damn sure. Pardon my French. But he's got iron ore and a low gold count. I'm not even saying there's not gold further in, but his samples sure don't show it." He claimed the women's burlap sack, distracted. "If you're going to be a *lady* prospector, you're going to have to be on the lookout. People will try to rob you blind. You two here to run samples?"

"Well, about that. We'll need you to extend us a small amount of credit for the firing."

His expression straightaway turned. "This ain't a bank or a mercantile. We don't extend credit unless you're a large mine, and half the time not even then."

"Couldn't you *please* make an exception in our case?" Maude batted her eyelashes a couple of extra times. He didn't yield, so she stuck out her chest instead.

Met with stony silence, she tried a different tactic. "The man who left wasn't any too pleased, you know. More than likely, he'll go around casting aspersions about how he got cheated. *By you.*"

Frowning, Sam drew himself up taller. He strutted out from behind the counter and hefted up the sack. In fact, acting as if he were doing them one hell of a favor. "What are you up to anyhow—asking all the women in town if they got any loose ore lying around?"

"No. I took a job at Madame de Silva's Fortune Emporium. And I'm telling you, this ore feels good."

Turning to *Mrs.* Harper for confirmation. The woman flicked her head in agreement, but that was as far as it went.

Halfway gobsmacked, Sam spluttered. "That sure is a first."

"I'm a fortune-teller. The point is that I may have other customers for you in the near future."

His eyes glinted like a pair of stolen dimes. "Five dollars will get you the results in four days."

Maude shifted her weight, digging in her position. "Three dollars now, and two on credit. Come on, Sam! You'll need someone on your side."

He hesitated. Taking advantage of that lull, Maude slapped down the assembled three dollars on the counter, coins dull from use and time. The assayer's hand dashed out and gathered them up in nothing flat, his shirt cuffs frayed along the edges.

"Oh, never let it be said that I turned away a pair of ladies," he grumbled.

Mrs. Harper piped up. "I'm not sure I have four days to wait."

He shrugged. "Take it or leave it. There're other samples ahead of yours. Ones that are paying the going price."

"Take it, I guess," Millicent replied with a half-shouldered shrug.

Maude received Sam's wink and smirk in return.

A wink and a smirk designed to make her feel low, but she'd take it. She had to.

CHAPTER TWENTY-TWO
HARD ROCK MINING

The Scavenger mine stood the same as any number of such operations—tailings spilling down the mountainside and no different from a dozen other workings. The crusher mills reverberated throughout the valley the same as always; the local newspapers continued to crow, bullish about the riches from Battle Mountain's holy ground. But the deep, extracting operations concealed a secret: a secret thrown out with the pulverized scrap. Nothing more than a single, solitary rock balancing atop a slag heap. All it took was one careless step, a momentary lapse. That dislodged fragment—careening downwards and picking up speed—collected other rocks and debris, until that one, falling piece became a landslide. An avalanche of discarded ore, annihilating anything and everything in its path.

Such accidents not only maimed, they killed.

No such devastation was anticipated on that day, but, then again, disasters seldom carried warnings. Everything appeared as it should, humming along with the natural flow of progress and the illusion of prosperity. No one, other than a very select few, suspected the Scavenger might be heading into decline. In fact, the entire operation teetered atop a precipice, yet the drone of machinery clanked along, oblivious as to whether the ore priced ten dollars per ton or a hundred. The compound crushers stamped an industrial percussion. A siren's song that mesmerized men and lured them either to fortune or doom. Investors, bankers, merchants, and entire towns might all end up in a slag heap at the bottom, when the choking dust settled.

All in the name of the yellow witch of gold.

Everett didn't waste time dawdling in the engine rooms for the simple fact there was nothing to be gained by doing so. Impressive machinery admirable in passing, it remained just another means to an end. Eyes trained upon the superintendent's office—through that door he knew his livelihood hung in the balance.

So, in he went.

The very man sat, all but barricaded, behind his desk shrouded in maps stacked half an inch deep. Unfurled documents lay before him, edges ruffled and curled from continual use.

"Looks like you're studying a hole in those drawings, Jim."

Skin the ashen hue of someone seldom exposed to the sun, the superintendent did not appear fighting fit. Probably overworked and underpaid as well, but that wasn't Ev's concern.

The man betrayed no hint of surprise but rather resignation. "Everett Stevenson. I figured you'd be by sooner or later. The Denver crowd send you?"

"Not yet." No invitation extended, Ev grabbed the arm of a nearby chair and dragged it right up to the desk. "Not as long as the dividends keep coming. Had to take a loan out to make that last distribution. Nothing more than borrowing from Peter to pay Paul—a hell of a way to run things."

The superintendent spat into a spittoon poised near the leg of his desk. "The content is slipping to the point where it's almost visible to the untrained eye. Take a gander at the ore carts for yourself if you have doubts on the matter. We're down around sixty dollars per ton, and you know what that means."

Opening a desk drawer, he pulled out a worn, green production ledger.

Everett took the tome, promptly abandoning it upon his lap. Like the superintendent, his attention was drawn to the maps on the desk: crisscrossed networks of various drifts and shafts that honeycombed the mountain's interior.

"While you're still extracting from the primary vein, sink one or two exploratory shafts. Maybe we'll luck out. There's got to be color left."

"What do you think I've been doing, sitting on my hands? The investors' expectations be damned; the loss of employment is what's got me bothered. To complicate matters, the miners are bellyaching as well, and now is not the time for it."

"*My* job's on the line," Ev grumbled. "To hell with them. What do the miners want anyhow?"

"And I'll probably be shown the door before you." Jim's clear gray eyes didn't waver or hold much regard. "Miners want more pay and a shorter workday, same as always. Knowing how this tale is about to unwind, do you care to offer specific direction?"

Everett splayed his fingers wide. "Tell the men to keep their heads down and keep tunneling: what'd you think? As far as production, keep it up as long as you can. Denver'll sure as hell tell you when to stop, if it comes to that."

"Or the miners will." Weary, he offered Everett a cigar from a box.

Making a show of choosing one and clipping off the tip, Ev concentrated as he drew from the proffered flame. "The investors'll bleed it dry. I don't want to be the one to break out the bad news, but I'll have to lay the groundwork. Sooner or later they'll notice the falling production. Right now, they are convinced, *to a man,* a simple spate of mechanical troubles and equipment failures is to blame."

The superintendent clenched the cigar between his teeth. "Operations were reduced a couple of days. Nothing more. While that didn't help, the equipment is not the root cause, as we both well know. The vein is petering out."

Everett puffed a smoke ring and studied its disintegrating form. "You keep drilling, and I'll aim for a new prospect before this one flops over, dead all the way. Heard any scuttlebutt worth pursuing?"

Rubbing his knuckles across beard stubble, the boss considered the question. "Nothing too interesting, other than a rip named Harper down in Cripple. He's been bragging pretty loud, but he's a lousy drunk and can't be trusted."

"New to town?" Everett leaned back in his chair, squinting in the forming blue haze.

"Nope. He's a sourdough but doesn't appear to be paying his bar credits if you take my meaning."

A wry smile. "And here all this time, I thought you didn't frequent saloons."

The chill of a gray-eyed stare that didn't waver. "I don't. There are enough fellows on the payroll that do— and, of course, word gets about."

The two men sized up the other's qualities. Personal habits notwithstanding, deep down they were more or less on the same side. For the time being.

"I'll try to draw a line on him, one way or another."

"Couldn't hurt. As I said, Harper's a drunk and full of hot air, but he's been around long enough to know what he's looking at. Provided, that is, he's sober enough at the time to see straight. The strange part is that no one, and I do mean no one, seems to know exactly where his claim is. It's got to be one of the best kept secrets in the district."

"There will be no pay rise for the miners."

The superintendent shook his head, weary. "Didn't expect there would be. We can't break ranks with the other mining concerns, anyhow."

"Not unless we want to get blackballed. Besides, that would eat into Denver's profits."

A flicker of distaste and doubt. "Which hotel are you staying at if I need to get word to you?"

"The Mikado." The name and all the associated implications tripped off his tongue.

"It's like that, is it?"

Everett puffed up, his chest expanding a couple of inches. "Coming down here to Cripple's my chance to cut loose. I tell you, I live a different life up in Denver. Hell, I'm a respectable family man there."

With a pronounced hardening of aspect, the superintendent turned as unyielding as a lump of solid granite.

Everett didn't care in the least. In fact, the disapproval made him proud.

———

The Mikado was building up steam when Everett rolled back into town, halfway toward discouraged. But Cripple Creek in the nighttime counted as fine a place as any on earth to unwind; it was a jaded man who didn't feel livelier at the prospect. Lights blazed from windows that offered intentional and tantalizing glimpses into another world. Bare arms and stockinged legs. Forced laughter tangled with piano music that tore through the night wind like a rusted razor. Whores' laughter had a penetrating, unpleasant quality to it that got the blood pumping, boy howdy. If only his wife would laugh like that on occasion...

He cast her from his mind. The last thing any man out for a good time needed was a reminder of his wife, Lord help us all.

The same as any other punter, he knocked on the Mikado's locked door. The thrill of the chase. Once the booze grabbed hold, the Mikado turned into a downright paradise.

The faint snap of the door unlocking promised a treasure chest of earthly delights. Music and lurid goings-on spilled on out as the door opened wide.

"Looking for a good time, sugar?" Red Florence purred, all come-on and come-hither. She knew what he was and didn't hold it against him. Not even the very specific fact that he was deemed Julia's *man*.

"Always," he replied as she stepped aside. She eyed him up and down in a positively indecent way.

Wishing he could have a good time with her, he passed by a bit closer than necessary, arm brushing against her breasts. Purely by accident, of course.

Enveloped into a flurry of female flattery that all successful whorehouses supplied—contrived and up for grabs—he stood a bit taller and more masculine, enjoying the special status Julia afforded. Conveniently forgetting who controlled the house in name and deed—and it wasn't him.

The professor hit a glaring wrong note on the piano. No one else even missed a beat. Everett pushed his way through the assembled bodies halfway through the front room when the madam veered toward him. His paradise began to tarnish.

"You might want to keep tabs on the company you invited, Ev. He's put a sizeable dent in that whiskey bottle in front of him. Whiskey loosens tongues, and men become careless. I'll tell *you* that for free, but things go missing, and the girls aren't saints."

"I thought you kept the hook-and-ladder business under control."

"And so I do! But you must understand," she glinted sharp and practiced, "that, when a fellow gets drunk, he tends to misplace items like watches and wallets. You know, *things of value*. And who's to say where they actually went astray? *Not* here. Let me assure you."

She belted out a startling, raucous laugh without the slightest provocation. Their conversation didn't warrant such a response. Maybe she wanted to get the ball rolling, acting like they were all happier than hell. Whatever the case, Ev could have sworn the music picked up tempo. Voices rose in response.

"He's in through there and is set up with the middling stuff."

Ev evaded Julia's eyes.

There indeed in the dining room sat Sam Evans, cigar clenched between his teeth, a half-empty bottle and a full glass of whiskey in front of him. A whore hovered over his left shoulder, ready to seat herself on his lap at the slightest encouragement.

"Later, darling," Sam said, catching sight of Everett. He started to rise.

"Don't get up on my account." Everett turned to one of the girls. "Fetch another glass, will you?"

He kicked out the chair nearest Sam and sat down. "The Scavenger's about played out, as suspected. I didn't bother with the figures but got the word straight from the super's mouth."

Sam's cheeks were flushed. "Never you mind that! Ore came into the office that assayed out at about one hundred dollars per ton." His words twisted, bent and strung together in unexpected places.

The girl returned, another glass in hand, and showed every sign of lingering.

"This is a private conversation," Everett told her, pouring a stiff measure.

She pouted, practiced and hardened. The uninitiated might even fall for it. Still, he marked her retreating figure, appraising the curve of her hips for hire. "Tell me more."

Sam shrugged. "Who can say where in the vein the sample was harvested—probably near the surface. But it might get richer further in." He laughed off-kilter. "Better still, it was brought in by two women, of all things. They haven't the slightest clue. One—listen to this—is a fortune-teller and a new arrival in town. Pretty, too. It's the second time she's come in for valuations; who knows what she might stumble onto next."

"A *fortune-teller*?" Everett laughed, although dead intent upon the information. "Is she any good?"

"Damned if I know, but she's young and good-looking. You don't believe in that stuff, do you, Ev?"

"Nah. Idle curiosity. Back to her samples: what's your feeling?"

Sam acted predisposed to overplaying his hand, or maybe he was just that drunk. "For stray ore coming in, it's interesting. Measuring against the big concerns, the content's worse, but not that far off. Whatever the case, those diggings are the best unknown prospect I've seen for a while. A *long* while."

"I want to get to them first. How am I going to go about that?"

Sam rubbed his jaw. "Don't know yet. I haven't given the ladies the results, so they don't know what they've got."

"Where's the claim, anyhow?" Everett leaned forward, making sure Sam understood how serious he took the matter.

The assayer shrugged, ran a finger underneath his collar, and tugged. "Don't know that part yet, either. Would have gotten that up front, but some blowhard was chewing on my ear." He raised his glass in a toast. "The fortune-teller's green enough that she might tell me straight out."

"And if she doesn't?"

Sam's eyes danced, skittery. "No matter. I'll come up with a plan. No need to borrow trouble. All you have to do is get ready to come on in and low-ball the selling price."

"What could go wrong?" Everett spoke to his glass, swirling the liquid catching the light. Taking Sam's measure over the rim. The assayer wasn't up to the task. Not in the long run. "Well, hurry it all up, will you? I haven't got time to hang around sitting on my hands."

The assayer came across as clueless. "I told them the results would take four days, and I've only used up the one."

"Speed it up. I can't wait around."

"Fine," Sam replied, attention wandering back to the circulating whores. "She's holed up at that crazy Rose's fortune parlor, or whatever the hell it's called."

Well, he wasn't made of stone either, by golly. Seeking out the lithe figure of Red Florence across the room, Ev crossed his legs and reclined back in his chair. Entangled in some jackass's embrace, her shoulder strap slipped down, and she locked into him over the jake's shoulder, eyes taunting.

He raised his glass in a salute. Then froze.

Julia.

The temperature of his blood plummeted. Standing a few feet away, she damned sure caught his actions and made her thoughts known without even saying a word.

He forced his mouth into either a smile or grimace; he couldn't tell which, but it would have to do.

The madam stood there for a long, hard moment with those narrow pig eyes that missed very little.

He turned his attention back to his guest because he sure as hell didn't want to get into it with Julia at the moment. He hadn't had enough to drink for that.

The assayer, oblivious to the drama, hooked a passing whore around the waist by the crook of his arm. "And what name do you go by, darling?"

"Long Lizzie," the girl replied, making herself comfortable on his lap with a little extra wiggling thrown in for good measure.

Everett rose to his feet. "I'll leave you two to it."

Once he got a paying claim, things would change come hell or high water, whether the old whore liked it or not. Still, he tossed another spineless simper in her general direction because he didn't have a pot of his own to piss in. A *temporary* situation, he assured himself with a pat on the stomach, feeling for his gold watch fob.

That Red Florence was a real looker. Younger than Julia, and firmer, too. Firmer, in all the right places.

That gave a man something he wanted to think about. Fob hanging in place, he sniggered.

CHAPTER TWENTY-THREE
DISILLUSIONMENT COMES IN MANY FORMS

A dirty-faced, dusty urchin thrust out the scrap of paper. A crude, scribbled note written in dull pencil.

Maude
The results are in.
Sam

This was it. Her stomach suddenly felt like live fish were swimming around inside. Everything she depended upon came down to those results.

Charlie radiated out a notion or warning, but she was in no mood to gather.

Maude flipped the sign to *Closed* and tore off to the assay office.

———

Sam labored green around the gills and the worse for wear in his shirtsleeves, furnaces blasting. A crapulous night beyond a doubt. No one who saw him that day would find him dapper in the least.

Maude rushed to the counter, not holding onto her words once she burst through the door. "The results are ready? Early, too."

"Yeah; just add that messenger's cost to the amount I'm already losing on this deal." He shuffled over to the cubbyholes on the wall, maddeningly slow about it. "I've got your results written down. It's not bad news, but it's not exactly good, either."

She stiffened.

He pulled out a sheet of paper. Scratched his head. "Fifty-two dollars per ton. Nobody's going to get excited about it, and you shouldn't either."

"*What?*"

Sam stared at her, hungover or not. "You heard me. I'll need the location of that claim to finish up the paperwork. Where'd you say it was?"

There had to be a mistake. "But we left out the rocks that didn't feel promising! Are you certain?"

"Not you, too. You can't tell ore content by *feeling* them! Good heavens, Maude. Stick to advising the lovelorn, why don't you? Now, location?"

She shook her head in shock. "I haven't the faintest idea."

Muttering something about a "skirted greenhorn" under his breath, again he pushed in a hard-nosed way. "Maude, I have to have that for the bookkeeping. We are required to maintain complete records of the ore tested, and that includes the location."

Maude wanted out of the assay. "I'm telling you: I don't know where it is."

"Yeah, right. And I'll bet I'm not going to see that money I fronted you, either." Sam's words came out cutting and cruel as they hit their mark.

Unlatching her purse, her fingers located the fifty cents within. She slapped the coins on the counter a bit harder than polite. "I'll come back with the rest of the money when I have it."

He picked up the coins, and his annoyance dried up a measure. "You, like everyone else, got your hopes up, that's all. And there's still the bead."

Opening a drawer, he pulled out a small tan envelope, *Maude* written on the face. He tilted it, and a tiny gold pellet rolled out, which he held up for her inspection. "This is why it's never a good idea to extend credit or loan money for assays. Everyone involved usually loses one way or another."

He dropped the bead back inside the envelope, which he proffered between two fingers. Casual and disinterested. The tiny sample was just that—tiny and beneath consideration.

The hard slap of disappointment left her diminished and small.

She mumbled a scattering of words that had no real meaning, words that never quite registered in her brain. Outside and closing the door behind her, it was all she could do not to wail or burst into tears. She stood outside, halfway towards gasping. *She had been so certain*. The familiar surroundings had turned strange in the course of less than ten minutes. Yes, the furnace and smokestacks stabbing the Cripple Creek sky remained—pretty much the same as the mills in Lowell when it came right down to it. But the similarities ended there. Gold changed everything. The rules that governed precious minerals were far different than those that applied to ordinary spools of cotton thread. Fortunes were, no doubt, to be made in both places. But, while Lowell produced the practical, Colorado produced dreams.

"Damn," she swore under her breath.

So much for easy money.

———

The depths of the hours came shrouded in blue, her room lit by silver shadows. Grasping the sides of the bed, she sat staring at her bare toes on the cold plank floor. Wrapped in both the old quilt and a blanket, the plummeting temperatures set her teeth to chattering. All the while the silence of that fragile hour pressed down as an unspoken accusation. She had no notion how long she simply sat in the small hours. Like everything else, her timepiece had long since been lost to pawn. The worst of it was plain— there was no one in that bed beside her. There was no one to hold her hand and tell her everything would come right in the end.

And she had been so damn certain about that ore.

She moved over to the window, restless and alone.

Blanketed in drifts, the street beyond was deserted, but the faint carry-on from Myers Avenue caught on the veil of the night wind and tempted. She exhaled onto the frigid glass, warm living breath crystallizing into frosted lace. The beauty wasn't lost on her, but the bitterness of the night's blue melancholy seeped deep into her bones and lodged in her heart.

The Mikado probably tilted full steam ahead.

Not yet, not yet. That wasn't the place for her—not yet.

In those unkind shadows, Maude held up her hands to the moonlight. She didn't need to consult her palms. She had shortcomings aplenty, any plans curling up and dying around her. Maybe like that ghost girl had done. Maybe like her marriage.

Her battered valise remained relegated to the corner— a solid reminder against heady natures running unchecked.

The wind shifted, taking the song of Myers Avenue along with it.

But the hair at the nape of her neck crept and tingled as the air crackled, a queer electricity like the moment right before a lightning storm sparked. Summoned by either Maude's unhappiness or some unknown calling, the ghost girl returned to visit.

"I can tell you're in here," Maude whispered into the darkness. "Why won't you pass on?"

She might have asked herself that very same question.

A small sound. The shade's crying came on the current from an inexplicable distance, rippled like lapping water.

And, just as abruptly, the essence of the girl dissipated, leaving lingering sadness and turmoil in her wake.

———

The following day rose pale and drained of possibility. Heavy footed, Maude turned up at the Emporium's door earlier than usual. Rose already puttered within, reading those damned newspapers.

She pushed on through, catching a whiff of perfume.

"The results came back bad." Her voice came out half strangled.

"Shit." Rose spat out the word and abandoned her reading. "What happened?"

Straight to the scratchy point. "I don't know. The test results spelled it all out: fifty-two dollars to the ton."

"Damn. You sure about that?"

A defeated shrug. "Sam said the tests don't lie."

Rose's kohl-rimmed eyes narrowed.

"Well, hell," she chewed on the thought. "I never did like that idea of yours anyhow but wanted to see if you could do it. Now we have that answer, for what it's worth."

Maude crumpled down at the fortune table. "Possibly."

"Possibly, my ass. And we can kiss the money we loaned to that washerwoman goodbye to boot."

Maude did her best not to wail. "We don't know that. Don't go borrowing more trouble than is already there."

Rose raised her eyebrows and looked down her nose at Maude, disagreeing.

All of which nettled. "You *really* never liked the idea of advising on ore? You usually like the idea of money, all right. Now you're just rubbing it in."

"If you could actually ferret out gold, that would be one thing. Sure, maybe you can tell when it's in your hand, but that's not where the game takes place. It's played deep inside the mountains. It's played by men who have a whole lot of money for real advisors and mining engineers. I assumed you meant on advising greenhorns. Not real mining men."

To that, Maude had nothing to say.

Rose patted her chest to calm herself down and tried another tack. "Now that you've got this nonsense out of your system, I've got a line on a fancy dress you can borrow. Maybe we'll show you off a bit. I'm thinking of parading you around the fancier saloons. That should do the trick."

"And then what—tell them that I *can't* sense ore? It will never work, Rose. Beyond that, there's still a problem. What about Millicent—I've got to tell her something..."

Rose tossed back her head like she found her excessively dim. "Tell her that she owes us five dollars, that's what!"

Maude deflated.

Rose softened her tone a touch. "We need a plan. Forget Millicent—we're out of that now. We can say that you advise on accidents and occupation. You know you can do both of those. That should work..."

"I guess it's all over then," Maude said.

"Look at me, girlie. A couple of fortunes, and we'll be square enough. Now get touting and draw some punters in." That crazy spark and whirling calculations. "Oh, and Maude? Try not to seem miserable. It tends to put people off."

Without another word, Maude returned to her position on the boardwalk and called out to passers-by who appeared like they might have an extra dollar to spend. But her heart sure wasn't in it. It was somewhere around her toes.

CHAPTER TWENTY-FOUR
IT AIN'T OVER—THOUGH IT SHOULD BE

*M*illicent, *Please stop by the Emporium this afternoon if possible.*

Maude grabbed a passing boy and gave him a coin to deliver the message to the National's laundry.

Sure enough, the laundress appeared in the distance as the fortune-teller touted and tried to rustle up customers. Maude marked her progress as the woman crossed the street and made a beeline for the Emporium.

Maude stood there waiting, heart hitched and gathering up her nerve.

Millicent, reading Maude's expression, faltered. "What?"

There was nothing for it, other than the truth. "The results came back. The ore didn't really test out. Fifty-two dollars to the ton."

Confusion visibly rippled. In fact, the laundress appeared incredulous. "But that can't be; it doesn't make sense."

In a lowered voice, Maude put her hand on her arm,

consoling. "I'm truly sorry, but those are the results. There's nothing further we can do."

Mrs. Harper's eyes calculated, refusing to believe. "But that can't be right."

"I know. I thought the same thing, but the tests don't lie. I have the bead for you, at least." Maude turned to enter the shop.

Millicent, stock-still and rooted, insisted. "Arthur knows what he's doing. He told me the ore is good."

"Come on." Maude opened the door for her.

"Damn it," Millicent swore as she swept in. "I should have known better. He acted so cocksure."

Darting behind the counter, Maude retrieved the small envelope and held it out. "Sam asked where the claim was. Said he needs it for the paperwork. I didn't know what to tell him."

Millicent withdrew the pellet, shaking her head. "That's it, then." A twitch of the mouth. Notions colliding in her mind. "What do I say if the sharper comes back?"

Rose, coming in from the back door, obviously caught that last part. "Sell it to him, if he still wants it."

Bothered, Millicent dropped the pellet back into the envelope and folded the top over one extra time.

"Here." She held it out to Maude. "Partial payment for the debt owed. But I gotta tell you, it don't even look a dollar to me."

Shrugging, Maude took the bead. "What should I tell Sam?"

Millicent shook her head, eyes locking into hers. "Tell him whatever you want. I don't give a continental about his records, and I don't know exactly where it is myself. Guess we'll have to figure out something else now."

She blinked a few times, eyes darting.

"What do you mean?" Maude asked. "The verdict is already in."

"Oh, nothing. Just hoping on a landslide of money, I guess."

Maude had been hoping on that, too.

———

That marked the point when a dangerous idea started taking hold.

Maybe she could help Clayton along. After all, women had been doing that for centuries.

That same evening, she set out upon another course. A different route, a different street...Maude passed along hoping for a chance at something better. Behind the mountains, the glowing western sky leached out gold as the sun declined. The forge came into view, the door ajar. Hammer blows ringing, decisive and clear.

She picked her way across the uneven yard, the spring run-off thawing and freezing in turns making a muddy mess to navigate. Clayton leaned back to see who approached, a rod and tong still in his hands.

"Maude! What brings you here?"

Intentionally vague. "A notion," she replied holding on to her skirt. Ruffling it and flirting, yes, but it also gave her something to do with her hands.

"Hang on a minute," he called, probably not noticing a damned thing about her attempted enticement.

He struck several more ringing blows, and she inspected him as he inspected his handiwork. Satisfied, he plunged the iron into a water bucket, hissing out a cloud of steam. She pretended a fascination with the tools hanging on the walls. A fascination she certainly didn't feel.

He smiled the question again.

"Oh, I was just passing and thought to stop." She bit her lower lip, pretending to consider her reasoning.

A wayward shock of hair tumbled over his brow. "I haven't got any tea to offer."

Heart thudding, it wasn't the time to go shy and bashful. Yet there she lingered, faltering. She had to come up with something.

"I was just wondering how long you've been here?" *Good heavens.* Now he'd know she was throwing herself at him.

"About three years now. Why?" A glance over his shoulder. "Here, hang on a second."

He went back to the irons in the fire, turning them one after the other, movements deliberate and practiced. Broad and strong shouldered, his suspenders emphasized the fact he was a real man's man.

Attention back on her. "Guess I'm not so good at social calls. Now, how was that?"

"Just making conversation, I guess." Searching. "Rose has an Indian skull in the shop, but you probably don't take too kindly to Indians, considering your father and all."

He furrowed his brow. "He didn't *die* in the raid. Sure, he had a couple of arrows in him, but he managed to run into the barn where he had his rifle. It was sickness that got him in the end. Why?"

Those injuries had weakened the man, but there was no good reason to bring all of that up. "Oh, I was just wondering what kind of Indian he might have been. Everyone deserves a proper burial or resting place..."

Lifted eyebrows and a downturn of the mouth. "Well, if he was a local Indian, maybe he was Ute or Arapahoe. Depends where he started out, I guess. You know, Maude, there are good people here if one overlooks the flash and get-rich-quick types."

That admonishment cut too close to the bone. "Those are the types I need to make a living."

He shrugged. "'Spect so, but there are other ways, too."

She shook her head. "No school-marming for me. But, back to the day I told your fortune—you thought I was stringing you along, didn't you?" She swayed willow-like, skirt fluttering in the gusts down the mountainsides—hoping he took notice. It wasn't certain that he did. "But you see, I wasn't. You'll have a change of location in your future, mark my words."

A flash of embarrassed curiosity as Clayton stiffened. "And, like I said, I don't plan on leaving. And, to set matters straight, I never thought you were a fraud."

Maude scanned the horizon, searching for something reasonable to say. "A lot of unsettled people come here—second chances and all of that."

He dipped his head to the side, still considering her. "Hoping for one?"

"Aren't we all?" It came across half strangled. "Well, I'd best be going."

He looked about ready say something else, but, waiting to hear what that might be, she lost her nerve and bolted.

———

Dear Mother:

Please don't read this letter aloud, as is your custom when unexpected word arrives. It is not my intent to cause upset, and I'm not much one for correspondence as time has proven.

I am writing from the wilds of Colorado—the gold camp of Cripple Creek, to be precise. I want you to know that I am well, but it is no picnic out here. The weather is cold, the living is hard, and the prices exorbitant. Still, I am managing to hold body and soul together and live in hope of something better coming around the corner soon.

As you warned all along, Charley left me in the lurch. I am not telling you this as an act of contrition. There are certain practical matters that need attending to—namely whether his parents know his location. I plan to file for a divorce but don't know where to aim. He might be in Cheyenne, or he might have moved on by now. Decrees get published in whatever local newspaper might serve. Since such notices cost money, and as I have very little, I can only afford to place one such notice and be done with it. Please find out what you can. People out here can leave marriages behind, but it doesn't seem right. Maybe I'll do something foursquare for once.

I have taken a room at the Morning Glory Boarding-house (where you may write to me). This is the first room I have ever had that is my own, and I don't know what I expected. I should have valued our home in Lowell more highly, but that's all said and done by this time. But rest assured that I am fine, and my accommodation is clean and safe. I also have a job telling run-of-the-mill fortunes, while I wait for something better to arrive. It pays the bills but doesn't leave much left over.

Cripple Creek is viewed as upstanding and fairly tame as far as such places go, which would give anyone cause to wonder. I'll get by. We always knew I was born under a dark star.

You are ever in my thoughts, Father and Maisie and Michael as well. Hope they do not turn out as willful as I have proven. For all of that, this is the first time I have the chance to cut my own path. I expect to prevail.

 Yours affectionately,
 Maude

CHAPTER TWENTY-FIVE
SKIRTING THE TRUTH

STILL APRIL 1896

She'd been prospecting, all right, and didn't have a damn thing to show for it. Her letter to her mother made her feel a bit better, but it didn't change things for the time being.

Of course, like any young woman and hoping against hope, it would have been better if Clayton had sought her out, coming straight up to the door and making his intentions clear.

But he didn't. Probably he didn't have any intentions toward her at all.

And she was still legally married, anyhow.

Despite herself, she kept watch for him. Hope still rubbing against a situation she doubted. The Emporium's oval-windowed door marked a border of sorts. A border between their shadow-filled world of innuendo and the workaday nature of the rest of the town. That other world got on with the business at hand. Wages that needed earning, meals that required cooking, and children that needed tending.

She wondered, and not for the first time, what it would be like to belong to that other world beyond the shop's closed door.

Distracted, it took a moment to home in on a boy. Approximating ten years old, he loitered on the boardwalk in front of the shop. Switching from one foot to the other, he didn't approach the door but hovered in front of the window. Children often peered in, curious. There was nothing so unusual in that. Figuring he'd run off like the others, Maude moved to the door and opened it. Craning around the corner to catch a better glimpse.

He saw her all right but didn't hightail it.

He had Maude puzzled. "Can I help you?" she asked.

"Gosh, I don't think so," he replied.

His awestruck tone forced a chuckle all the same. "Well, what are you doing, hopping around out here like a bird?"

A glimmer of purpose surfacing. "I've got a message for, um, Maude."

Her breath hitched. "I'm Maude. What message?"

"The fancy lady, Mrs. Mikado, said to tell you she has something, um...no. But maybe she wants to tell you... huh. Whatever it is, she wants to see you. She paid me to come and deliver this here message."

A garbled message from the wrong person.

Oblivious, the boy peered past her into the Emporium. "Do you have magic in there?"

Glancing over her shoulder into the shop, the contents struck her as tatty in the clear light of day. Even the skull just sat on the shelf, giving off nothing at all.

"No," she replied, "I'm sorry. There's no magic in here."

Her words struck deep. Perhaps, like the boy, she had been searching for magic where there was none to be had.

The madam herself opened the door as the clear-sky sun melted the icicles and started the spring runoff.

"Glad you could make it." Julia stood aside to let her enter, never offering to take her coat.

"Your errand boy left a bit to be desired."

"Oh? Seems to have done the trick to me." Julia turned back into the interior, leaving Maude to close the door. "You've stirred up talk; I'll say that much for you, fortune-teller. One of the local assayers was in here drinking more than he should, blathering on about a batch of queered test results. Laughing about two women who didn't know their asses from their elbows, and one of them sure fit your description. He's latched onto the idea that you are some sort of female prospector going around Cripple Creek nosing for easy pickings. Sound familiar?"

A jolt. "Sam Evans."

Julia folded her arms. "I don't give out names. But let's say that he claimed the ore tested out better than expected. He proceeded to spend a fair amount of time bragging about how he downplayed it."

A nerve twitched at the corner of Maude's mouth, and the madam caught it. "So that bothers you a bit. Well, well, well."

"Who was Sam talking to?" Maude lightened her voice as best she could.

That got the madam's interest. "You're on a first-name basis, is that it? I might start to wonder about the company you are actually keeping..."

"I thought he liked me," Maude murmured.

"Well, think again," Julia snapped. "Or he's got a real funny way of showing it. And I forget who he was talking to, but it doesn't matter."

An obvious lie. Julia never forgot who anyone was talking to. "Protecting someone?" Maude countered.

"Always and forever more." The madam puffed up, proud. "Secrets have value, if a woman's smart. And I sure hope you are."

Maude hoped so as well. "I am."

What the hell, it was worth a shot.

"Stow it. I can see I haven't wasted your time." The madam glinted, sharp as a shard of glass. "And a deal is a deal. In return, you're going to advise a friend of mine. Being a man, he'll be reluctant to accept the help, of course."

Rose's warnings rippled.

"As you like," Maude responded, wary around the edges. "But if the outcome's supposed to land a specific way, you might as well tell me right now."

Julia cackled and took a step closer. "I want you to steer him. *I* don't *care* if things might be looking up; there's no need to give him any information that doesn't go my way. In fact, the last thing I need is for him to catch wind of any reprieve. I want him to stay put right here, where I can keep tabs on him. Understood?"

"Are you sure that's best?"

Julia's gaze flickered. "I am. Now, wait here. I'll be right back."

Maude unfastened her coat and shrugged it off, slinging it over the back of a chair. She sat down to wait. A long five minutes later, Julia returned with a companion in tow, color high in her cheeks. The man—rude, unwashed, and in his shirtsleeves—stank of stale whiskey. His suspenders hung down around his haunches, too lazy or uncaring to pull them up.

Hands stuck in pockets, he made his opinion plain without uttering a single word.

"This is *my man*, Everett. I've told him about your...abilities."

A double-crossing current circulated in the room. "My name is Maude..."

"I don't really care, darlin', and I've already heard about you. I can't say I credit this type of mumbo-jumbo much, so prove me wrong." He sprawled down in the nearest chair, legs stuck out in front of him, wide. Bare bony ankles peeked between his cuffs and his shoes. Hardened or oblivious to the cold.

"Charge him the going rate." Julia clamped her hand on Everett's shoulder.

"Five dollars," Maude replied without skipping a beat.

His eyes shot daggers at Julia, who countered them with a steel clash of her own. Irritated, he fished around in his shirt pocket, found a gold piece, and tossed it onto the table, where it clattered.

Five dollars cash. She snatched it, fingers closing around that sweet coin. If anyone noticed her reaction they didn't say, too busy being locked into each other, and not in a friendly way.

Maude slipped the money into her bag as casually as she could and focused her attention on Julia's *man*. "What would you like to know?"

"I want to know if I'm going to get lucky tonight."

Julia hauled off and belted him on the shoulder. A glancing blow and the dull thud off the bone—the man all but reared up, nostrils flaring.

He flung his weight back in the chair, churlish and mean. If Maude hadn't been standing in front of them, there would have been more to the confrontation than mere words. "Give me a whiskey, woman. If I'm going to have to do this, I'm going to have a drink, by golly."

Julia lunged at the sideboard, poured with impatient determination, and shoved the glass into his hand, whiskey sloshing over. "There," she said to him but turned to Maude. "Get on with it."

A loud thump and the sound of breaking glass came from upstairs. Dead silence hung for a brief moment, broken by two rising voices. Accusatory and hard.

Julia eyed the ceiling like she could see through the lathe and plaster.

The crack of a slap.

"Son of a bitch." Gathering up handfuls of her skirts, she bolted from the room and rushed up the stairs to the accompaniment of caterwauling and bickering. Below, Maude and the man charted the staccato of the madam's heels overhead.

Julia's voice slashed across the others. A door slammed, the quarrel muffled.

Any interest in the drama upstairs dissipated like free whiskey. Leaning forward and expelling liquor fumes, the man's eyes bolted onto Maude's. "Getting laid in a whorehouse is like shooting fish in a barrel. Rumor is circulating that you have something to do with mining. Is that so?"

She recoiled from more than the smell. "I can advise on ore and claims. As well as read fortunes."

"*This* is none of Julia's business. So, let's get that part straight. That five dollars you gobbled up is mine, and I want to make sure I understand this. People bring you ore, and you do what with it exactly?"

"Sense it." She did her best not to squirm.

"Bullshit." He laughed outright.

She had to take control of the situation so pulled her chair up directly in front of his. Pretending nothing was amiss in the entire situation. "Put your hand in mine, palm up."

"Nothing you say will hold any water with me, not unless someone's told you of a good claim." Yet he gave her his hand. Vanity, as usual, won out in the end.

Skin soft to the touch. A flash of treachery.

Pressing down on his hand, old calluses lingered beneath the padding. His lines were deep and decisive in the main, splitting off and intertwining as they branched out.

"Physical labor is in your past and has brought you a fair measure of success."

He snorted.

"See that strong line here?" Pointing out one of the creases, she paused for effect. "Along the way, your success ceased to be yours alone. Other people became involved. The more people are interested, the more difficult any future success is to control. This weakening line means a weakening of confidence."

A rude exhale. "Bullshit again."

Still, the telltale flush rose in her cheeks, and she could feel it. He noticed it, too.

Julia bustled back into the room, glancing from Everett to Maude and back again. "What did I miss?"

"A whole bunch of nothing," Everett claimed, kicking his chair back as he stood, scraping the wooden floor. An insult half out of hearing as he stalked from the room; churlish steps climbing back up the stairs.

Julia twisted her hands into claws, poised to strike. "Could you tell anything about romance?"

"Romance?" Maude recoiled. For a split second, she assumed it a joke she didn't understand. The madam's expression put that notion to bed. "Not in the conventional sense. I did see three women, however."

"Three?"

Maude wet her lips. "Maybe one of them is his mother."

Julia unfurled a measure. Her demeanor changed into something a little less...predatory.

"I bet you he'll want another consultation." Julia

stepped closer, giving Maude a smile approximating encouragement, if one overlooked the fangs. "What else did you see?"

"A tangled mess."

"Sounds about right." Julia leaned her backside against the table, calculating. "Remember, you've got absolutely no reason to gloss over his fortune. With luck, whatever you say will rattle him, and rattle him good."

"Why don't I take a quick glance at your palm for confirmation?"

For a split second, the madam turned into glass. "No. Not today. There's no need to go dredging up anything else."

CHAPTER TWENTY-SIX
UNEXPECTED COMPETITION IS NEVER WELCOME

One hell of a mess was bound to kick off.

Off-kilter, Maude was relieved to find Rose at the Emporium.

"Good. I'm glad you're here," Maude panted, breathless and winded.

"First you'd better listen to this." Scrunching the newspaper, Rose gave it a good shake and Maude a sharp look.

The mystery of two hemispheres, special arrival and first visit to this city, the Occult Wonder and Clairvoyant—Madam McClure—will be available for consultation. She asks no questions but reads your life like an open book. And, before you can utter a word, she tells you YOUR NAME in full. She gives valuable information on all mining matters, tells you whether it is worth the time and expense to work your claim. How much it will cost. Whether it is best to sink shafts and, if so, where. She will tell you how far it is to bedrock and how best to work your mine. You do not pay a cent until the reading is over and you are satisfied. Business is sacred and confidential...

Flapping the newspaper, Rose jabbed the print with a long forefinger. "How can *that* clairvoyant tell a punter their name in full? You've got competition, my girl, serious competition if that's true."

That pulled Maude up short, but she'd deal with that later.

"I was just at the Mikado. The assayer who ran the tests was in there drinking. Julia said he devalued the results."

Rose stopped rustling the paper and froze. "Well, that's a new angle. I had hoped that you had cut your ties down there. Guess that was foolish on my part."

Maude ignored the barb. "The question is what to do about it."

"*Do* about it? Why, nothing at all. We're done."

"He's trying to swindle us."

Rose was having none of it. "'Us'? Who is that 'us' you refer to? You're overlooking the point that we're only involved in a *fortune-telling* capacity..."

Maude rolled her eyes.

"Well, I guess it proves you can make out good ore. Beyond that, the problem is the Harpers'. *Not* ours. It doesn't say 'We'll solve all your problems for you' in that window, does it?" Rose relented, but only a fraction.

Maude wasn't convinced. "It's not right, all the same."

"A lot of things in this world aren't right." Still, Rose's wheels kept turning. "What I don't understand is *why* Julia's passing you information in the first place. That don't sound like her. And now that you've learned not to take people at face value in these parts, who's to say she's even telling you the truth?"

"I'm fairly—"

Rose cut her off. "Fairly ain't good enough. I don't understand why you're in each other's pockets. You have something over on her, or does she have something over on *you*?"

"It's just an arrangement. No one has anything over on anyone."

A sharp-eyed assessment. "If you insist," Rose sniffed.

Maude was halfway toward pleading. "But I *believe* Julia. This is it. This is *the chance*."

"Well, if you're bound and determined, I'll give you some advice, and I'll give it to you for free. You have *got* to suspect her motives. Especially if it involves her cadet."

A twang of conscience—she owed Rose at least the partial truth. "He needs a new strike."

"Well, hell," Rose crowed. "Don't we all?"

"You don't understand. She wants to keep him dependent upon her. Any fortune I read for him has got to lean toward the bad. I can't see what she'd gain by lying about assay tests in these circumstances. Can you?"

"My, my, my." Rose eyed her, shrewd. "It didn't take long for your high and mighty to tumble, did it? But no. I don't see what she'd have to gain, but trust me: it's gotta be there. She does nothing for free."

"Her man is no prize. He deserves to be brought down a peg or two."

"And for some odd reason, you're the one who's going to do it, is that it? But distinctions sure are starting to slip, ain't they?"

Maude retrieved her coat, defiance rising. "I'm going to go find Millicent to tell her what's happened."

"Bef—er..." Rose got out half a word before stopping.

"What?" Maude's hand already rested on the doorknob.

"No matter, Maude," Rose replied. "It'll keep. Let's just see what happens next, shall we? I, for one, can hardly wait. And I was only joshing on that last part. I would hate for it to get misconstrued."

The laundry's windows, steam-fogged from the inside, were a grayed-out white. Glimpses of monotone white within—a body struggled with a sheet and mangle. More gray billowed out from under the door, the overall impression drear. The brick walls were the same as the mills of Lowell, dirty and damp and backbreaking. The overcast sky did nothing to jolly matters along.

Maude pounded on the door to be heard over the thunking and thudding machinery.

"Come in," a woman's voice bellowed.

She pushed through. The temperature inside warmed by twenty degrees.

"I'm looking for Millicent Harper," she told the nearest woman, who didn't take much interest, one way or another.

"Millicent!"

Other voices passed the message down into the back. "Millicent Harper! Someone's here to see you!"

The laundress emerged, bedraggled and perspiring. A frown and furrowing brow at recognition. "Has something happened?"

Conscious of the women listening in, Maude smiled carefree and broad, not wanting to set rumors swirling. Or to get Millicent docked. "Nothing serious. Can you step outside for a quick moment?"

Millicent gestured back out the way Maude had entered. Passing through to the street, they shut the door on the curiosity.

"What's this about?" Steam rose from the laundress's damp skin.

"The assay test came back wrong."

"Oh!" A sheepish laugh followed. "That explains it, then. How'd you figure that out?"

Strange reaction, Maude thought. "Explains what?"

A nervous half laugh. "I don't know. It's hard to believe Arthur had been *that* mistaken. Go on—tell me how you got that all sorted out."

"I'm not at liberty to give the particulars," Maude caged. "At any rate, I thought you ought to know."

"Uh-huh." Suspicion rippled, going both ways. "Well, thanks all the same."

About to leave, Maude hesitated. All she could read on Millicent was pure calculation. "Say, did that sharper ever return?" The question was poised as an afterthought, although it wasn't.

The laundress shook her head. "No, not yet. Maybe not ever. But, now that the claim's got value, I'd best think it over. Don't suppose your...person... said how much it's valued, did they?"

"No. How could they know such a thing?"

Millicent wrinkled up her nose and eyed her. "I've no idea because I don't know who they are. Well. I'll talk to Arthur about this. Listen, I'd best get back to work."

"Rose said to remind you that you owe us for the assay."

A flick of the head. "I know. Besides, if the claim's valuable, paying her back shouldn't be that difficult at all. Should it?"

Maude shook her head *no.*

The laundress turned back inside, shutting Maude out in the alley with dirty drifts of snow.

CHAPTER TWENTY-SEVEN
PREMONITIONS CAN PAY, ESPECIALLY IF PHRASED RIGHT

I n this case, shit rolled uphill.

It didn't take long for Julia's *man* to find his own ill-humored way to the Fortune Emporium. Worse the wear from drink, he had stubble on his cheeks and bloodshot eyes as he pushed in through the door. Maude remained seated at the table. Out of principle. "Anything in particular make you change your mind?"

The skull set off those low humming sounds only Maude could hear.

Everett's demeanor hadn't changed one jot from the other day, still wretched and aggressive. "Those ore samples you brought in. Where'd they come from?"

She offered a dry laugh. "So, you heard the talk at the brothel, too."

An off-guard flinch. "How do *you* know about that?"

"I'm clairvoyant," she preened, superior. Still, she'd better watch what she said.

"Yeah, and I'm Andrew Carnegie's younger brother."

She paused while the skull hissed. "What do you want from me?"

"Isn't it obvious? I already asked the question."

Maude shifted in her seat, rearranged her skirt. "I don't know the location of the mine, if that's what you are asking."

"That's exactly what I'm asking you. And, failing that, I'll settle for the name of the owner."

"My clients are confidential."

"Bullshit." He leaned in close enough that she could see the individual veins in his eyes. "Of course, I'm not expecting to get this information for free."

Maude held her ground, waiting him out.

"You don't have to like me, and I don't have to like you. This would be a business arrangement." He made a pointed inventory of the Emporium's contents, unimpressed. "How much money would you say comes in here?"

The skull continued humming low. Everett fidgeted, feeling for his watch and checking it was still there.

Rising from her chair, she drifted over to rub Charley —in part to make Julia's man nervous, and in part to settle the energy down. All she got for her troubles was an irritated electric shock.

The man pulled out another five-dollar gold piece from his vest pocket, slapping it on the table without a shard of manners. "So, you like to play games, is that it? This five-dollar piece is payment. Payment for you to tell me what you're doing."

"I act as an advisor. Nothing more." Maude returned to the table and picked up the money, thinking how easily she could tell him about the dose of clap he would get.

"Meaning?"

"Exactly that. You don't give a fig about Julia, but you love acting the big man."

He rose and stepped close, breath stale. "I don't give a continental about your opinion on such matters. And you might want to watch that mouth of yours. Unless you don't mind making enemies, that is."

She pretended not to have caught the threat. "You fall in love with...mines."

"I do if they've got good features." His chuckle came out lewd. "If you help me, I'll pay you far more than five dollars a go."

Forget any steering; Maude would have to gain control first. "I'll have to think about it."

"Well," his gray eyes bore into her. "You'd better think fast, darling. Opportunity has a nasty way of drying up and disappearing. You must not make much here, 'cause I know you straggle down to Julia's begging for scraps." He checked his pocket watch yet again and clicked it emphatically shut.

His attention landed on the all-seeing eye. "Masons bug the shit out of me these days. Don't tell me they run this place, too?"

"They don't. Rose just keeps that for decoration."

He didn't look convinced. "They think they own the entire goddamned district."

He stomped out in a huff, near slamming the door. And the skull calmed down, vibrations slowing. Other than for that warning hum.

CHAPTER TWENTY-EIGHT

SOMETIMES THE ROAD TO HELL IS PAVED WITH GOOD INTENTIONS

Circumstances be damned. Ev might not believe Maude had *abilities*, but Julia sure as hell did.

Mulling that all over and looking at it twice, the girl was bound to need the cash Everett would surely offer. As she stood there planning on just how she would cut him off from *that*, by golly, a ring jangled at the front door. Far too early for punters.

Irritated, Julia answered it herself. On the stoop a messenger stood, holding out an envelope.

"Can I help you?" She made certain it didn't sound like a genuine offer. Experience had taught her that questions needed to be proffered with care. Especially when answering a whorehouse door.

"You the landlady, Julia Robinson?"

"One and the same," she swaggered.

"In that case, this is for you." The man thrust out the envelope stiff armed, but he touched his cap as he left.

All the same, it couldn't be considered good or fortunate. People did not send notes to brothels. Not without sound, incriminating reasons. And there it was. Her name scrawled across the front of the brown envelope.

In my official capacity, I am required to alert the authorities in all matters concerning public health. In the same interest of public health, the Mikado should be placed under strict quarantine. It is my considered opinion that an outbreak has started within that location; resulting in the death of one of the inmates.

If you prefer to discuss matters and to provide evidence of good health for each of said inmates, please meet me prior to Tuesday noon when my report shall be submitted to the proper authorities.

J. F. Blake, Esq.

Splendid. Just goddamned splendid.

The undertaker acted the part of the bastard she assumed him to be. Over at the safe, she tossed his missive inside where it landed right next to her little black book. It would keep. But not for long.

Hell. She turned and marched back over to the safe, twirled the combination dial and pulled the paper out again. The same way as she'd worry a loose tooth. His words gave her exactly the same sensation.

She read it over again. Nothing would stick to him the way he wrote it. Well, she'd see what she could do about that.

It all boiled down to money, one way or another.

But damn it, there was no contagion in the house.

Be that as it may, the man would have the outcome rigged three ways to Sunday.

That's what sentimentality got a person. Blackmailed in the end.

CHAPTER TWENTY-NINE
BARROOM BANTER

S urprisingly enough, Millicent returned to the Emporium, distraught and panting to catch her breath. "The claim deed's gone! It's supposed to be in the tin box under the bed, but it's not there now. And Arthur didn't come home..."

Rose piped up, in no mood. "And what is it *exactly* that you expect us to do?"

"I...don't know..." The laundress deflated.

Maude scowled at Rose before turning her attention to Millicent. "He usually comes home, right?"

"Unless he's on a spree. Maybe that sharper came back while I was away and took the paper." Millicent blocked out Rose.

Maude sighed. "Well, that doesn't sound likely, does it?" Still, something wasn't sitting right.

"Well, at least it's an idea! I need that money, and Arthur's probably drunk again somewhere. You can't see where he is, can you?"

So that was what the woman wanted. "No," Maude replied, thinking on how that would have come in handy in the past. "I've never been able to do that."

"Well, I'd best start hunting him down. I've got to let him know the deed is missing, drunk or sober."

Rose and Maude exchanged quick glances. Rose remaining adamant.

But Maude had a softer spot. "Nothing much is happening here yet. I'll come with you to help."

Relief washed over the laundress. "That's good of you. I mean it."

Rose rolled her eyes. "Don't worry about our business," she muttered as Maude pulled on her coat.

Together the two women stepped out into the frozen morning sky—searing blue without a cloud in sight. The crested snow sparkled, glimmering like a million scattered mica flakes.

"It's bright," Maude groused.

Millicent didn't reply, only gathered her skirts in a pronounced manner and kept on walking.

Again, Maude eyed her companion. "Where did you live before you came here?"

"Leadville. The weather's worse, and the town livelier." Millicent paused, hand on hip, scanning the street and coming across as practiced. "The one time I've needed him, he's nowhere to be found. Take my advice and don't marry a man who drinks."

"Wasn't planning on it," Maude replied. That would just be the icing.

"I love him, but it's the damnedest thing. Guess I got lucky."

Taken aback, she guessed luck came in all different stripes, and Millicent held firm. They trudged on, snow crunching beneath their boots.

A few blocks later, Millicent lingered at the mouth of an alley. Peering down into the shadowed alley was no treat: castoff debris and dregs strewn about; outhouses, yellow snow, discarded lumber, and saints-only-knew what else, and none of it good.

"We'd best take a pass down here right quick. Just to make sure he's not dead in a drift."

They hadn't ventured but about ten steps before a hard case stumbled from an outhouse, fumbling with his fly. A lewd grin spread when he cottoned on to them. Swaying in the middle of the alley ruts, he waited, undone and laughing loud. Still drunk from the night before. Instinctively, the women took a couple of steps back.

"That's right! Run away, you pair of bitches, seeing as how a real man scares you!"

He took a couple of reeling steps toward them, none too steady.

Millicent snatched up a discarded board propped up against a wall and brandished it. "I won't hesitate to whack the living daylights out of you if you come any closer!"

He might have been drunk, but he thought twice.

"Hell, bet I wouldn't feel it a t'all..." he muttered as he slunk away into the back of a saloon.

Millicent surveyed the alley one more time. "Well, chances are Arthur would have heard my voice if he were down there, anyhow."

She pulled up short at Maude's expression. "What?"

"Nothing," Maude replied, bothered. "You handled that well."

"Huh," Mrs. Harper snorted. "Guess I've had enough practice. You've got to toughen up, girl!"

Which felt kind of rich, all things considered.

By the time they'd made a circuit through six miserable and hostile saloons, hope dwindled down to next to nothing. Standing across the street from the prominent Palace Hotel lording over the corner of Second and Bennett Avenues, the women hesitated in front of the vaulted, etched windows. Crowded and indistinct, nothing registered beyond the fact that the customers were all men.

"He wouldn't go into such a fancy place, would he?"

Millicent's mouth compressed into a tight line. "God, I hope not. Come on."

In they scuttled and for a few fleeting moments went unnoticed.

Suited men, for the most part—the odd dungaree-wearing miner thrown in for good effect. A liberal smattering of greenhorns, trying to act accustomed to such surroundings, gave themselves away by their eagerness to fit in. The ornate bar was dark and carved; liquor bottles beckoned and tempted neat in front of a fifteen-foot mirror. A rich and cleaned-up version of Myers Avenue, the well-heeled patronized the establishment for more reasons than one. But at that early hour, the purpose of morning indulgence brought them together in camaraderie, a mountain custom that seldom resulted in anything productive.

Voices and conversations carried on, liquor-loud and boasting.

"The Scavenger is back up and running; they say it was a fluke...and are chasing for a new vein...that's got to be why Stevenson's back in town."

"Either that or it's the Mikado..." Snide laughter burst out.

The barman, in clean white shirtsleeves and sporting garters, first spied their presence. A pointed nod in their direction to the assembled cast of drinkers. Irritated and unwelcoming scowls were cast over shoulders, no matter how trimmed the beards and mustachios.

"Begging your pardon, ladies, but are you supposed to be in here?" The barman kept drying the glass in his hand.

"Son of a bitch," Millicent spat, before anyone had the chance to do or say anything further. Making a beeline for a scrawny fellow sitting next to the potbellied stove, she heaved the sot by his collar and up to his drunken feet.

"Why, there's my bride!" He tried to give her a kiss, but she ducked away, and laughter rippled.

"Arthur Harper, we've been robbed!"

"Robbed? Robbed of what?" He struggled to focus on her face.

"The claim deed is missing from the box!" She didn't relax her grip from his collar one jot.

"Oh. That. I sold it, Millie. We got seventy-five dollars. Can you believe it?" A slow grin spread over his face.

Millicent released her hold, and, while he teetered, she hauled off and whomped him on the shoulder. Hard.

He staggered backwards, knocking into the wall. "What'd you do that for?"

"Because I'm mad, damn it! Now empty out your pockets."

More laughter at the floor show. To his credit, Arthur didn't argue but pulled out wads of bills from his pockets, slow and drunk.

Millicent counted out the money in plain sight for everyone to see. "Well, I'll be damned. There's seventy dollars here."

He laid a finger aside his nose, his answer a high, drunken laugh. "I've got a secret!"

Millicent, ignoring his drunken ramblings, folded the bills nice and neat and stuffed them down the front of her dress. She turned, nearly colliding with Maude. "Wonders never cease. Let's go. We've got what we came for; no need to put on a show as well."

"Hey!" Arthur called out. "Leave me two dollars, will you?"

Millicent fished in her pocket, brandishing small coins, which she slapped into her husband's outstretched hand. "Twenty cents for beer. And then you come home, got it?"

Again, he tried for a kiss, but she pushed him away. Acting the source of amusement, Arthur remained in the center of the floor swaying drunk, beaming in the general direction of his wife's departure.

Maude wasn't laughing. Claims sold for a fraction of their worth were no laughing matter. If Harper'd been in his right mind, he would have known as much as well. Or so she thought.

CHAPTER THIRTY

EASY MONEY IS
ANYTHING BUT

(AND THERE'S MORE TO THAT THAN
MEETS THE EYE)

"How *do* we get hold of that claim?" Everett posed in a casual way, his voice almost singing the question. Patently false in the level of disinterest he conveyed. Leaning against the assay counter without a care in the world, yet his mind dripped poison.

Sam coiled back from instinct, wary. "It's turning out more convoluted than expected. The fortune-teller brought in the prospector's wife, but nothing is clear as far as who all the players are."

"*The fortune-teller,*" Everett muttered, convinced he should never have trusted Sam with anything of this magnitude in the first place.

"Don't you worry. She owes me a favor, and I intend to collect." Sam, doing the one-armed lean against the battered wood surface, pretended the conversation was nothing more than shooting the breeze. But his eyes skittered about, worried. As well he should be.

Ev did his best to stare him down, but the assayer had the advantage of height, which made the proposition a bit more skewed than ideal. "And what favor might that be?"

"I gave her some pointers on prospecting."

Ev acted amused, but that's all it was. An act. The clairvoyant didn't like him, and open dislike tended to make that person an enemy. Or, at the very least, a person that needed watching. Either way, he now had this mess to sort out.

Sam yakked on, oblivious. "Yeah, none of this is anything that can't be handled."

Everett drew a bead back on him. "You sure? Because I'm not. You don't know who has the claim deed is the upshot of all of this, correct?"

Sam leaned forward, kept his voice level and unconcerned. But it was an act; nothing could have been further from the truth. "More or less, but I'll get to the bottom of it. You'll see."

He'd see, all right. "How d'you plan on doing that, since you haven't already?"

The assayer laid a finger aside his nose—a gesture that always set Everett's teeth on edge. "Leave it to me. Now, it's time to re-discuss our financial arrangements. The way I see it, I've provided a valuable service to you. I found the ore and had enough wherewithal to discount the content."

Everett's gut clenched. He'd be damned if the scoundrel wasn't about to try to bleed him. He held his voice steady, with mounting difficulty. "We already have an agreement, along with a plan. You were to find good-looking ore. Once that happened, you were to lead me to the owner and *after* a *successful* business transaction concluded—in this case meaning *the sale* of the claim to the consortium—you were to receive a finder's fee of five hundred dollars." Everett stuck his hands in his pockets. "*That* was our agreement."

Sam shifted his weight. "And it still is. Nothing's straightforward on this one, that's all."

"That's plenty. You don't even know where the claim is located, or who owns it for sure. It's a small matter." Ev checked his watch before snapping it shut. "But one that needs resolution."

Everett made sure there was no mistaking the tone, right before he took his leave, destined for the Palace Hotel's bar rail. Snow danced along in the currents before it floated down toward the inevitable.

The fact of the matter remained: while they were blundering about, another investor might seize the opportunity and leave him empty handed. And he couldn't have that. Well, he'd see what was being bantered about inside the Palace. Maybe he'd acquire a nugget of value. Maybe there was a greenhorn with money to invest.

———

The skull's insistent chatter got her attention.

There Sam stood, framed by the Emporium's doorway one minute and slipping in like an eel the next. Taking the empty seat, he didn't face Maude square across the expanse of the fortune table. Instead, he sat tilted side-ways, ready to bolt should the need arise.

As a tested method of discouragement, she waited for him to speak first.

"You look real nice today," he claimed, for want of anything better.

Her coat covered the same threadbare clothes as always. "Meaning I don't normally?"

"No, of course not." He fidgeted, all angles and elbows. "You happen to get hold of that claim location? For my paperwork, you understand."

She shrugged, nice and dainty. Too feminine to be true. "You know, Sam, I've been thinking. You helped me on my first day in town, and you granted us a bit of credit when needed. Why don't I do a favor for you now. Let me read your palm. It's possible the answer will come from there."

A few rapid blinks. "Really?"

"It's been known to happen." She proffered her hand, turning her wrist just *so.*

He didn't take it.

That set her back, and she dropped the charade. "What's the matter? Give me your hand."

"Nah. I might fall in love." He seemed to find that funny.

Maude's rising glare was trained right between the assayer's eyes. "Fine. Cards, then. You like gambling, don't you?"

"Sure, but I don't see how one thing has anything to do with the other." He had at least enough sense to look worried.

She thrust out the deck of cards. "Shuffle them and draw one out. You have time for that, don't you?"

Scowling, he wedged his hands under his armpits.

She toyed with telling him his increasing reliance on booze didn't escape notice. But that would scare him off for damn sure. And that wasn't her purpose. For the moment.

"Come on, Sam. It's the only way, if you feel you *really* need that answer."

Against his better judgment, he relented and drew out a card. Before he did so, she caught a flash of a red joker in her mind's eye. *Unexpected events.*

Sam drew out a two of clubs.

Light and darkness. Cooperation and associations.

She bit her lip, pretending to be perplexed by the meaning. "No, that's not enough to go on. Draw another one."

"You said this wasn't going to take long."

"Then quit arguing and draw!" She tossed her head for added emphasis.

The ace of hearts. *Intimidation and death.* Eroticism if he had the chance, which he sure as hell wouldn't get with her.

Well. She got what she needed out of the reading, confirming what she suspected all along.

With a rising sense of triumph, she locked into Sam. "Nah. Nothing in there tells me more than the claim is nearby and in a dark hole."

"Shit, Maude. Now you are funning me. I need that information for the assay's records."

She pursed her lips, pretending to think it over, really hoping to cause a note of shame. "That's not why you want it, and we both know as much."

He swallowed, left eye twitching. "There's no need to be like that. Not when I've been a friend to you all along, as you said. I've got a prospective client for your lady friend. He wants to buy her claim, and he's good for the money. What d'you say?"

Maude set the cards down on the table. "I say I don't believe the assay results you gave us were true. Now, why might that be?"

Having practice with that particular complaint, he didn't flinch, nor did he color. He didn't even bother to appear concerned in the slightest. "It's science, Maude. The tests can't pick up minerals that are simply not there."

"Nothing more to it than that?"

"Nothing more."

"Well, as it is, you're too late," Maude glinted. "It's already gone and sold."

His mouth opened and shut without a sound. It took him a moment and a couple of tries. "Sold?"

"Sold."

"Why, who'd she sell it to?"

Maude sat back in her chair and studied his distress, detached. "How should I know?"

Sam ran his fingers through his hair, ruffling it. "Well, you must know something since you told me it's sold!"

"I'm a clairvoyant. Of course I know things like that. It's all part of the trade."

He gawped. "That's impossible."

"Prove it."

Sam shifted before rising to his feet. "I'm kind of in a tough spot, you see."

Maude picked the cards back up and shuffled them, signaling she was finished, unwavering eyes still trained on him.

He shook his head, looked at her hand, and left.

Alone, Maude turned over the top card and threw it down on the table in front of her. The five of hearts—a warning of jealousy and ill will.

The shop bell jingled before she formed a clear impression, and up another prospector shuffled, tracking snow in along with him. Maude picked up the card, stuck it deep in the middle of the deck, and offered the punter a smile.

CHAPTER THIRTY-ONE

ULTERIOR MOTIVES AND STRANGE TWISTS OF FATE

Upon the side table, just inside the door of the Morning Glory, a letter waited. A letter addressed in her mother's hand. Maude made it back to her room in five long strides. It was definitely a "closed door" letter. A lecture expected, but for once it was almost welcomed.

Fingers fumbling, she tore at the envelope—the words a lifeline and a tether.

Dear Maude:

I didn't know whether to laugh or to cry when I received your letter, so I did a bit of both. I'm not surprised but was still sad to hear the way it is with you. I did as you asked and went to Charley's parents' home. Of course, they didn't want to hear any criticism of their son. They don't know his whereabouts, as he's never been in the habit of keeping in touch regularly. So, we all have that much in common. They asked why I'd come, and I said I was worried. Nothing more. If they had raised their son better, you wouldn't be in your predicament. If you had listened better, all of this could have

been avoided as well. His mother said if she hears anything,
she will let me know. I believe she will keep her word.

I felt next to sorry for her, the way she crumpled when I
told her about your letter. Even if her son is a no-account,
blood is still blood.

You are ever in my thoughts, and if I went in much for
praying, you'd be there, too. Maybe your headstrong nature
will prove an asset in Colorado. Surely, I do not know. What
I fear most for you, is your tendency to want the wrong
things. Maybe this has changed over time and circumstance.

Your mother

After the initial flare up, she reread the letter and felt
shamed. But, more than anything, she wished she could
tell her mother the truth. She wished she could tell her
that she was lonely and cold.

————

The laundress returned to the Emporium bearing four
dollars tied up in a handkerchief.

"It's all there." Millicent shifted her weight from one
foot to the other, watching Maude from underneath her
lashes. "Well, I subtracted a dollar for the bead, so there
you have it. One debt cleared."

Maude, leaning against the fortune table, kept her
arms folded, so the laundress placed the handkerchief on
the table. For her part, the clairvoyant made no move to
claim it. "There can't be all that much left over from the
sale."

Millicent flushed. "There isn't. Even that had to be
helped out with part of my wages."

"Take a seat, why don't you?" Maude pulled herself
upright and sat down on the business end. "Let's see if the
chain of events has clarified with time and details. It's

possible, you know, and the cards might spell your solution out better."

The laundress shook her head. "I don't have the money to pay for another consultation."

"On the house." Maude did her best to radiate encouragement.

Millicent made no move toward the chair but clasped her hands together and held them against her chest. "I don't have time to stay on right now. Some other day, perhaps."

"Everything all right?" Rose asked, coming in from outside.

"Of course it isn't," Millicent said, glaring, "but now you two are square. And I'm still working in the laundry, ain't I?"

Maybe, in a way, that summed it all up. Leaving those words hanging, the laundress slid on out, head down but steps determined.

Her figure disappeared down the street. Leaning back against the door, Maude explained. "She wouldn't let me read her fortune."

"I guess that's her business, nor do I care in the long run," Rose countered. "Now that she's paid us back, these banjaxed dealings are none of our concern. But let me tell you what I *have* done. I took out an advertisement," she crowed. "And it'll come out in the paper tomorrow!"

She gestured grandly, a performer on stage. "*Maude Sinclair! The wonder of Cripple Creek is available to advise on matters of the heart and the pocket.* What do you think?"

Maude felt her eyes widen. "You might have asked me first."

"And you'd only have said no." Rose folded her arms across her chest. "I predict we're going to have a busy week upcoming."

A last-ditch effort. "But is it the type of business we want?"

"Oh, pish." Rose waved the suggestion away. "Paying customers, you bet! You're just feeling blue on account of...whatever it is that you feel blue about. Things don't come exactly easy out here. Hell, they never did. Nobody ever writes about that part."

"There'd be a caution in Millicent's fortune, guaranteed," Maude grumbled.

"And no matter," claimed Rose, "because it don't involve us any longer. She never was the clientele we were going after in the first place. You and I"—she nodded with a beady-eyed gleam—"are in this for the money."

———

What they got was notoriety.

Miners coming off their shift on a Friday or Saturday night had entertainment in mind, and it sure went beyond fortunes.

And a pretty young woman sitting on display drew all sorts of interest, as intended all along. Without question, many of them, washed or unwashed, paid their dollar just to have her hold their work-roughened hands and gaze into their eyes, searching for a glimmer. Of course, the women did nothing to curtail such activities.

"Who the hell cares," was Rose's usual response to Maude's grumbling.

"They aren't taking it seriously, and I do have a level of pride. Did you hear that last one? 'I want to know if I'm going to get lucky' indeed! He was laughing in my face, Rose."

"You took his money, didn't you? After you told him *no*, I stopped listening." Rose laughed, shaking her head.

"Yeah, well. He quit laughing when I told him about the possibility of the influenza."

"And was it there?"

A shiver along her spine. "No. Not specifically. 'Asshole' was written all over his lines and in his eyes. One of those Rocky Mountain canaries, as you call them."

Rose sashayed over to the money box. Her shaking it produced the gratifying clatter of multiple silver dollars within. "Make you feel better?"

True; for the first time, money in Cripple Creek panned out well, and Maude wouldn't need to scrape together her weekly rent. She might even save money by making monthly payments. She *could* use that money for the divorce...maybe she would. It was all becoming so much more distant now. The plan would be first to purchase a new skirt and blouse; no young woman liked to dress in rags if she could help it.

"If you'd put on some kohl and a spangly scarf, you'd have them dropping at your feet," Rose offered.

"Like you, you mean," Maude shot back. "And I could tell most of these new punters any darn thing, and they wouldn't even bat an eye."

Funny how a bit of money made people more discriminate in their dealings.

One week after the newspaper run, business had kept her hopping, but an undercurrent still pulled. Following a late night involving plenty of hand-holding fortunes, Maude walked home, dead tired. A nocturnal visitation from the ghostly girl disturbed her further. This time the girl did nothing more than sob; maybe it was a warning of sorts, or maybe the girl was just sad.

———

Drained, she dragged herself to the Emporium later than usual the following morning. The skull gave off an annoyed vibration.

"Yes, Charley, I'm late." But Rose wasn't within, so none living would be any the wiser.

Hanging up her coat, she hesitated, her blood creeping for no particular reason she could discern. Unnerved, she sniffed. The Fortune Emporium smelled a different kind of musty and stale.

Maude placed her hands on the top of the skull, allowing a heavy atmosphere of bad memories to travel up the side of her neck like a ghost's otherworldly fingernail.

She brushed at it, but traces of another person remained. Male. It sensed male.

Humming a wobbly tune to bolster her spirits, the shop came across as unnaturally cavernous despite the daylight. Her voice wavered, flat and uncertain.

The floorboards creaked too loud underfoot.

She bolted toward the rear door like hell was a-popping. Outside on the wooden landing, hands pressed against her thudding ribcage, she peered back inside. Nothing appeared physically amiss.

But the hair at the nape of her neck told another story.

Gripping the rough-hewn balustrade, her knuckles standing out white, the rickety steps down to the yard offered yet further escape. A wall of gray-steel storm rose behind the western mountains, wind-scoured snow pierced through by grass bowing low. She focused on that grass, and those Nebraska swells came to mind as wisps of her hair caught in the currents, a brown veil tangling around her face.

Struggle lay ahead.

A door slammed—a dog's bark carried from the distance. And the wind did not relent.

Too cold, she didn't linger. Feeling foolish all told, she returned inside, but it still didn't feel exactly right. Nerves twanging, in two strides she swooped down again upon Charley, lifting him from his shelf and holding him at eye level.

A floorboard creaked behind her. Not the settling sort of a noise, but a shifting of weight. Stomach washing over cold, she didn't want to, but she glanced over her shoulder.

Nothing.

Relaxing a mite, she tapped one of the skull's front teeth as he hummed, insistent in a way she hadn't heard before. But, then again, they weren't always on speaking terms. "You're not going to bite me, are you?"

"He won't, but I might," came a familiar voice.

A pent-up scream welled from deep inside. She spun around, clutching the skull to her chest.

Skiptown Charley emerged from behind one of the long, heavy drapes.

"What...what are you doing here?" She continued to clasp the skull in a death grip.

The same old smirk. "What if I said...I was hunting for...a fortune? Of course, you were out back, mooning about. Seems nothing much has changed where you're concerned."

The skull flared, hissing. The living Charley stopped dead in his tracks. Eyes shifting, uneasy and not knowing why.

A split second later, he smoothed over any misgivings, and his face returned to that old mask he wore when he prepared to fleece. "An old geezer directed me straight to you. Our paths crossing in Cripple Creek was a stroke of sheer unforeseen luck, but you didn't have to scream."

"Bad luck, you mean. What do you want?" Setting the skull down; the vibrations settled a notch.

Charley, the man and the con, folded his arms across his chest in a casual way, but in truth there was nothing casual about it.

"Well, not that I owe you any explanations, but mining has a nice ring to it, wouldn't you say? As far as what I want from you, nothing more than to catch up. For old times' sake. You've grown thin. You been pining away for me?"

"I've grown thin because I don't always have enough food to eat," she snapped.

A brief flicker and a throbbing vein. "I suppose I could buy you dinner tonight."

She wanted to fling it back in his face but wouldn't. "If that dinner is in a public restaurant."

He laughed with a dangerous confidence that had always served him well. "Don't worry so much. I'm not going to seduce you. And, on the face of things, your reputation is on a downhill slope while here I am, itching to get started. Try to choose a restaurant where you're not a curiosity. I, for one, plan on starting with a clean slate."

CHAPTER THIRTY-TWO
CROSSED PATHS AND CROSSED PURPOSES

Maude's firsthand knowledge of restaurants remained limited, so the threadbare establishment Lizzie brought her to would have to do. From the outside it didn't look as bad as she recalled, but falling snow had a way of softening things. The flat light shadows smoothed the splinters and rough edges, maybe on more than just buildings. With a disingenuous gallantry, her husband opened the door for her.

The customary ripple when a woman wandered in.

Skiptown claimed his place at a vacant table, ignorantly confident in the rustic surroundings. A small kerosene lamp stood in the center, its flame a flicker that got swallowed up along the edges. The five other tables were occupied by solitary men tucking into their meals. A place of scant conversation, striking utensils and masticating carried.

The proprietor sidled up to them, with a tired and determined cheerfulness. "We ain't got much for choice, but what we've got is fresh."

"Order what you want, Maude. Unless you want me to do it for you. For old times' sake."

She concentrated on the waiting pad of paper and pencil that promised food. "I'll have a steak, two eggs and a potato."

He wrote out her order, concentration exaggerated.

She ignored Skiptown, knowing what she'd find.

Sure enough. "It's like you got a damned hollow leg," he muttered.

The man kept his eyes on that pad of paper until he pointedly raised them to Skiptown.

"Steak and potatoes. And a glass of whiskey," he drawled.

Maude latched onto that and chimed in, "I'll have whiskey, too."

The man nodded and stepped away as the couple sat in estrangement, sizing each other up. Two glasses of whiskey were quickly placed before them without benefit of a spoken word.

Wanting to wound, Maude lifted her glass in a mock toast. "What happened to the other woman. She get tired of you?"

A snicker of irritation, but his posture didn't change. "Never you mind about that."

The liquor burned her chapped lips, right before the warmth hit her belly.

Skiptown sat forward, secretive and beady in turns. "It might interest you to know that I have possession of a claim. One that's going to pay. How does that strike you?"

The clanging of non-coincidental chance. "Arthur Harper's claim?"

Caught off guard, he flinched, scared enough that he patted his breast pocket. Still there. "Glad you haven't lost your touch—well, what there is of it. How'd you know, and don't think for a minute you can fool me into believing some damn second-sight bullshit."

It would be so easy to string him along. "I know his wife in passing. How'd you get it?"

"Why, how do you think? I bought it from the geezer fair and square."

There had to be more to it than that. "You've never struck me as a pick and shovel type of fellow."

"Very funny. I'm going to sell it on to deeper pockets. That's the plan in a nutshell."

The serving man reappeared, cutting the conversation off. Tin plates were set before them, barely touching the table before Maude dug in.

"No one's going to take it away from you," her *husband* chided.

Chewing, she appraised him. "Why are you telling me about your dealings?"

"Now, why do you think? Just to put your mind at ease, the plan is to find a buyer and move on. You wouldn't happen to know of anyone who's on the lookout for a claim, would you?"

"And if I did?"

He tugged on his shirt cuff flaunting a gold cufflink. "In that case I'd hope you'd introduce us. For a cut, of course."

Maude glared at the gold. "I know someone. And he's got money, too. I'd want a cut *and* a divorce. Your fancy woman give you those?"

"A formal divorce? My, my. Never knew you were so hard-over on details. As for a cut *and* a divorce. Well. I'd have to think about that for a while. I'm not exactly sure I could see my way clear to do that, Maude."

"And I'm not so certain I could see my way toward providing an introduction, otherwise. How much you plan on selling it for?"

That sly old grin. "Five thousand dollars."

It kind of rolled off his tongue, the way he said it.

"You come up with that yourself?" Maude challenged.

"Nah," he replied. "I've asked around. Seems reasonable, and it's a pretty good return for what I've got into it."

"Well? Meet my terms, or you're on your own."

"Well, maybe I don't want my name linked with yours. You ever stopped to consider that? You know, there's a curious story making the rounds. About how a woman matching your description has been seen going in and out of the Mikado during daylight hours, and without the slightest regard for the ordinances. How does that strike you?"

It struck her as inconvenient but nowhere near as upsetting as he assumed. "Sounds like nothing more than drunken imaginings."

He sneered and offered a wink. "Hard to say."

Maude tucked back into her food, enjoyment dwindling.

The restaurant door opened, and a man entered. Something about his build struck her, causing a second glance. Of all the rotten luck, *Clayton* lingered by the door.

A split second later and he tracked her. Sitting with another man. He turned right around and left without a word.

"Wait here." Maude's utensils clattered onto the plate as she rushed out behind him. Chasing him down in the street and skittering as she went.

"Clayton, wait!"

He stopped, squared his shoulders, and paused on the weathered boards. He didn't turn around.

"Please. Let me explain," she pleaded, grabbing his coat sleeve and propelling herself in front of him. "It's not what you think."

Her breath came out in gray clouds in the cold night air.

"You don't owe me any explanations." His voice came out strained and exasperated.

"That man, well, there's nothing left between us but a divorce to be had. And I'm working on that part."

"You're *married*?" He reared back. "You sure don't act married!"

Again, Maude reached out for his coat sleeve, but this time he brushed her off.

Her hand hung in the air. "He abandoned me in Nebraska, and now he's turned up here out of the blue! I let him buy me dinner because I was hungry. Nothing more."

He squinted down at her. "*You're going hungry?* You could have said."

A shamed laugh welled. "You never came calling."

"You ran off! I was getting ready to ask you that other day, when you stopped by talking about Indians! Look, I'll buy your dinner, Maude. There's no need to lower yourself down."

Cheeks stinging in the darkened street, her back stiffened. "Lower myself down? I haven't lowered myself down. Is that what you think? I'm out here as an honest woman..."

Distrust rippled through his expression. "If you say." A shrug. "I've already been shamed once. I don't plan on going through all of that again."

"We've all got pasts, and not all of them are nice. Now, I've got to go back. It'll go harder on me if Charley thinks there's something between us."

"But there's not, is there." It was a statement, not a question. The blacksmith peered down at her in a way designed to make her feel small.

When she didn't answer he stalked off into the darkened street, leaving her standing alone.

———

The look she got from Skiptown was one of pure condescension.

"Who was that? Either you've moved on, too, or he owes you money. Judging by the way you went tearing out after him, I'd hope it was money. Otherwise, it comes across as pretty damned desperate. Doesn't he feed you?"

Maude glared. "None of your business."

Picking up her fork, she stabbed at the food in front of her. Ill-mannered for emphasis, without comment or permission, she snatched a slice of bread from Skiptown's plate and made a show of sopping up the juices.

In between mouthfuls, she bothered a few points. "I'll broker your damn deal, but in return you'll grant me the divorce and pay the fees." Another bite of bread. "And, before you start to argue, don't. It won't work unless I step in to help. You may not know it right now, but I sure as hell do."

"Fine," Charley agreed, over a barrel. "But a divorce seems nothing more than a waste of good money to me."

Disagreeing, she shook her head as he signaled for the bill.

PART THREE
A MINING SWINDLE

PART THREE

A MIND ASUNDER

CHAPTER THIRTY-THREE
GAMES OF CHANCE ARE USUALLY RIGGED

Striding straight up to the Mikado's door, Maude twisted the bell key. The sound severed any illusion of tranquility. Tentative footsteps approached, wary. Those steps didn't belong to Julia. Hers would be decisive, no matter the hour.

Gretchen, the housekeeper, cracked open the door about three inches. With a spark of recognition, she opened wide, weary bleach-blue eyes magnified behind spectacle lenses.

"Is Julia in?" Maude asked.

The fish-eyes challenged. "Where else would she be? It's too early for them lot."

"It can't be helped." Maude's voice dropped. "Listen, Gretchen, if that Everett is around, don't mention I'm down here if you can help it."

A derisive snort at the mention of Ev. The woman stood aside, and Maude passed into the half-light. Last night's carry-on hung in the stale air, ripe and none too refined. Slashes of the morning penetrated through disorderly gaps in the curtains. Glasses with remnants and bottles lay strewn about, spittoons and ashtrays brimming foul.

"You don't see him dropping dead by chance, do you?" Gretchen wasn't joking.

The twinge of caution rose from Maude's tailbone. She offered a mere shake of the head.

The fish-eyes challenged, shrewd. "Who will this benefit, then?"

That was the ninety-four-dollar question. "If this all works out, Mr. Stevenson will probably move on."

Gretchen tossed her head at the mess in the front room. "I've got to get cleaning."

Maude considered the stairs and what lay above, and the woman followed her gaze.

An exhale. "Oh, shoot fire. I guess I'll handle them lot upstairs for you. Mind you, I don't usually go there myself. Not until past the noon hour."

The housekeeper took a suck of air as she set foot on the stair's tread. Grasping the bannister in that old-woman way of climbing, she took one determined step at a time.

Left alone with her reflection in the diamond-dust mirror, Maude shook off the woolies. She could end up jaded—near as jaded as the inmates above. And that jaded lot upstairs grumbled and stirred. The thread of a cutting temper...muffled voices in strained, harsh tones. The heel-strikes of a woman who had an ax to grind.

Julia leaned over the railing, peering down, tangled crimson locks cascading. "Heard of decent calling hours? This had better be good." Her voice rasped, jagged and thick.

She made plenty of bones about the inconvenience, clomping down the stairs in shoes hastily put on but unfastened, a dressing gown loosely tied and frilly undergarments poking through. If she couldn't sleep, she was bound and determined that none of the others could either.

"Julia, shhh! I need to talk to you. In *private*."

"Don't you shush me in my own house." Except for her hair, the madam came across faded in the pigeon-gray light. Less imposing, in a steel-corset kind of way.

"It's important, or I would have waited. I've come about a business matter. A *confidential* business matter that shouldn't be overheard."

Sticky underfoot, Maude's boot soles gummed on the wooden floor. *Hopefully nothing worse than spilled liquor.*

Expression pained, Julia brushed past Maude and opened her office door. "Get in here, and let's get whatever this is over with."

Maude had never ventured into the small, tight room before. Nor had she been invited. The yellow cabbage rose-and-trellis wallpaper struck her as out of place. Misguidedly innocent, even. Of course, any such naiveté was slapped into place by the masculine desk that claimed most of the floor space. An artfully rendered mountain landscape decorated a massive safe set into the far wall.

Drawn to the gold-stenciled letters on it, Maude blinked.

John A. Hamlin, Agent, Kansas City & Denver.
Detroit Safe Company

Hangover or annoyance be damned, for Julia followed her eyes and crowed, "Ain't she a beauty? And that, my friend, is what this business is all about."

Shutting the office door, the latch clicked into place. Julia leaned back against the door and sized up Maude, smirking and blocking any escape. "If you're expecting coffee, that's too damn bad. Let's have it."

Maude sat deep in the chair, her spine against the spokes. "Just so you know, I'm playing this straight with you. So, hear me out."

The madam flicked her fingers before launching herself to the larger chair behind the desk. "You sure have a lot to learn about enticement."

Maude ignored the taunt. "The devalued claim has come up for sale, and it's falling to me to find a buyer. I want to offer it to *your* man, hoping that he takes it."

A wry flicker. "So far that ore has caused nothing but trouble."

"Does it matter? One way or another, it's going to be sold."

The madam inspected her nails, eyes beady when she finally latched onto Maude's. "If it's a winner, you know I can't have that."

Maude's knuckles turned white; she gripped the armrests that hard. "He'll think it's a winner, and that's the point. He came to see me the other day, as you said he would."

Hands pressed together in a mercenary prayer, Julia studied the ceiling, the constant wheels turning. "And you want to off-load it on Everett. Well. That might work in a run-around type of way. What's in it for me?"

Maude shifted in her seat, without a ready answer.

The madam leaned forward, all sharp angles. "If the claim's a winner, that's the last I'll see of Everett Stevenson, and we both know it."

"Speaking of missing men, guess who holds the claim deed."

A blink.

"Shit," the madam hooted, slapping the desktop. "You're joshing me."

Pursing her lips, Maude sought to keep her tone even. "Well, it changes things on my end."

"Does it?"

Sprawled in the chair, the madam listened and listened close.

"This presents an opportunity. Part of the deal is that he'll agree to a divorce and even pay the fees." Maude heard the hope lurking and quashed it back down. Her hopes were her own business, and nothing she wanted the madam to latch onto.

"That's it? That's what you're banking on? Can't see how it's much of a deal on your side."

Maude's pride flared, and she puffed up indignant. "I'm going to pad the selling price."

"How much are we talking?"

That damned mercenary glimmer, sparking a notion of a steep slagheap poised to give way.

"Well," Maude stalled. "He wants five thousand. I'm making it ten on the quiet."

Underwhelmed, the madam puckered her mouth. "So, let me see if I've got this right. Your—husband—is going to sell the claim, and Everett hands him a bank draft for twice the amount. How's that going to work?"

"I'll figure it out." Maude again shifted in her seat.

Julia smirked. "You'd better. You'll need to figure out a plan. A real one with teeth." She sat up straighter, suddenly impatient. "You didn't see Ev becoming rich, did you?"

That invisible shove. Maude's purse slipped to the floor, coins clinking. Coins that could disappear oh so easily.

She snatched the purse up, set it back square in her lap. "No. I did not."

The madam drummed her fingers on the desk. Stopping abrupt, she opened the center desk drawer and pulled out a *carte de visite*. Tapping it against her thumbnail like it didn't matter.

Maude caught a glimpse of a scant-clad dolly. "Who's that?" No one within the walls of the Mikado, that much was certain.

"Who the hell cares! This was in his pants pockets, which means he's wandering. If he's noticed it's missing, he hasn't had the balls to ask."

Julia tossed it back into the drawer like an unpaid bill, slamming it shut. "I'll take one thousand dollars for the loss of my investment and the help I'm about to provide. Do your worst, and we'll see how it lands."

A few rapid blinks. "A thousand dollars! For what?"

"Banking. You're going to need help on that end; I guarantee it."

Maude hid her gasp at the unforeseen complication. "That's a hefty cut." A pregnant pause. "Three hundred dollars *if* I get the five thousand."

The flick of the madam's head. "Five hundred, and not a penny less."

Silence.

The madam clarified her position. "At this point—and I can see the question roiling in your brain—you're paying for experience in dealings that you don't have, but I certainly do. Unless the unforeseeable goes wrong, and that's where *you and your abilities* are supposed to come in, Everett's going to have himself another mine. So, I'll take your five hundred dollars on account of how I consider you a *friend*. For anyone less, it would be half of your takings."

Maude shifted in her seat, unhappy. "And if it goes wrong?"

Julia shook her head. "I'll handle it. Like I said, I've got experience."

And so another wary Cripple Creek deal was brokered, with neither party completely satisfied.

CHAPTER THIRTY-FOUR

SOURED ROMANCES
(AND CHOOSE YOUR COMPANY WISELY)

M aude couldn't get out of the Mikado fast enough. An early morning as far as Myers Avenue was concerned, the denizens lurched into the day in varying shades of dress and inebriation. The whoop-up was already stirring, but an uncanny sensation travelled her spine and brushed across the nape of her neck. Eyes were upon her. She scanned the street and saw the culprit. A sharper of some sort, lounging against a doorframe and staring straight at her. He tipped his hat in the southern style.

Knowing better, she still nodded in response.

She took a few more steps, and her blood damn near stopped.

Clayton, of all people. Making a delivery to a saloon, he stood rooted outside of the door, a metal implement in his hands.

Judging by the expression on his face, he'd either seen her come out of the Mikado, seen the exchange with the sharper, or, even worse, both.

Cold blue eyes scanned her face, followed by a slow, disappointed shake of the head. He entered the side door of the saloon and shut it behind him without looking at her again.

The wind knocked out of her, she cast about, and her gaze collided with that of the sharper. He smirked, but she didn't care.

Clayton. Well. He'd never think anything good about her now.

———

Cheeks stinging, heart racing, and shame sorely creeping, she didn't tarry any longer. Desperately wanting a sympathetic ear—Rose's version would have to do—she rushed to the Emporium, but from the distance she could see no movement. Just a gnarled miner waiting in front, no doubt wondering why the shop was still closed.

"It's gone past eleven o'clock," he boomed in that hard-of-hearing way underground miners had.

Rattled, she fumbled with the key. When the door opened, he trailed on in after her.

"Not working today?" she asked, turning to him direct-on so he could read her lips if needed.

"Nah. Going drinking after this. But I figured to check whether I should be drinking beer or drinking whiskey. I guess it depends on how this here fortune spins."

"What can I do for you?"

"Prognosticate," he replied, like she was dim. "That's what you do, ain't it?"

And so she did, but her heart wasn't in it.

———

Two dollars later, Rose bustled in, oblivious or uncaring as to the time.

"Morning, Sunshine," she chirped.

"More like afternoon." Maude muttered, still feeling hangdog.

Rose gestured, wide and grand—no doubt a relic from her theatrical days. "The sky is blue, the temperature is on its way up, and spring is around the corner. What's wrong with *you*?"

"Plenty."

Rose laughed but broke it off, turning a shade toward cautious. "Such as?"

Maude flailed her hands about. "Kind of hard to know where to begin. Yesterday my husband found me. I sure wish you'd been here..."

"Did he *hurt* you, Maude?"

A stab of memory. "No. Nothing like that." The words tumbled out, just a bit too fast.

"You're sure?"

A miserable nod from Maude.

The sharp glint of appraisal from an unconvinced Rose. "So, what's the problem—second thoughts?"

"No," Maude replied, grappling for safer ground. "Said he heard tell of a seeress and followed the lead. Turns out he has a mining claim he wants to sell."

"Stay out of it." Rose frowned, still studying Maude.

"The claim he's trying to offload is Arthur Harper's."

Rose reared back. "Shit. That thing's got legs on it..."

Maude stared into the corner before searching Rose's eyes. "Clayton saw me coming out of the Mikado."

Rose pressed her lips together thin enough to almost disappear, the unspoken I-told-you-so clear.

A hint of defiance sparked. "Julia's man wants a claim, and Julia wants a cut of the selling price." A pause. "Aren't you going to yell, or tell me that you warned me, or a caution along those lines?"

Rose's exasperated laugh died halfway out. "This is all

too far gone for that. Word'll get out about you and the Mikado, mind. Like I always said it would."

Another stab of shame. "You also told me that Clayton wasn't the kind to go shooting his mouth off."

"Maybe he's not. But don't you worry on that count, for others certainly will." Rose folded her arms, like that settled matters once and for all.

Flushing, Maude tried pleading. "I need your help, Rose. Honestly. Skiptown's planning on naming the price as five thousand dollars. Does that sound right?"

"Maybe. It's a prospect hole. But a prospect hole in a good area." Rose shrugged, more interested in the drama rather than her words.

Maude, wanting help and expertise, felt Rose wasn't forthcoming. She tried again. "He'll give me the divorce and ten percent of the selling price. A commission of sorts."

Rose, latching onto a different point, snorted. "So, you've decided to let bygones be bygones, is that it? And, while we're at it, how does Julia fit into this exactly?"

A zing of caution. "I've told you: Julia passed on word about the assay results, which is how I know it's valuable. Now"—she took a slight step to the side—"I'll admit I shouldn't have told her about padding the selling price, but it's too late for that now. As for Skiptown, maybe for once I can hold my own."

Rose put both hands atop her scarf and smoothed it back. "Revenge, is it? And pad the selling price how?"

She'd stepped in it again. "Skiptown thinks he's getting five thousand. I'll tell Julia's man the price is ten. I'll tell Charlie to never bring up the selling price again. Pretty good, huh? Julia's figuring out the details as we speak."

"Well, that's a nifty trick, if you lot can pull it off. And

I'll take the same for my troubles." She folded her arms across her chest, matter settled in her mind.

That shocked Maude cold. "What do you mean?"

"If you're paying Julia, and I'm pretty sure you must be somehow, you can spread money my way as well. After all, we've been partners for a time now, and I'm worth every bit as much as that old whore is, if not more."

Judging by Rose's stance, there was little point in arguing. "I'm only going to pay if this works," Maude spat. "That's the same deal Julia got. But I feel you both are taking advantage of me."

Charlie started chattering from his shelf, catching Maude's attention.

"And throw in Charlie, too. He's no good to you, and I want to at least make something in this mess right."

"So be it." Rose's voice tightened. "The skull will belong to you. Now, we'd best locate that no-account of yours. Before someone else gets the notion to go a-helping him with that claim."

———

The woman walked downhill and rounded a corner.

"It's fairly disreputable," Rose half sang as a low-down affair came into view, "but I've always liked it."

They stopped square in front of a gambling establishment. No sign, no name, and not much of a welcome.

But men were going in, heedless.

And, it was true, few of the local gambling hells bothered advertising for the simple fact that they didn't need to.

Maude took its measure, clutching her purse tight. "Well, it looks a place Skiptown might frequent..."

Rose, needing no encouragement whatsoever, pushed in like she belonged.

The women entered a deep blue-gray veil of smoke. Packed to the brim with punters itching to lose their money; faro, poker games, and roulette wheels clattered along beneath choking gas lights struggling to dispel the gloom.

Red number 5, Gentlemen!

The spinning ball whirled in the roulette wheel: the fateful bounce followed by a stunned silence, then muttering and muffled curses when no winner emerged.

"Roulette's a dupe's game," Maude muttered.

Rose seemed half impressed that she knew anything about such dealings at all.

Games of chance radiated from the potbelly stove set plunk in the middle of the room. *Step right up and take your chances* crooned the universal come-on, each game a splintering spoke in a crooked wheel.

The punters displayed a remarkable disinterest in the women's presence, a disregard that bordered on insulting. Women had their place, and, in their minds, Crumley's Gambling Hall wasn't it. Yet, nevertheless, the gambling fraternity offered a queer sense of equality, with any and all participants equally poised to lose. The dealers and the ringers took their measure, eyes flashing in impassive faces. Watching. Always waiting for the inevitable slip to turn the odds in favor of their own personal gain. Or the house's. At times, the two were damned near inseparable.

Dimly lit or not, Maude located Skiptown out of an old, half-forgotten instinct. She turned her back to him, hoping he wouldn't mark her just yet.

"He's the one over there." A backwards, dismissive toss of her head. "Slouched against the wall near the corner, wearing an Eastern suit."

The din of the dealers singing out and men's voices continued, unabated.

It was a hell of a way to blow off steam.

"At least now I know he's not one of your damn wraiths." Rose's demeanor changed on a dime as a half-kempt man ambled over in their general direction.

"How's Lady Luck treating you?" she bellowed, in her element and displaying the wry recognition of a partner of sorts.

"About like a woman," he replied with the tinge of a smile, bitter around the edges.

Jolly old Rose when it suited her, reeling someone in. "Well, it's about time you got put in your place! Seems to me you take more out of here than you pay in. All the same, hope the gambling doesn't treat you too rough."

The man chuckled as he tipped his hat and shuffled off in search of more ways to lose his money.

Of course, by that time, Skiptown had spotted them. Just another fixture awaiting any chance to strike, he propelled himself from the wall and appeared at their sides in a jiff. "Ladies, care for a drink?"

Rose lit up at the prospect. His eyes flickered over her getup. She caught it and positively beamed, putting him on the back foot.

Good for Rose, Maude thought but still cut her off from answering. "This isn't a social call. We're here for business reasons only. And I'd sure hate to have what I'm about to say get overheard."

A pointed flicker of interest. The old, polished conde-scension that had worn so thin. "In that case, let's take this outside, shall we?"

He herded them out the door.

On the uneven boards, Maude waited for passers-by to clear. After checking up and down the street again, she lowered her voice. "There's a man interested in your claim, and he doesn't want his name to get out, hands to get dirty, or be associated with any of it."

Skiptown aimed a barb in Rose's direction. He never did care for witnesses.

Maude flashed their old sign, flicking her left earring. "He's got backers in Denver. Rose knows the ins and outs of what's going on in the district, and he's the best bet you're going to find."

"Is that so." That same old deadpan.

"I take it you have a plan?" Maude tapped the toe of her boot against the boards, growing impatient.

Hands on hips and pushing the sides of his coat back, his posture remained confident. Too confident. "Point me in his direction, and I'll have it done with."

"It's not that simple. He has a history in mining and knows what he's looking at. Like I said, he's fair skittish. You got that claim deed on you?"

He patted his breast pocket.

"Let me see it." Maude thrust out her hand.

He rolled his eyes, pulling out the document with a sarcastic flourish, pinched between his fingertips. Poised to pull a trick.

Maude snatched the paper, pressing it between her palms before reading the contents. Concentrating and sensing. "It's had a fair amount of handling. Any idea why that might be?"

That cautious, tense stare. "No. And quit that mumbo-jumbo bullshit. What're you getting at?"

It wasn't as if they were exactly on the same side.

But the plat number was written there in black and white.

Plat S Section 13 T 15 R 70.

She flourished it at Rose, who caught the number with a practiced eye.

"You told the swell the price, right?" Shifting his

weight ever so slightly from one foot to the other, he was bothered. Bothered, but that was none of Maude's concern.

She bared her teeth, attempting Julia's mercenary smile—a smile that put men in their places. In return, he offered a derisive glare.

Maude dropped the game. "Five thousand dollars. Now, that's a figure *you* need to be careful of. Don't *ever* bring up the selling price again. To anyone."

Sensing deep waters, Skiptown's guard rose. "That's ridiculous. Why the hell not?"

A feigned air of superiority. "Because that's not how it's done out here. If you start tossing figures about, they'll take you for a greenhorn, in which case you're *really* fair game. The sale price has already been agreed. All you do is collect. Think you can manage?"

"Oh, I can manage all right. You've got the meeting set up?"

"Of course not." She put her hands on her hips. "How could I? I don't exactly know how to find you."

"You never could, could you?"

Back to his sneaking around with the other woman...a hated, stinging flush in her cheeks. A sudden vulnerability she didn't welcome. "Well, I did just now."

He eyed her. "It was doubtless your friend there that figured it out, little girl. But let's not quibble. I'm staying at the American Boardinghouse. For the time being."

Rose wrinkled her nose and cackled. "You'd best sleep with that deed on you, if that's really where you're holed up."

He threw her a cutting expression and turned back to Maude. "How do we make the deal?"

"It'll have to be set up, won't it? Stop by the Emporium at five o'clock tomorrow evening, and I'll have something figured out."

He mock saluted the two women and returned inside Crumley's with a newfound spring in his step.

"It's next to worthless," Rose urged in a low tone, taking his measure. "Not signed over like that."

Maude marked his progress, separated by a thin glass pane and miles in outlook.

"But he doesn't know that," she replied and, for some as yet unknown reason, felt slightly better.

CHAPTER THIRTY-FIVE
SORDID COMPANIONS
AND HANGERS-ON

I n a foul mood bordering on murderous, Julia had plenty of problems of her own. The most pressing of which, strangely, had nothing to do with Everett. What she held in her hands was far more immediate, and the threat spelled out for her was real. Underlined, in fact. Just in case she missed it.

> *I've got it on good <u>authority</u> that your house poses a public health hazard. It is my duty to <u>report</u> such matters to the proper authorities, unless you can <u>provide</u> evidence that there is no contagion emanating from your establishment. A man, whose identity shall remain <u>protected</u>, claims otherwise. Based upon past history, there is <u>merit</u> to his account, which must be <u>considered</u>. The <u>penalties</u> for running a pest house can be <u>substantial</u>. It is a known fact that women of ill-fame spread disease.*

So, another twenty dollars wasn't going to fix it this time.

There were only so many times a body could re-read a note; the underlined words emphasized the consequences for ignoring him. That asshole undertaker was far too enterprising for his own good, and *hers*. The intimidation had to be answered, head on.

Well, hell. She could blackmail him in return. If he had backing in City Hall, *she* had ammunition in her little black book. Names of those who *ran* the town and district, if not beyond. The asshole hadn't stopped to figure that far. True, those men of noted preferences might not be all that willing, but they could be brought around with a carefully aimed word or two.

The thing to do was to invite him into the house to discuss matters. Once that front door swung shut, he would be smack dab in the middle of her territory, and it would be her word against his. And if one of the girls took him for a twirl, so much the better.

Speaking of girls, that drugged-out Lizzie seemed slow on getting up. It was nigh on three o'clock in the afternoon.

Julia dropped the note back inside the safe, shut the door, and spun the wheel. She came out from behind her desk, left her office, and minced her way up the stairs, careful of her footfalls. Creeping up to Lizzie's door, she noted in passing it could use another coat of paint.

She hauled off and palm-slapped the dingy surface, making sure the sound carried good and loud. Hoping to startle the hell out of Lizzie, but it didn't hurt to put the other girls on notice, too.

"Lizzie! You up in there?"

No answer. Julia jiggled the doorknob. "Hope you're decent, 'cause I'm coming in!"

Another girl stuck her head out into the hallway. "She ain't going to hear you, if last night was any indication."

Julia shot the girl a nasty look that told her to mind her own goddamned business, then pushed on through. Clothes were strewn about, expensive clothes at that; the girl lying in bed, passed out, head flung back and mouth open. But breathing. In three quick strides Julia was at her side, slapping her on the cheeks as if she had fainted, when what she wanted to do was haul off and belt her one.

"Goddamn it, Lizzie! Get on up, you hear me? I've about had enough of this shit..."

The girl opened her unfocused eyes and blinked, still half in the bag.

"Julia...what is it?"

"I've got better things to do than spend my time rousing you. Now get the hell off that bed and clean up this mess!"

Lizzie propped herself up on one elbow, not near as upset as she ought to be. "What time is it?"

"Time for you quit the dope. If you can't get a handle on your habit, I'll throw you out on your ear. Then it'll be the cribs for you, my girl."

A dainty yawn and a stretch, although the whore appeared green around the gills. "That won't happen."

"It might," Julia snapped. "That's where faded-out dope fiends end their days, one way or another."

That comment registered in depths of the dolly's befuddled brain. Swinging her feet to the floor, she managed to concentrate enough to cast a glare in Julia's general direction, not quite focused. "I'm the best-looking whore you've got in this rat hole, and I sure haven't heard any complaints."

"Rat hole, is it? And you're hearing an important complaint right now, because I'm the *one who's making it*. Get up, get dressed, and be downstairs in time for the midday supper. I shouldn't have to mollycoddle you. And the drugs, they are a-telling. You know, the monthly docs are tomorrow. And I sure as hell don't want your name or any other problem cropping up. Understand me?"

The dolly mumbled something or other. Right before she spewed.

"Clean it up," Julia hissed as she left the room and headed back down the stairs. "Everyone had better be up and getting ready to start another bang-up shooting match! And someone get in there and make sure Lizzie cleans up her puke and airs the room out."

Voices rose in complaint, but they didn't deter her in the slightest.

Julia marched back into her office, slamming the door behind her.

They would damn well do as they were told.

She twirled the combination and opened the safe, pulled out her black book and the most recent ledgers. Reading the two in tandem always gave her a fine sense of perspective. After scanning the latest takings, she opened the black book and considered the contents within. Names of the clientele and preferences noted. She considered the names of those who might be willing to bend certain rules to her advantage. A more careful consideration of those men with *specialized* proclivities they would be desperate to keep hidden. Of course, those would be the most profitable of all.

Thus assured, she wrote out a card that would probably do the trick.

Mr. Blake,

    Please stop by the Mikado to discuss the complaint at your earliest convenience. No doubt you will want to inspect the premises yourself before making such important accusations. Of course, I hope to resolve the matter between the two of us and have it extend no further. Please call any time after 2:00 in the afternoon. The evening might be the most beneficial, but, of course, the choice is entirely yours.

    Consider this an invitation extended.

> *Your servant,*
> *Julia Robinson*

"Servant, my ass," she spluttered under her breath.

Men such as Blake liked nothing better than to see women kowtow. Funny thing about that. She felt exactly the same way, but in reverse. She would like nothing better than to see him grovel instead.

CHAPTER THIRTY-SIX
TRANSACTIONS IN THE HALF LIGHT

TUESDAY, APRIL 14, 1896

It was becoming a regular habit—sidestepping drunks and eyeing the dregs from the previous night. There was no respectable time along Myers Avenue, and ten thirty in the morning could be taken as fair game.

Straight to the brothel door she strode, the twist of the bell-key answered near straight away. A tousled half-decent denizen opened the door wide enough for the entire world to see and stood halfway draped upon it. In fact, the door held her upright—still drunk and reeling from the night before.

"You're late to the party," she slurred. "And now it's all over. I'm going to bed."

Maude nodded at the girl and tried to get into her good graces, muddled though they might have been. "You're Lill, aren't you?"

The girl tried to focus. "Yeah, that's right. And you're the crystal-ball gazer, ain't you? I've been here two *very* long weeks, now." The last part a drunken whisper that came across plenty loud.

Maude glanced up at the stairs. Mercifully, no one was around to catch it.

"Say, Lill, on your way to your room, could you *please* tell Everett Stevenson that I need to talk to him? It's important."

The dolly leaned forward, offering another exaggerated whisper that came out on her breath as straight liquor. "Don't tell me he's got you on the string, too."

"Of course not," Maude snapped. "What would give you that idea?"

A drunken giggle faded, drained away. "Because you're asking for him, and I've seen you...talking...to him before." A half stagger and a finger pointed in Maude's direction. "He's a fox in a chicken coop, that one. But he's Julia's..."

Depositing those tainted nuggets, the dolly trailed off up the stairs, an unpromising messenger at best.

Maude crossed the threshold. The clock read 10:34, and she figured she'd give it five minutes before resorting to another plan. In no way did she want to climb up those stairs herself. But she could. *If* she had to.

As it turned out, luck struck in her favor, and, apparently, Lill did her bidding. A few moments later, Everett Stevenson clomped down the stairs as ill-humored as ever.

"I thought you and I had an understanding." His tone wasn't promising. "What part didn't you understand...darlin'?"

That word *darlin* came out near to a threat.

"Apparently, the part about how I *wasn't* supposed to contact you when I found a good prospect." She put her hands on her hips. "If you expected a *telegram,* you should have said so. Now, where *exactly* do you want to conduct this conversation, because the news won't keep. And, let me put it this way: if I'm not having the conversation with you, I'll be having it with someone else."

Everett tossed a shifty-eyed glance up the stairs. "Keep your voice down, will you?"

He was nervous. Good.

"Where's Julia?" Maude asked, rubbing it in.

"Upstairs, but maybe not for much longer. Now, out with it." He grabbed her arm hard, clamping on like a damned mongrel.

A half-formed yelp through clenched teeth, but not loud enough to summon anyone. "You're hurting me!"

His eyes were as determined as death. But he let her go without saying a damned thing, contempt plain.

Maude made a show of rubbing her arm. "I don't take kindly to bruising."

"And I don't take kindly to playing games."

She was losing ground. "Sam Evans—you know him —stopped by, wanting to know about a mine location, of all things. His interest, of course, stems from the ore I brought in. Would you believe the results came back *bad*?"

The man's eyes narrowed.

Straightening her sleeve, she lied. "I took the ore to another assayer, who had far better results. Does that catch your interest? If it doesn't, it sure will someone else's."

Those dead eyes hardened. "What's the asking price?"

"Ten thousand dollars." She never once blinked.

He sneered. "For a *prospect* hole?"

"For a prospect hole with *good,* assayed results. Some might even say it's a bargain. You know what I've heard? I've heard that the day of the lone miner is gone. Companies hold most everything these years. Where do you think you're going to find a better chance?"

Surveying her up and down, he weighed out her value, never mind the ore. "What's your part in all of this?"

Shifting uncomfortable, she could still manage. "Isn't it obvious?"

"No."

From the periphery, she glimpsed Julia listening in, but the madam had enough sense to pull back.

She returned her attention square on the fancy man. "I'm acting as a go-between. As such, I'll expect a finder's fee. Say, seven hundred dollars?"

Flinging his head back, he laughed at the ceiling. "What do you take me for, an idiot?"

"Fine. Have it your way. It's all the same to me." She took a decisive step toward the door.

Again, he grabbed her arm, lowered his voice. "Not so fast. Say I pay a portion of your finder's fee. Two hundred dollars tops, and maybe not even that. I'm still going to want to see that mine for myself. Due diligence, it's called. Heard of it?"

She hadn't.

"A trip to the mine can be arranged," Maude replied, staring pointedly at his fingers. A flare of certainty came with the contact—he would get what he deserved in the end. And that case of the clap she'd seen earlier.

"Tomorrow," he replied. "Make it tomorrow at noon."

CHAPTER THIRTY-SEVEN
WITNESSES CAN BE BENEFICIAL...OR NOT

Skiptown whistled his way to the Emporium, like he hadn't a care in the world. He pushed through the door, the bell tinkling bright and the skull rumbling low. It was a quarter past five in the evening.

A quarter of an hour late just to show who was boss.

"Pawn your watch along the line?" Maude shot across at him.

He clasped his hands over his heart, staggered back a step or two for effect. "No," he replied with a grin, flashing his pocket watch at her.

Maude took his measure. Pointedly. "The buyer wants to visit the mine as a condition of the sale."

That caused him to quit joking around. "Hell, I haven't even seen it yet myself."

"You do have the quitclaim, don't you?" Maude asked point-blank.

He faltered, like he'd been clipped. "How's that?"

Maude did nothing to tamp down the wry smile that played upon her lips as his spark of superiority fell, dashed to pieces.

Equally, she knew none of it was a laughing matter.

Everything *could* come crashing down, and all too easily. "Proof that Harper has relinquished all claims to the mine."

She could see he didn't understand. "If all you've got is the deed, well, you're probably in for a fair amount of trouble if you're *really* trying to sell it on."

"That's not funny, Maude."

"I'm not laughing, Charley."

He'd never been the kind to strike a woman but looked on the verge. A vein in his neck throbbed, and his voice came out tight. "You had better tell me what you are talking about, or, so help me, you can kiss that divorce goodbye."

"Your deed isn't signed over. Now maybe he was drunk and forgetful, or maybe he hoodwinked you. You know how to find Harper? If I were you, that's what I would be doing, right now. And I'd start out talking real nice to him, too."

He put his hands on his hips, annoyed. "And if he doesn't give me a quitclaim?"

"Then you'd better make him. It's your word against his. But, while he's a drunk, no one knows *you* here. It'd cost you money to get it sorted out in a legal way, if it came to that. Rose thinks the deal might come down to witnesses. People who saw the transaction."

His eyes narrowed. "I don't have their names, Maude. The Abbey barman might remember the exchange, but I don't want to return there with my tail between my legs. What am I supposed to do—go in and ask, 'Did you see a miner about yay high sell me a claim, and did you notice the money exchanging hands?' No one is going to want to get involved with anything like that, and I can't blame them." He ran his fingers through his hair, pacing. "What if I sold it at a discount?"

"It might not help." Maude shrugged. "The prospective buyer knows what he's doing. Maybe if the price came cheap enough, he'd drag it through the courts for you. But those things take time, and time is one thing he doesn't seem to have much of."

"Well, then. I'd best go locate Harper." He paused. "Don't suppose you'd care to accompany me?"

He'd never wanted her around for any of his maneuverings before, and Maude frowned. "What good would it do?"

"Don't know, but hell. Maybe you could spook him or something."

Desperate enough to agree, Maude sighed. She worried about whatever it was Millicent was hiding.

She would have felt better if the washerwoman had let her re-read her fortune. But she hadn't. And Maude rose to her feet.

———

The Abbey Saloon stood at the corner of Third and Myers, one block over from the Mikado and far too close for comfort.

Sparrows and crows, sparrows and crows.

Those words kept repeating through her mind, although she couldn't have said why. "They aren't partial to having women in saloons out here."

A derisive snort. "Since when has any of that ever bothered you?"

Since North Platte. "Maybe I've wised up a bit," she replied.

Startled, he considered her a second time before an abrupt laugh. She could almost swear there was regret behind it, but it was too late for that now.

Her pace lagged. Trailing a step or two behind, until

his arm reached back, and he grabbed hold of her. "What is it with you, anyhow?" he asked, pulling her alongside.

He even hooked his arm through hers, a proprietary action that sparked a flare of misguided pride. For once, she wasn't on her own.

"This is no place to be mooning about," he admonished, the underlying assumption—that he understood such matters far better than her—obvious. "The darker it gets, the rougher it gets."

As if she didn't know all about that firsthand.

The Abbey's door stood a few yards away, a saloon as downtrodden as the rest. Skiptown opened the door for her, and the rabble glanced up from their cups as they entered.

There was nothing like stale liquor spills, wet wool, and unwashed socks to get the stomach a-churning. The spittoons were brimming full and foul. Of course, it suited the punters just fine. The same low-down assembly of grizzled men that drew the likes of Arthur Harper to them.

And there he stood.

Arthur Harper, drinking at the bar rail, eyes glazing but not entirely befogged.

Skiptown flashed her the "don't draw attention" signal, one splayed hand and a quick flick of his fingers. Considering how everyone stared at her, the odds of that working were next to none.

The regulars latched upon her as the enemy, and a chorus of grumbled complaints murmured. Not so with Arthur Harper, who was far more interested in the contents of his glass than women.

Skiptown sidled right up next to him. "I'll need that quitclaim on the mine you sold me."

Harper heard him all right but didn't turn his head. He tossed back the remnants of his whiskey and set the glass down with a measured slowness. Then, and only then, he turned to square with Skiptown. "Well, that ain't for sale."

So Arthur Harper had steel cord in him after all. His eyes flickered at Maude and returned to Skiptown square.

He knew what he was doing. Skiptown just couldn't see it.

Instead, her husband leered predatory, leaning against the bar sideways, his back blocking out the others as best he could.

"You know," he began, "the deed is useless as it is. That is, unless you plan on signing the back of it, with the explicit words that you relinquish all rights to the claim."

"I don't know that I want to do that." Harper weaved ever so slightly.

Skiptown signaled for the barman—a sullen, surly fellow. "A shot of whiskey, and one for Harper here. Maude, what would you like?"

A slow wag of the barman's greasy head. "We don't serve women here. Especially not one of her kind."

"Her kind?" A nerve twitched in Skiptown's cheek.

Drying a glass with a dingy towel, the barkeep didn't bother to pause. "I've seen her going into the Mikado, straight through the front door."

Maude's heart stuttered. "Only to tell fortunes!" That damn flush rose, although in the gloom it likely passed unnoticed. "I tell fortunes in there."

Skiptown pulled back his shoulders. "There you have it. My *wife* tells fortunes."

The man snickered. "We don't serve sarsaparilla, if that's what you're hoping for."

Skiptown's hand darted out and caught the barman's forearm, hard and unpleasant. "You'll serve her what she wants. Maude?"

"Whiskey. I'll have a glass of whiskey."

Skiptown released the man's arm. "You heard her."

Judging by the exchange, the barman wasn't a witness from the previous night.

The barkeep glared but did as told, pouring out the three whiskeys without another word to the contrary.

The other customers held no such qualms. "You don't mean to be serving her, do you?" one sniped in their direction.

Skiptown scowled, but it made no odds.

Glass within reach—Harper's hand was halfway there when Skiptown clamped his palm down on the rim with those lightning reflexes. "Not so fast. I paid you seventy-five dollars for that claim and bought you a few drinks besides. Now, I'm going to sell that claim on. And to do so, I'll need a document in writing that proves you've sold it on. *To me.*"

Watery blue eyes sized the pair of them up and down. "It's worth more than seventy-five dollars."

"You sure about that?" Skiptown brushed aside his jacket. A large knife holster stood out, fastened onto his belt.

Maude did a double take.

Skiptown let the fabric fall back into place, just as cool as could be.

Half sober, Harper had enough wherewithal for concern. "There's no need to get all riled up or hasty. I am a reasonable man. But you see, I was drunk that night..."

"You're drunk most nights, aren't you?" Maude shot across the pair of them.

Skiptown pulled up straight and tall. "There's no telling what a cheated man will do."

Wary, Harper turned his attention to Maude. "I remember you from before, just couldn't place it. You were with my bride, coming to check up on me." Harper shook his head. A spark. "Which is why I can't see my way straight to do it, selling it on at a fraction of its value."

Skiptown moved a step closer. "You'd best find a way."

A shifty squint from the prospector. "You got a buyer?"

"Maybe. If the mine looks good and the paperwork's square."

Harper stopped shuffling and shifting. "Another five hundred dollars, and you have yourself a deal."

Skiptown tensed. "Four hundred dollars, once the deal goes through. Not a bleeding moment before."

The drunk licked his lips, features relaxing. "I believe I'll take that whiskey now. To seal the deal, that is. I'll even go up to the mine to make sure everything is prettied up."

"Fine," Skiptown agreed, picking up his glass. "It's settled. We'll bring the man to the claim tomorrow at noon."

"That don't leave me much time..."

Skiptown shook his head, gauging the drunk's reflection in the mirror behind the bar. "Make it work. And be at the Fortune Emporium tomorrow at eleven thirty, and in a decent state to conduct business. Last thing I need is you falling over drunk."

Unoffended, Arthur Harper finished his drink and shuffled out of the saloon with something approximating purpose.

———

Outside, Maude fell into step with Skiptown as two crows winged overhead, loudly harassing a magpie. The magpie sailed straight into a plate glass window with a terrific *thwack* and landed on the boardwalk, stunned and twitching.

She stopped dead in her tracks, staring.

"You aren't going to turn all hinky, are you?"

Maude shook her head. "Not a good sign," she murmured. "We ought to get the bird out of the way."

He could have cared less. "Suit yourself," he jeered, "but I don't want to get bird shit on my hands."

Scooping up the bird, its heart fluttered. Just stunned, Maude guessed, as she set it safely by a wall.

All without a speck of bird shit on *her* hands.

"We both need that money," Maude cautioned. "Make sure you handle all of that money, or neither one of us will be seeing anything but Arthur Harper's back end."

"That another one of your otherworldly visions?"

"No. It's simple common sense," she replied.

Skiptown doffed his hat once they reached Bennett Avenue. "I've got other business to attend to now, thank God. And we'll need a conveyance for tomorrow."

He took a few strides, then stopped. "Maude? Make sure you get something suitable. Impressions are important, you know."

Sure. Maude stuck her tongue in her cheek. She knew impressions were important. Especially those that others could not see.

CHAPTER THIRTY-EIGHT

SPRING IS FICKLE, AND SO ARE FORTUNES

S uitability be damned. They'd be lucky to get something that rolled, because it would have to be hired on credit.

No matter how hard she tried to stuff down the growing unease, the last time she'd seen Clayton Davis she'd been caught red-handed coming out of the Mikado.

And now she needed a favor. Splendid.

Shadows lengthened from the mountains, the sun lowering in the west. The night was building steam, but its manner so much more civilized than just a few streets over. Swanks were swanning, and their well-dressed ladies' noses were stuck up in the air as if the smelter fumes did not exist. Money, real and otherwise, sure seemed to flow in that part of Cripple Creek—pouring out from storefronts and including a high-falutin' livery she didn't even need to try.

It was a completely different story a few streets over where the houses were low slung and where the living came hard. Miners' houses and a dark existence underground. All for three dollars a day.

Hard choices—hard outcomes.

An uncomfortable certainty zinged along her spine. Cripple Creek wasn't for her, ultimately. Not in the long run.

And she had better take what she could, while she could get it.

The avenue bustled along heedless of any misgivings. Laughter spilled out from the myriad of "choice" saloons that charged more for the same old swill. Glancing in through the window of one lamp-lit establishment, who should she see but Rose de Silva holding court like the Queen of Siam. Indeed, a crown of gossamer smoke wisped around her head. Gesticulating with a striking grace, she held a passel of men enrapt, hanging on to her every word.

So. The rumors had been true, and Maude could feel the smile tugging. How Rose got away with drinking in a saloon was another mystery, but there she was. As for her part, Rose appeared at ease. Well. Maybe for her it was natural.

As fate turned, Rose glanced over her shoulder and latched onto Maude lingering outside. A theatrical turn so that Maude couldn't read her lips, a quick comment, and laughter erupted. Every single man stared at the window where she hesitated.

Rose beckoned for her to join them inside.

Offering the briefest of waves and a shake of her head, Maude took off down the boardwalk, drawing her shawl tighter as she went.

"Maude!" Rose's voice pierced the carry-on.

She'd only made it as far as the corner. Turning around, Maude laughed. "You sure can be fast when you want to be. I've got to arrange transportation to Harper's mine for tomorrow."

Rose came up to within about six feet of her, eyes twinkling. "Sounds like a date with destiny to me!"

More like a reckoning, Maude thought and turned the conversation. "Those friends of yours in there?"

"They are now." Rose laughed in a flirtatious way. "Actually, I knew one of them before. I was extolling your clairvoyance virtues."

Maude's stomach tightened, and memories needled. "If you say so. Well, I shouldn't tarry, and Clayton's bound to close soon."

"Pride before a fall and all that," Rose countered, as happy as a meadowlark in spring. "What *did* you do to him, anyhow?"

Maude checked her hair in the window reflection. Half of her wondered why she bothered; the other half knew damn well. "Nothing, but I told you he'd seen me."

The gypsy folded her arms across her chest. "Any ghosts been whispering in your ear?"

"Oh, not in a clear way. Something's swirling, that's for sure. Did you lock up the shop? I've heard there's been a rash of petty thefts."

"Locked tight with Charley guarding." Rose took a step closer, leaning in and lowering her voice. "I've set my cap on one of those men inside. Wish me luck!"

Indeed, Rose gleamed cocky. She turned on her heel and swaggered into the saloon, hips swaying in suggestion.

In that soft spot beneath her shoulder blades, Maude knew full well Rose's romance would come to pass. She didn't need to consult any damn lines to see that one coming.

Again, she pulled her shawl tighter around her shoulders. So even Rose had a sweetheart. That was just damn ducky.

———

The last rays of falling color smudged across the evening sky, the surrounding slopes swallowed by shadows and fading to dark. The forge and stable were bathed in muted gray, but the embers within glowed an invitation.

The truth of the matter was she was tired of being cold. Alone.

"Hello," she called, a trifle too soon, a trifle too desperate.

Clayton stuck his head out the door, features closing down. "Maude. Hello."

She took a few steps closer, but he stayed rooted. If anything, impatient at the intrusion. *Her* intrusion of crossing a line in more ways than one.

Breaking the stalemate, a youth emerged from the shadows whistling a jaunty tune. Relief visible, Clayton turned his attention toward the young man.

"That's Fred. He's my cousin. Fred, this is Miss...er, Maude. Guess I don't know your second name."

A stab of panic. The darting of eyes. "Hays," she expelled. Not Montgomery, not Sinclair, but her father's name. Hell, she'd have a ways to go before she could claim that back.

"Got more work these days than I counted on," Clayton mumbled after chewing on that nugget. Like he owed her an explanation.

"And that's where I come in," Fred remarked, still cheerful, picking up a pitchfork and sending a veiled glance over.

"Make sure you get the back stalls good while you're at it." A slightly lowered voice. "Hope he works out OK."

"He'll be just fine," she proffered with an unasked-for weight in her words. As if her opinion resolved matters once and for all.

Nerves. Her nerves were showing, and she cringed.

"Uh-huh. Well, that'd be good," Clayton remarked.

Silence fell between them, and it was down to Maude to state her purpose. "I need to hire a horse and buggy for tomorrow."

He grimaced. "We're more of a boarding stable. How long d'you need it for?"

"Not long." She ventured another half step. "Just a few hours tomorrow afternoon."

He shrugged those strong shoulders, rubbed a hand behind his neck. "There's a wagon you can use, but it's nothing fancy. The horse is another matter, however."

Distrust and guilt seeped in. "Oh?"

A shuffle, but his expression held level and firm. "He's hard to handle if you're not used to him. Can't say I'd feel good about having anyone driving him, and especially not along busy roads."

"We can pay." Maude shifted from one foot to the other.

"*We.*" He made it sound foregone.

"Yes. The buyer for the mine, my...former husband, and the prospector. It's at the back side of Bull Hill...from what I understand." A tongue-tied silence. "Like I said, I can pay. I've got two dollars right now."

He shook his head, jutted his chin out. "You sure you don't have more money than that?"

"Wh—" Confusion rippled.

He cut her off. "I'm not a fool, Maude. So, when did you fall?"

She recoiled. "I never did!"

He shrugged the words off, voice dead. "That a fact? You know I saw you coming out of the Mikado."

She bit her lip. "It's complicated."

A laugh, disgusted and abrupt. Strangled. "Complicated. I see. *Complicated.*"

Maude searched his eyes for the slightest glimmer of

understanding. "The madam's man is the buyer. I'm brokering this mining deal. That's *all*."

Conflicted, he wagged his head, eyed her hard. "If you say so."

She pressed her hands against her stomach. It was up to him whether he believed her or not. "Look, if the claim gets sold, Charley will take his money and go. I'll get my divorce, uncontested."

Deep down, she wanted to be held.

"Then I'm your huckleberry, I guess." His doubt lingered despite his words.

To hide the flush rising in her cheeks, she turned to face out toward the yard, away from Clayton. Peering past the dark silhouettes of the cold mountains, searching for the rare trace of promise. "Nothing is straightforward out here."

"I'm not sure I agree," he countered.

She turned to him. "And your marriage? Rose mentioned something about one."

"I was a fool. It won't happen that way again."

So much hung in the balance at that moment. And she felt so alone.

"Please come to the Emporium at one o'clock tomorrow," she finalized, stepping into the darkened yard, mud hard and uneven underfoot.

The evening chill pressed down as he grunted his reluctant assent.

CHAPTER THIRTY-NINE
PROSPECT HOLES AND INTRODUCTIONS

WEDNESDAY APRIL 15, 1896

"I hope he doesn't say anything stupid," Skiptown groused.

And she, for one, hoped Skiptown didn't say anything stupid either. It was bad enough that Clayton would meet him at all. None of it struck her as particularly promising as Harper made his way in their direction, rubbery about the knees. Hat clamped so far down on his head it was a wonder he could see at all and thumbs stuck in his belt loops.

He peered up at them from under his hat brim. "Yeah, I'm here."

He launched a stream of tobacco liquid into the street.

"Does Millicent know about all this?" Maude asked.

"Only what she needs to know," he replied, guarded.

"Never mind about that," Skiptown cut in. "Did you get done whatever needed doing?"

Harper exhaled; his bleary eyes darted. "Mostly."

Maude caught sight of Everett Stevenson approaching, coming up the hill and almost within earshot.

"That's him now," she hissed.

The fancy man kept his eyes on the party, sizing everyone up. Eyes hard as steel bits, he took the measure of the men but dismissed her out of hand.

Nevertheless, the introductions fell to her. "Allow me to present—"

Julia's *man* cut her off. "Let me go first. I'm the one holding the money, and, as far as I'm concerned, that's all you need to know for right now. Anyone have a problem with that?"

That smooth snake-oil smile. "We understand completely," Skiptown said. "I'm Charles Montgomery, the owner of the claim, and this is Harper, the prospector."

"Why sell?" the fancy man challenged, eyes shrewd.

Again, Arthur Harper hitched up his pants, and Skiptown clamped a hand on his shoulder. "A man's reasons are his own business, as is his bank balance. That said, I'm looking to move further west. Arthur is my partner, and we've decided to sell. It's as simple as that."

"Uh-huh." Everett, for one, clearly wasn't sold on that story.

So Skiptown tried again. "There's no shame in admitting that neither Harper nor I have the capital required to invest in such a large-scale endeavor. We'd rather sell out, take the money and run, as they say. Let deeper pockets do the real expansion."

That seemed to do the trick, and the tension ratcheted down a notch or two.

Punctual, Clayton drove up right at the stroke of one. The horse snorted and blew, the whites of its eyes showing wild.

Maude did her best not to linger on Clayton, and she waved without meeting his gaze.

"What are we waiting for?" Ev grumbled.

Harper hitched his pants upwards and spat out another glob of tobacco juice.

Skiptown came across as relaxed and easy as if it were a Sunday drive. He attempted to play the proper gentleman and help her up into the wagon, but she rebuffed his hand and clambered up on her own. All for Clayton's benefit.

A lost gesture, since he never glanced her way. Instead, he flicked up his coat collar against a chill no one else felt.

As everyone settled into the wagon bed floor, fingers grasped the Emporium's sign and flipped it over to *Closed*.

"Wait for me," Rose hollered, pulling the door shut and fiddling with the key. "I'd hate to miss out. On the outing, of course."

"Didn't know this was a sightseeing tour," Everett groused to no one in particular, claiming the front seat alongside Clayton as his right.

Skiptown offered his hand to Rose. Of course, she took it, preening.

A vein throbbed in Clayton's cheek.

A queer, silent errand, no pleasantries were exchanged as the wagon rolled in the direction of Bull Hill.

———

Loud, loud, loud, the honeycomb of mines and industry clanked and pummeled along. The clattering and belching landscape vibrated. Smelter smoke hung trapped in the basin by the mountain walls; ore belts rumbled along overhead trestles spanning the road. The reverberations chugged and blasted from every direction, punctuated by detonations at indeterminate intervals.

Thundering mining traffic careened down the dirt

roads, hauling loads of raw ore and machinery. The notion of easy money seemed even more far-fetched than before.

Meanwhile, Arthur Harper turned twitchy the nearer they got to the claim. Possibly just the effects of the alcohol wearing off, but something had gotten to him.

Skiptown under-handed him a flask. Eyes trained on the back of Ev's head, Harper took a pull before slipping the flask back. "There she is," Harper crowed.

A five-foot hole bored into the side of the low mountain, tailings scant and unimpressive. A crude wooden sign carrying the warning: *Keep Out – Dynamited*

Anyone with an ounce of logic could surmise this was one hole that hadn't been worked all that hard.

Ev exhaled, rude. "Hell, I've seen bigger holes in outhouses."

Skiptown kept his poker face, but Maude figured he was worried.

Harper bristled, offended. "Goes further back than it looks, and, besides, there're two partial drifts. No sense calling attention. I've got lamps right inside the mouth so you can see for yerselves."

"Nothing's going to go off, is it?" Skiptown asked, making a joke of it.

Harper looked at him as if he were thick. "I cleaned it up last night."

Ev muttered something uncomplimentary, stalking forward. The other men followed.

"Wait for us," Maude called, clambering down.

"No ladies allowed." Everett's tone was clear. "Davis, you coming?"

"Sure, why not."

Maude took Clayton's response to mean that he didn't want to stay in her company.

He looped the reins around the wagon brake and

jumped down, light and graceful. A glance in Maude's direction. "Mind the horse, will you?"

Rose waited for the men to move off. "Reminds me of the early days, is what this does."

The men still lingered at the entrance; their words were indistinct, swallowed in the thrum of the district.

When they moved further in, Maude stepped up to the entrance, running her hands over the jagged rock walls. The interior smelled of damp and raw minerals, but the actual facing felt like nothing much at all.

Turning and rubbing her hands together, she shook her head *no* to Rose, who hovered behind.

"Keep trying," Rose urged in a low voice. "If nothing's there, you'd best prepare to lie."

———

No one asked Maude's opinion at all.

A silent ride back to the Fortune Emporium followed, but Everett had a gleam he couldn't quite hide. The men all wore poker faces once the wagon stopped. But, from Maude's perspective, nothing was sitting right about the entire business as far as she could tell.

The men shook hands and mumbled goodbyes. Said how they would be in touch.

Clayton drove off like he couldn't get away from the lot of them fast enough, leaving Maude and Rose standing out front of the shop.

"What did you make of that?" Rose murmured.

Maude shook her head. "Don't know. Let's see what the cards have to say."

Inside the Emporium, Maude picked up a deck of cards on the fortune table. She shuffled them over and over, until she felt that slight release in the deck—the cards signaling that they were ready to give up at least some of their secrets.

Rose hovering over her shoulder, Maude laid out three cards, face up and one after the other.

The Jack of clubs, the eight of diamonds, and the six of clubs.

A sure sign of business success, the ability to gather needed knowledge, and—the six of clubs—the card of a psychic.

That six of clubs was aimed square at her.

Her hand hovered five inches over them, the cards staring at her from the table. Rose moved closer, peered over her shoulder. Maude marshalled her concentration and dealt out three additional cards, straight down and face up.

The eight of spades, the ten of diamonds, and the six of spades.

The meaning, the meaning. What was the meaning? *Success.* Professional success, success after a period of difficulty, and a recent situation linked to an unpredictable event.

She turned to face Rose. "I need to go back to the mine."

CHAPTER FORTY
THE TABLES TURN ALL AROUND, AND IT AIN'T PRETTY

E verett was quite clear in his mind. Others be damned, he headed straight to the Palace for the purpose of availing himself of the telegraph office there. Not to mention a celebratory drink or two that he so richly deserved. Of course, he could have placed a telephone call to cut to the chase, but it lacked the element of drama. And drama was what the occasion inspired and so richly deserved.

> *April 15—Claim found promising. Assay at $100 per ton.*
> *Gold visible in mine. Asking price ten thousand dollars.*
> *Advise immediate acquisition before word spreads.*
>   *—E. Stevenson*

Ev slid his telegraph fee across the counter to the operator. "I'll trust your discretion. Bring me the response at the bar."

He whistled under his breath as he swaggered out of the office, across the lobby, and up to the bar rail. All he had left to do was sit back and wait. After all, it wasn't every day that a man found a gold mine ripe for the picking.

Inexplicably, the telegram from Denver wasn't immediately forthcoming.

A few drinks later and tired of holding his tongue lest the claim get stolen out from under him, he returned into the telegraph office. "Say, didn't you forget something?" he asked, startling the clerk.

"No, sir," the man stammered. "Nothing's come through."

Ev bit the fringe of his mustache. "No matter—they're pulling together the offer. Send their reply to the Mikado on Myers Avenue. I've got better things to do than stand around waiting."

Truthfully, that was *all* he had to do.

———

Everett rattled the doorknob on the off chance it was unlocked. It wasn't. He gave it an unholy jangle before twisting the bell. Requiring admittance was getting mighty old. Especially in the daylight for the world to see.

Gretchen opened the door and had enough sense not to say a damned word.

He stepped into the parlor and headed for the back cupboard, where he fished around among the bottles and extracted the one he liked best.

Julia swished into the room but swished right back out. He'd sit down to wait and drink her whiskey while he was at it. Hell, he'd drink the whole house dry if he had the notion. *Funny,* he thought in passing, *she didn't even say two words to me.* But her eyes sure as hell registered the whiskey label. Usually, she had more fight in her than that.

Several drinks in, a messenger came to the door.

"It's for you." One of the girls sashayed over, bearing an envelope, tantalizing for a moment but then thinking better of it. "What'cha celebrating?"

He didn't owe her an answer. He snatched the envelope and tore it open.

Then he swore. "Son of a bitch."

CHAPTER FORTY-ONE
SHOWING YOUR CARDS AND LAYING DOWN YOUR HAND

Maude skedaddled down to the forge, aware Clayton had better things to do than spend his day driving up and down to the same prospect hole. All on account of her and her abilities—*or lack thereof.*

Fred, lugging a bale of hay, greeted her with that same toothy grin. "Didn't he just drop you all off?"

A shrug of embarrassment. "That's right. Say, is he around?"

The wagon stood unhitched off to the side.

"Back in the—"

Hearing their voices, Clayton came out of the barn. "Is everything all right?"

"Yes," she replied, proffering a bright smile. "Knowing it's a lot to ask, could you drive me back up to the claim?"

He pulled up short. "What for? It wasn't that interesting in the first place."

She edged closer. "You'll think I'm unbalanced, but I really need to go inside, female or not."

He pressed his lips together, not exactly jumping for

joy. "Well, I'd have to hitch up the wagon again, and I just got the horse rubbed down—"

"*Please*. You'd be doing me a huge favor."

Fred smirked. "Hey, Clay. Didn't your mother ever tell you it was rude to turn a lady down?"

"Why don't you mind your own business?" the black-smith snapped, although he didn't mean it.

"It's nowhere near as entertaining." Another grin. "Want me to go fetch the horse and hitch him up for you?"

"Well—"

She laid her hand on his arm. "Please, Clayton."

He took off his hat, wiped his forearm against his brow. "Well, hell. It's an awful lot of bother over something no one should be excited about in the first place. I saw a vein and some scattered color. Sloppy at best, suspicious at worst."

Either way, that was all the encouragement Fred needed. He jogged off to get the horse, leaving the two of them standing there—unspoken words hanging heavy.

Clayton squinted, unconvinced and unmoved. "Now, what's this about. *Really*."

"A hunch from the cards. And the fact that I couldn't feel anything outside."

Utter disbelief. "Those cards told you to go *inside* the mine?"

She shrugged. "Well, no. But I've already tried outside. You don't have to go in..."

A slow wag of his head. "Nothin' doin'. I'm not letting you go inside by yourself in case you trip or something." At length, he shrugged. "Guess I'll get a lantern."

Maude waited by the wagon, watching Clayton retreat and Fred bounce forward. The youth looked over at her as he put the horse in the traces. "Can't help but mention there are nicer roads with better scenery than Bull Hill. If anyone was asking me, that is."

Maude laughed, climbing up onto the wagon seat. "This, I'm afraid, is business."

"Business, huh? Ain't many women interested in mining."

Lantern in one hand and a pick in the other, Clayton returned and put them in the wagon's utility box. Smirking, Fred ran his fingers through his hair, smart enough not to laugh.

"You seem to be hangin' around an awful lot—don't you have work to do?" Clayton climbed onto the seat and untied the reins looped around the brake.

A flick of the ribbons and the wagon lurched forward. Fred shook his head, bemused and amused in no certain order.

———

Seated right next to Clayton, she managed to make the seat a bit smaller than it actually was. Every time the wagon hit a rut or pothole they jostled together, and there she sat, thrilling at the contact. So solid and stable. She had no idea how the close proximity was affecting him.

It was now or never, so she took a deep breath. "I'm souring on ore advising."

A blue, long-eyed stare from the corner of his eyes. "Oh? Kind of hard to tell, seeing as how we're heading back up there."

The din of mining operations clattered and thrummed, mounting as they rolled onward.

"Yes. Well. I know you don't exactly believe in fortunes, but I laid out the cards when we got back to the Emporium. It was made clear that I had to go back and try again. This time without the distractions of the investors and Skiptown."

"That's what you call him...Skiptown?"

Maude shrugged but didn't waver. "It seems about right."

A sigh that made it clear he wasn't won over. "What are you looking for?"

"Men or mines?" She shouldn't have been so plain. Flushing, she tried to explain. "This isn't a goose chase. There's just a lot of turmoil surrounding, well, everything."

Another doubt-laced look.

That got her back up a bit. "My *husband* abandoned me in Nebraska. North Platte, to be exact. Ever since, I've had to figure out things and take my chances. That mining deal is going to go through from what I can tell, and I don't understand why."

A slight shrug from the blacksmith. "Wouldn't you be better off just to stay out of it?"

She raised her voice to be heard over the thundering of a nearby stamp mill. "And lose the divorce? No." She twisted away from him, the din drowning out further conversation.

A quarter mile further, the roar of pulverizing rock retreated. If ever anything was to work between them, she'd have to offer up a truth. "My parents warned me away from him, but I didn't listen. Turns out they were right all along. Fancy that."

Clayton inhaled and kept on staring straight ahead.

His lack of response was getting to her. "My family are honest people. I just thought things would come easier in the marriage. He said they would."

"I was raised knowing that what was easy wasn't worth having."

Maude turned away from the criticism, peering over the edge of a drop-off alongside the road. It was steep, and likely fatal.

She glanced over at him, then back down over the edge. "I made a mistake. I'll own up to that."

"Well, we've all made mistakes," Clayton replied, his words measured and strangled. "I was plenty rattled when Susan snuck away. It wasn't so much her past that bothered me—I could've lived that down. But she couldn't settle. Maybe *wouldn't* settle. Especially not after the boy died. Said she didn't want to be tethered down."

Maude didn't exactly want to be tethered down herself. Not in the traditional way that it sounded. "Why aren't women supposed to go into mines?"

A half-cocked smile. "Back to that, huh? Don't rightly know; tradition, likely. They're dangerous, for starters. Accidents happen and happen frequently. I'm sure you've heard your share of tales. You name it, and it can go wrong."

And that telltale zing along her spine told her in no uncertain terms that he was right.

And the machinery ground on, air vibrating as they neared Harper's claim.

He glanced at her. "Now, you're sure..."

"I am," she replied. "I didn't bring you out here to back down."

He laughed. "Never thought you would, I guess. Especially not now, now that I know a little more about you."

They pulled up in front of the entrance, wagon wheels scraping over the rock-strewn road. He hopped down and grabbed the lantern, struck a match, and lit the wick without fanfare. Grabbed the pick. "Ready?"

He didn't offer to help her down.

"I hope," she replied, meeting his eyes, which challenged her.

They walked to the adit side by side, sharing glances between them. Self-conscious, Maude placed her hands on the stones at the entrance, the same as before. Nothing but uncertainty in the pit of her stomach.

"Nothing," she murmured. "Absolutely nothing."

"I'll lead the way." Clayton stooped to enter. "This one just doesn't feel right."

"Oh?" A flash of humor.

"Yeah..." he muttered, "I heard what I said."

Inside the adit portal, he straightened. "It's not really much more than a prospector's pit. Goes up a bit higher than usual so a man doesn't have to stoop, but that's about it."

Clayton lifted the lantern high overhead so she could get a better look. The rough walls had been hacked away, angular and jagged. The surfaces weren't uniform: rust-colored bands, lighter portions, and dark strata. The inside of the mine smelled of old pennies—bringing to mind her first day in camp, right after the rain and snow.

Clayton stepped further in, snapping her memories. "When mines get opened, they have to clear out the debris as they go. See how this one has remnants scattered around? I'm not saying every fragment gets picked up, but still. Sloppy is what it is."

Glancing around, Maude wasn't too keen to go further in. "It seems a bit tight."

"Had enough?" Clayton looked back at her.

"No," she answered, picking up one of those fragments. The current rippled through her fingertips. "This one is like what Millicent brought in."

"Try another." He held the lantern higher. The light didn't cast far, swallowed up in the craggy outcroppings. A dripping ping came from further back in the darkness.

"You hear that?" she asked.

"Snow melt," he replied.

She took a few steps toward another rock, crouched down, and laid her hand on it. She nodded. It was good as well.

"Further back is that vein, but it's really not much. But who's to say, I guess. It might widen further in. Watch where you step. Like that Denver blowhard said, there's not all that much to it. Harper is not the most industrious of individuals."

Ten more steps deeper. Again, Clayton hefted the pick to point out a streak. "See that dark tail there? That's probably something and is what's causing the stir. The question is how much of it is there. That's the part that has me stumped."

It was out of Maude's reach by about two feet.

Clayton adjusted his hat. "I could lift you up if you want to touch it. If that wouldn't be too strange."

Maude grinned. "I'll never tell."

Clayton lifted her up, arms wrapped most improperly around her thighs. Yes, he was strong. And she could touch the vein. "It feels okay. Different, not as strong. But maybe..."

He set her back down, their arms resting around each other a moment longer than necessary.

For the briefest of moments, she thought he would kiss her. But he didn't. Men never did when you wanted them to.

"What comes next?" he asked instead.

She shrugged. "I guess let it all unfurl as it is going to. I need that sale to go through."

CHAPTER FORTY-TWO
MORE THAN A LITTLE DROP OF MORPHINE

J ulia kept her office door open a crack, just to make sure she didn't miss a damn thing.

She heard Everett swear and caught the tone.

So she plastered on a smile and sallied forth into the parlor. "What the hell is wrong with you? I thought I heard the door." She eyed the level of the whiskey—the good stuff. One she could get an arm and a leg for, and maybe some other body parts thrown in for good measure.

He spluttered. "I'm going to drink enough to get drunk. Problem?"

Obviously, was the first thought that crossed her mind. The night was poised to kick off, and provoking a nasty quarrel would linger and put everyone off their game. Instead, she tamped down the smile and tried a neutral approach. Well, one that might pass as such.

"Out with it. I thought you found yourself a new mine. Are you celebrating or drowning your sorrows?"

"Yes." He picked up the glass and bolted it, slamming it back down on the table to emphasize his point.

So he was going to be a pain in the ass. *Just wonderful.*

The doorbell clattered, and Julia gave him a final stare to make sure her point was taken. From the looks of things, he didn't care.

She clapped her hands to muster the girls. "Here we go! Make sure the lot of you act happy about the whole goddamned shootin' match."

The girls assembled into whatever positions they chose, some lolling around like sides of beef, which might not be all that grand upon second thought.

"Pull yourselves upright, to start out with at least..." She called that last bit over her shoulder as she went to the door and opened wide.

"Howdy, boys!" she belted out in a whore's rough voice. "What can we do you for?"

————

Men filed in, as they always did, singly or in prowling pairs. Their reception always amounted to pretty much the same damned thing—the more ambitious girls got up and circled, false smiles plastered on and glinting with those hard little calculations that passed as whorehouse flirtations.

And Ev sat drinking, black mood firmly in place. Two steps toward him, the bell rang again. Julia turned to see the undertaker and all-around good, public-minded citizen mooch into the parlor. *Asshole.*

He hadn't cottoned on to her yet. Prevaricating, rotating his hat in his sweaty mitts, and turning a trifle toward the florid, he was caught up explaining why he was there to the whore who hovered by his side. The girl could have cared less. Never cared, in fact. None of them did, and why should they?

Of course, he hadn't latched on to that part. "I have important business to discuss with Mrs. Robinson."

Ev and his mood could damned well wait.

Still on the sober side of the evening, it was late enough to make cleanliness inspections damn near unlikely. And there he stood, another victim of curiosity or his own desires. Either of which played into her hands just fine.

"I'll take it from here," Julia said to the hovering girl, sweeping up and all but knocking her aside. "Mr. Blake," she crooned. "How good of you to come for a...visit."

With an expansive gesture, she ushered him deeper into the front room, the girls affording far more interest than usual. Draped along the settees and straddling chairs, their availability came across as raw and blatant.

"Girls! This is Mr. Blake," she announced. "He's a special guest this evening. Show him whatever he wants." She bowed in his direction as hardened laughter rippled. "Shall we start this all off with a drink?"

Ev glowered enough to attract her attention and poured himself another glass.

Blake gathered himself, towering over and looking down at the madam, as men had a way of doing when they wanted to impress. Or maybe he just wanted to see her flinch.

"Bourbon, if you've got it," he replied as she held her ground.

Apparently, this was the night for the expensive stuff. Blast it. She clicked over to the sideboard and poured out two stiff measures. One for him, and one for her.

A dolly sidled up to hang on his arm.

"Now, should I show you the house, or would you prefer another guide?" Julia held out his glass, feigning indifference.

Lizzie chose that moment to drift into the parlor, eyes glassy and bright. Unfathomably, those eyes lit upon the overweight mortician. She sunk her fingers into the other girl's arm and pulled her off like a tick. It had to be the dope, Julia reckoned.

"I can show you around," Lizzie murmured as if nothing had happened in the slightest, pressing into him for effect.

"Oh, that's not what Mr. Blake is here for," Julia taunted, forcing him to make a choice.

"Well, since this lovely young lady offered..."

Julia responded with a venom-laced smile. "By all means," the madam replied, as the doorbell rang again.

In sauntered one of the district judges, who recognized the undertaker at once.

"Why, George," he bellowed, "fancy meeting you here! I won't tell if you don't tell..." He guffawed as another dolly came up and took his hat.

Julia smirked. What a damn fortunate chain of events for her.

And Lizzie led the undertaker upstairs by the hand.

———

The undertaker returned to the parlor with the gait of a satisfied man. Another charade involving a fake appraisal of the downstairs surroundings—it took a tick longer than expected, but he eventually caught the fact that Julia was watching and waiting.

He cleared his throat and crossed over to her. "Well, Mrs. Robinson, that Lizzie sure is pretty, but she seems a bit...languid. Not that I minded; I like a girl who lets a man just get on with it."

Julia's breath hitched, but she hid it well. "And your assessment of the house's condition? In your professional capacity, of course."

Changing strategies, he half bowed. "What's good enough for the judge, I 'spect is good enough for me."

Too damn straight.

But now that her point was proven, it was time to get a move on and get that man out of her house. She needed to go check on her star earner. *Languid* was not a term that lent itself to confidence.

But, no. The mortician droned on. "I think I'll have another glass of bourbon, if you don't mind."

She minded all right, especially since no money was changing hands. "Of course, but if you're waiting to see the judge, he's staying the night and likely won't come down."

What the hell. Discretion was always the first thing to go.

———

Julia lifted her skirts by the fistful in the rush to Lizzie's room. She needed that girl downstairs *tout suite.*

The madam rapped on the door, sharp. And was awarded with silence.

She outright pounded. "Lizzie!"

Still no answer.

Whorehouse doors didn't have locks for a reason, and she barged on in.

As half expected, the girl lay in a state of undress and sprawled across the bed in a heap, a vial still clutched in one hand. Julia snatched it away. Of course, there wasn't any label. She took a sniff and figured it for morphine. Slapping the dolly's cheeks, she started out soft enough at first, blows growing harder as panic set in.

"Lizzie? Shit! Get up, I tell you."

The girl only whimpered. Pulling her dangling arm, the limp ragdoll body halfway followed. Desperate, the madam grabbed both the girl's hands and tugged, dragging her almost upright.

When Julia loosened her grip, the girl slumped back over, face down onto the bed. The madam, huffing and hair escaping from pins, finally got the dolly turned onto her back. Eyes, nothing more than slits, showed white and rolling back in her head.

"Do you hear me at all? Hell..."

But the girl wouldn't, or couldn't, come around.

Julia bolted from the room. Music and voices competed, blurred and running roughshod over each other. Clambering down the stairs, she cornered a girl without a jake in tow.

"Bella! Go upstairs with Lizzie, *right now*. Keep trying to rouse her while I call a doctor."

Bella, wild-eyed and shocked, stammered, "She ain't dying, is she?"

"Of course not," Julia lied, giving her a hard shove that sent her on her way.

———

The doctor arrived in good time at the rear of the Mikado, catching his breath and a bit put out as Julia threw the door wide.

"She's upstairs. Follow me." The madam led the way, dodging bodies and elbows as she hurried. The crowd had spilled out from the parlor into the entryway.

"Red Florence," she shouted above the general melee.

The girl left the side of a jake, curious enough at the summons.

"Get all the punters back in the front room. Do a strip-tease or whatever it takes. Understand me?"

The girl's eyes flickered between the madam and the doctor. The passel of people milled about, oblivious and in the way. So Red bellowed, "Come into the parlor, said the spider to the fly! I just might have something for all of you..."

With the crowd drifting back to the front room, the doctor followed on Julia's heels. Together they burst into Lizzie's room, startling a tear-stained Bella, her makeup ruined and running. "I'm not sure she's even breathing..."

Julia pushed the dolly away. "That's enough, now. Good girl. Go fix your face, then start pulling. Whatever you do, don't mention this to anyone. Lizzie will snap out of it. You'll see."

Bella didn't need to be told twice. She bolted from the room, slamming the door behind her.

Lizzie's rasping breath came out shallow and labored. Her lips were taking on a bluish tinge. The doctor picked up the dolly's wrist, checking.

"How long has she been like this?" He pulled a stethoscope from his bag.

"Don't rightly know," Julia replied, on the defensive, toe-tapping nervous. "Maybe a half hour or so. By the time I got here, I couldn't get her up."

The doctor frowned. "Seems a common affliction of your lot."

"I'm sure it was an accident," the madam lied, her tone even and clear.

He shook his head, tired and bitter. "We both know better. Her heart might stop altogether. That ruckus downstairs isn't helping matters any."

True, the piano still banged out a tune below, with laughter and conversations rumbling in a rising swell. Razor-sharp comments and laughter pierced and splintered.

The sound of a whorehouse running well.

And so the whoop-up continued, as Lizzie clung to life upstairs in a closed room that sure as hell could have used a good airing. Nothing put a damper on an evening like a corpse in an upstairs room.

"I want her admitted to the hospital," Julia concluded.

"She might not survive the trip. It's a gamble, either way."

That was all the encouragement the madam needed. She scarpered from the room, returning with Ev and one of the larger girls in tow. Together, Julia and the girl managed to stuff Lizzie into her coat and stick boots on her feet.

"Between the four of us," Julia directed, "we should be able to get her out. Everyone downstairs is occupied. Come on now! On the count of three..."

"Jesus Christ, get out of my way." Ev pushed the others aside as he half lifted the girl from the bed, staggering backwards and none too steady on his feet.

The whiskey, it was a-telling.

The doctor thrust his bag at Julia and hastened to Everett's aid. Or the girl's. It was hard to tell which. Together the two men carried the limp girl out into the empty hallway and down the stairs.

The whooping and catcalls from Florence's striptease roared.

A wagon had the misfortune of passing at the wrong moment, and Julia waved her arms as if hell itself chased at her heels.

The driver stopped, cautious and curious.

"We need you to drive a girl to the hospital right now," she panted.

"I guess," he replied as Ev and the doctor came up from behind, carrying Lizzie like a large sack of potatoes. And, like a sack of potatoes, she got dumped in the back with a thud.

If she'd been conscious, it would have hurt.

———

As it turned out, the girl was pronounced dead at the Sisters of Mercy hospital.

The call came right after two o'clock in the morning as the customary whoop-up carried on. Julia answered the jangling telephone, with no one in the house any the wiser.

Of course, the news would keep until morning. If not a bit longer.

She wondered if the same could be said for Ev's *problem*. It had to be the fortune-teller's mine. Whatever the case, it likely could bite her in the ass, and bite her in the ass hard.

CHAPTER FORTY-THREE
PICK YOUR POISON
(CHANCES ARE THE RESULTS WILL END UP THE SAME)

THURSDAY, APRIL 16, 1896

The Denver crowd should have been singing Ev's praises to high heaven, and, yet, there they were, doubting his word. That part didn't sit well. No indeed. Required to play host to the lot of them. Men who didn't understand a damn thing about mining beyond the dividends that filled their pockets.

That stupid girl Lizzie was just the cherry on a rotten deal.

He made his hot-tempered, hungover way to the Scavenger. The door to the superintendent's office was closed. His head throbbed. *From the altitude*, he told himself. But it wasn't.

About to march straight in, Ev paused. He needed all the friends he could get, and antagonizing the man within wouldn't get him anything useful, even if it did make him feel better.

So, with considerable personal restraint, he knocked.

"Come." Jim's voice sounded about the same. Of

course, it was damn near impossible to tell from a solitary syllable.

The man's furrowed brow greeted his arrival. "You've been making yourself scarce."

The superintendent didn't come across anywhere near as accepting or impressed as Everett hoped. "Been attending to other prospects. As a matter of fact, I've even found a good claim."

Wilson had the effrontery to stretch out. "I heard something along those very lines."

Ev remained standing, clinging to the advantage of height over the man behind the desk. "Is that a fact? Good news travels fast it seems."

A dismissive half shrug. "We'll see."

Ev lounged against the doorframe to show his confidence and building disdain. "Care to elaborate?"

"Not really." Wilson leaned back in his chair, still taking Ev's measure.

"So, it's going to be like that, is it?"

The superintendent's eyes turned to steel. "For a man on the payroll, you have a notable way of disappearing. The Denver crowd's taken an interest in you. Personally. And that can't be considered good on your part. Too much the flimflammer for their liking."

"Flimflammer? That's the word they used?"

A dismissive shrug, but it was clear the man didn't disagree. "Their word, not mine. Anyhow, I shouldn't have said that. Seat?"

Everett had half a mind to walk out then and there, but he didn't. He stared daggers at the super, who didn't have the good graces to waver.

He took the proffered seat, reluctant but hoping to turn the tone. "Harper's claim. Yes. You told me he was a solid prospector. Turns out you were right...on *that* count."

"And, I believe I told you he was a drunk," Jim countered.

Ev stuck his hands in his pockets for added emphasis. "That has nothing to do with the business at hand."

"You haven't asked about recent production," Wilson drawled.

The old cat and mouse game. Well, Ev could play that, too. "I stood right here just the other week, as you well know. Have it your way. How's production?"

"An uptick, as a matter of fact." The superintendent appeared well satisfied.

That caught Everett. "An uptick."

The man glared back.

Everett cracked first. "So. One of those exploratory shafts that I suggested you drill paid off. Is that what you are trying to tell me?"

"I don't sit on my hands." The superintendent gestured around at the contents of his office and the larger property beyond. "Any mining engineer would already know as much. As I was saying, production figures aren't as desperate as they once were. Of course, you would know that for yourself if you took a stronger interest. Seems one of us works, while the other is...carrying on."

Sanctimonious bastard. "I don't answer to you," Ev reminded him.

The superintendent didn't confirm or deny that statement but left it hanging.

A sense of disquiet arose, with the most peculiar sensation of ground giving way. Ev stood up and tugged on his lapels. "I'll see you when they arrive. If you're asked along."

Wilson flicked his fingers.

Everett strode out of the office. "Those maps ain't going to save you," he called over his shoulder.

Wilson offered no reply.

———

Ev thundered back to the Mikado—the best choice in a list of sorry options as he currently saw it. He needed to pull together a plan. Julia might be getting long in the tooth—not to mention thickening in other places—but sometimes she had ideas worth chasing.

Some hair of the dog wouldn't hurt matters, either.

He paused outside of the Mikado for a long, hard moment before climbing the outside steps and pushing on through.

Unlocked in the daylight hours, the previous night's fragrance lingered. Not that the place ever smelled exactly clean. What the hell. It suited.

Julia was up and about. Eyeing him over the expanse of ledgers on her desk. Going over accounts or whatever the hell it was that she did.

"You're out early," she remarked.

Somehow that woman made even simple comments sound next to a full-blown accusation.

"I went up to the Scavenger to check things out." One thing for certain, he sure as hell wished he could see her accounts. He attempted an olive branch. "Care to have an eye-opener with me? We could catch up on...things. Heard anything about that girl?"

"Lizzie?" She gave a dark flash of something. "Still at the hospital."

He shrugged, uncaring.

Julia bit her lip before smiling, dark around the edges. "It's been a long time since you've...we've...Sure, why not have that drink?"

She got up from her desk, snapping the ledgers shut. The old duck thought his interest in her might be returning. *Fat chance* unless things really turned south.

She poured out two drinks straight from the bottle, not bothering about that decanter crap.

"Here's to morning drinking." She held up her glass in a toast.

He bolted the liquor. Once it hit and took hold, the pressure in his head eased up.

"Another?"

He thrust out his glass. With it refilled, he claimed one of the divans. "I've got a lot on my mind as of late."

She gave him the beady-eye look of a bird of prey ready to swoop. "You aren't the only one. Something amiss?"

"Oh, another annoyance. Denver's turned jittery. No matter—I've got it under control."

Julia didn't quite buy it, and that rubbed him the wrong way.

He decided to try it again. "I take my prospects seriously. Always have...Just another layer to work through, but it chaps my butt. Hell. But I might have one or two surprises up my sleeve yet."

She poured another splash into his glass—a lesser one in hers. "Sounds interesting."

"Damn straight," he replied, knowing she wasn't interested in the slightest.

Julia stared out the window to the muck of Myers Avenue beyond. "Springtime in the Rockies is always such a fickle thing, but at least the roads are drying out." Her voice trailed off. "How are they paying you, anyhow?"

Rising irritation at an afterthought of a question—a question ventured for the sake of keeping the conversation moving. "My salary, same as always. And a locator's bonus. Why?"

A shrug. "Just making polite conversation. One person talks, the other listens and asks questions. Or did you have something else in mind?"

His hackles were rising again. "Here we go. What else do you *think* I have in mind?"

She threw a dagger-like glance straight at him. The kind that landed straight between the eyes. "How could I *possibly* know? You're a hard man to figure out, Everett Stevenson. But I've got to wonder, why are you telling me all this?"

He was now asking himself that same damned question. "Because I have to meet their train on Monday. Hell's bells, you make everything hard."

"Do I?" Julia asked, voice sweet.

But again, it was a calculated question. He could see it. Like she said, he was *smart*. "You know it's intentional on your part."

But those damn wheels of hers were a-turning. He'd been a fool for bringing up any of his business in the first place.

Julia offered a twisted smile. "Well, do you know who's coming down?"

"I'd guess Mike Henderson, Thomas Mercer, Stephen Detweiler, and I don't know who else. Why?"

"Business. Extend them an invitation to come down here. Say we'll offer a discount. Call it a 'discovery celebration' or some such bullshit. What bank are you all using?"

"The Bi-Metallic. Got an opinion on that, too?"

A shrug. "I don't know. Silly question, I suppose."

"Too straight," he replied with a definite downturn. "What bank is it that *you* use?"

"Oh, I don't," she replied, airy yet decisive. "Never have and never will. Besides, I don't really know anything about them."

Some matters were best left to the darker sex, and banking was surely one of them.

"Yeah, well. I do," he replied, rising.

She'd got caught out, not knowing any better. So he chuckled at her confusion. Or maybe it was the alcohol. Either way, it lifted his spirits a notch. Everything would work out right in the end.

He really shouldn't doubt himself so much.

CHAPTER FORTY-FOUR
DON'T SHOOT THE MESSENGER

A grubby messenger boy thrust a note into Maude's hand, and she unfolded it.

"It's from Julia," she announced before reading aloud:

Meet me this afternoon at 2:00 at the mouth of the alley behind the Topic Dance Hall. Important information to share. Only send word if you can't.

Julia

"Where's that no-account of yours?" Rose asked by way of a response.

Glancing up from the message in her hands, Maude frowned. "Probably at his boardinghouse or out skulking around. Why?"

Hands on hips, Rose looked out the window before turning back to Maude. "Well, that's the point. Julia is trying to keep this quiet if she's taken to meeting in alleyways. Either that, or she intends to kill you. Which do you reckon?"

"Very funny, Rose."

"Things are afoot. Can't you feel it, or whatever it is that you do?"

Maude had been asking herself that same damned question, and more than once. "You mean the distinct sensation of a noose tightening?"

Rose squinted. "That's a bit extreme, but hell. Maybe you should find out what that husband of yours has to say."

Standing motionless, Maude inhaled, trying to pick up on...anything. "You can come with me, you know. Maybe you should."

"Maybe I will. I can't help but wonder if something has gone wrong, fresh out of the chutes."

It did have that feel about it, Maude thought but didn't want to say.

———

The American Boardinghouse certainly was nothing to write home about. A downtrodden affair, it clung low, listing on a hill. A whiskey barrel stood near the front entrance collecting runoff. Various stovepipes poked through the roof, none straight; a two-story addition was tacked onto the back like a hangover.

The two women paused outside.

Maude sniffed. "It's further down the ladder, all right. Guess we should still knock."

So they did.

A man in a dirty undershirt and a three-day growth answered. Maude smiled at him. "Is Charles Montgomery within?"

Oblivious to her charms, the man muttered, "How the hell should I know?"

"Well," Maude replied as sweet as she could make it, "could you ask?"

"*Montgomery!*" the man bellowed without moving an inch, scratching his stomach without a shred of couth.

A pause, then Skiptown's voice. "Keep your shirt on."

Maude fervently wished he would.

"Some um...ladies are here!" With that, he retreated inside, leaving the door wide open and them standing there flat-footed.

Skiptown appeared in his shirtsleeves, taking his own sweet time about it. "Figured it had to be you two. Something up?"

Stepping outside, he closed the door behind him. He looked tired, although passably clean.

"That's why we're here," Rose ventured.

Maude added, "We're asking you that very same question."

He didn't appear overly concerned. "I'd expect today to be the day. Stevenson wired Denver yesterday. Can't imagine they'd sit too long before making a decision. You know, there's nothing that says we *have* to sell to them. If the deal goes amiss, I mean."

Rose's eyes narrowed. Maude spoke up. "How is this all supposed to go? Does he even know where to contact you? Do you know where to find Harper? I found you the buyer, but it's down to you to close the deal."

"Relax, Maude. I've got it covered. When did you get so nervous?"

"Since North Platte," she snapped. "Now, are you planning to send word once this gets moving again, or do we have to track you down?"

He radiated the smug insinuation that she was overreacting. "All right, Mrs. Montgomery. I shall, indeed, send word."

"Not a Montgomery for much longer," she hissed, grabbing Rose by the arm and hauling her away.

When they made it out of his line of sight, Maude muttered, "This isn't going the way I expected."

"Amen to that, sister," came Rose's only reply.

———

Rose and Maude leaned against the rear clapboard of the Topic Dance Hall soaking up the heat of the sun. The happenings within might not have been full bore, but tin-pan piano music still carried. An approximation of the "Virginia Reel," the jangly tune was something to listen to even if unsteady. In time Julia glided up, dressed all fine and fancy. Both Maude's and Rose's outfits were shoddy in comparison.

"Ah, Rose. I wondered when our paths would cross." A pointed look over to Maude. "Need reinforcements?"

Maude offered a perfunctory smile. "No, that's not why she's here. She hears enough to help steer things. You know, she's even allowed in saloons."

Julia acted put out. "Is that a fact? Good old Rose, just one of the boys. Ain't that so? Before we get started on all of that, there's something I ought to tell you." She turned toward Maude. "You aren't superstitious by chance, are you?"

"Like hell she's not," Rose replied.

"Things are coming undone, at least from Ev's perspective," Julia continued. She turned her attention over to Rose. "Hmmm. This is starting to feel familiar..."

"Stow it," Rose snapped.

Julia snickered and landed her attention square back on Maude. "Seems Ev has fallen out of favor. They're sending down a delegation, which means your man is going to have to look pretty sharp to pull this off. The important part of this tale is that they'll move the money through the Bi-Metallic Bank."

A blank stare in response.

Julia frowned, finding Maude thick. "You'll want your cut, rosebud. It just so happens I know one of the bankers there and have already had a word. Two drafts will be distributed. One handed over to me, and one to your husband."

"One handed to *you*?" Rose snorted.

"This is what happens when too many people get involved," Julia pointedly explained to Maude in her sweetest voice, which wasn't all that sweet when it came right down to it. "Yes, Rose. One draft is coming to me for the simple reason that I made the contact in the banking field. If I didn't have the connections, there would be one single draft, and the full amount would go to Maude's husband to pay out *as he chooses*. How'd that suit you?"

"Hell," Rose spluttered. "That ain't saying much, either way."

Maude laid a steadying hand on Rose's arm. "You said you could handle things like this, and so you have."

Rose glared. "Of all the—"

Julia cut her off, smirking. "I'll bet Rose never explained our past history, did she? You see, Rose and I were once rivals for the affections of a foot racer in camp. Back in the early days. And you might not know it, but those fellows tend to throw races..."

"Oh, give me a break. That was three years ago, and, like I told you, I never was the one holding the money..."

And they were off. No one could call it friendly.

CHAPTER FORTY-FIVE
FISHING AND PAY DIRT DEALINGS

Ev had no reason to trust that Julia would *help* him, even if she could. But, damn it, he could help himself. The old vulture had mentioned something about stepping out on an errand, not that he had bothered to listen to the full discourse. Time, after all, was ticking down.

Red Florence lolled around in the front room when he passed through. Hungry, he headed toward the kitchen hoping Gretchen would rustle up something for him. That would be an arm-wrestling in itself.

He passed through the swinging door when the notion hit him.

"I'll be back in a minute," he said to Gretchen, who was poised to be put out. He retraced his steps back into the parlor.

Good. The girl still drifted about.

"Say, Florence. How'd you like to make some extra money—just between the two of us?"

A wary expression washed over her. "No, thanks. I don't want to get tossed out on my ear."

He laughed. "No, no. Nothing even near that. Can you write?"

Snorting, she figured he was putting her on. "Yes. Can you?"

"Of course, but that's not the point. I need you to write a letter for me. I'll tell you what to say and everything, and I'll give you two dollars for your trouble. How about it?"

She shrugged. "I'd say I need a pen and some paper, I guess."

"Fine," he replied and tried the office door to get it. Locked, damn her. "I'll be right back," he said. He jogged up the stairs and straight back down, holding the implements out for her. "Let's sit at the dining room table to do this. Don't mention it to anyone, will you?"

"And if they see us?"

"Well then, we'd better hurry." He'd deal with Gretchen later, if she even bothered to come out.

Together they sat down, and he dictated.

Cripple Creek Morning Journal

Mining Desk

It has come to our attention that a substantial new strike has been located along a previously overlooked claim on Bull Mountain. We have it on good authority that investment backing is sought, and the claim is up for sale. Any parties with a genuine interest, please contact Mr. Robert M. Smith in care of this newspaper.

"Who's Robert M. Smith?"

He smirked, superior. "Me, of course."

Going against whorehouse convention, she broached a forbidden subject. "Is that your real name?"

"No. But in case someone asks to see the letter, I don't want them to notice that it's in my handwriting."

"I guess that's real smart."

He leaned closer toward her, voice lowered. "You know, when this mining issue gets resolved, I'll have a fair amount of money of my own."

"And why would you be telling me that?" She tugged at her bodice to show a bit more cleavage.

"Because I've always...admired you."

"And I've admired you as well," she replied, with as much sincerity as whores in whorehouses ever mustered.

He winked at her. "Now that we have that settled, address the envelope like it's a letter going through the regular mail, and have some boy deliver it to the newspaper office. I've got to run now, before Julia gets back. Here's the two dollars for you, and two bits for the messenger. Make sure the kid's a reliable one."

Red Florence smiled at the money, watching him go about his way. With a steady hand she wrote out: *Editor, Cripple Creek Morning Journal*

He'd *said* to address the envelope. So, with a slight shrug, she wrote down a return address: *407 Myers Avenue, Cripple Creek* and stuck her head out the door to hail a boy to deliver it, pleased that she still remembered the finer details of another life.

———

The following day, Ev got up far earlier than his custom, hangover be damned. He left the Mikado with a very particular and peculiar errand: in search of a newspaper. *The Morning Journal,* to be exact. He paid a nickel at the newsstand and eyed the paper. The letter didn't make the first page as hoped, but it sure made the second. Satisfied in a roundabout way, he read the contents and found nothing amiss.

With the briefest of nods, he acknowledged the seller and decided to go to the Palace to see if the letter had struck pay dirt.

Tucking the newspaper under his arm, he made sure the masthead stood out as he ambled his way over, thinking how, for once, the morning light showed pretty darn shiny despite his throbbing head.

He thought he caught sight of the fortune-teller, but it was probably just another skirt.

Passing through the heavy door with an extra spring in his step, he sauntered right up to the bar rail. "Give me a whiskey and a coffee chaser," he ordered. "Or maybe that's the other way around!"

That earned a genial chuckle from the barman serving drinks, and more than a couple of eavesdroppers.

"I was reading how another strike has been located," he prompted. Offered as a general topic of conversation, of course.

"That story is already making the rounds," one patron replied.

"Me, I don't buy it," another morning drinker inserted. "I mean, hell's bells, where have they been hiding it?"

And the conversation sparked off, excitement and doubt intertwined. Either way, Ev's objective was met. That letter had gotten everyone talking. And he was fair on convinced that he could find other investors. *If* he had to.

CHAPTER FORTY-SIX
THE DAY OF RECKONING, AND THE ANGELS ARE TAKING BETS

Monday morning rolled around, with Everett and Skiptown dressed for business and awaiting the train's arrival. Arthur Harper, a few steps behind them, swayed in the breeze like some sort of tipsy bellwether.

"Don't get too close to them, unless you can't help it," Skiptown advised the prospector, before sticking his hands in his pockets and rocking back on his heels. Ev chewed the inside of his cheek out of habit, near enough to stoic, but anger roiled right beneath the surface. Skiptown marked it, and Arthur...well, he might not have even noticed.

Back turned toward the prospector, Ev said in a lowered voice, "If for some reason this deal doesn't work out, we'll just sell it on to a different set of advisors. I've already begun testing the waters."

"I'd rather get it concluded today, if it's all the same to you," Skiptown replied, his smile terse.

"That's the plan," Ev agreed. "That crystal ball–gazing wife of yours say anything toward that end?"

"Maude? Nah. She wants to get rid of me." He flashed a grin. "She never knew a good thing when she saw it."

Ev laughed, bitter. "I never went in for all the fortune-telling mumbo jumbo. Shit."

That didn't sit so well with Charley. "I'll admit she misses every now and again, but some of the predictions she makes are enough to raise the hair on my neck."

"*Hmph.* Time will tell, I reckon," Ev countered, unwilling to back down. "But she hasn't said much that's useful about any of this."

"She's best when she's not personally involved," Skiptown replied, smoothing his lapels.

"Well, she's not all that involved here." Ev spat on the tracks as the train came into view. "Why the hell we can't just sign the papers up at the Scavenger is beyond me. Bloody Masons. Watch out for all of them, but Henderson in particular."

The train huffed into the station, and its metal wheels screeched to a stop like nothing at all was different than any other day. Everett and Skiptown exchanged slight nods of unspoken agreement. Three men in quality suits disembarked from the first-class carriage and gathered upon the platform, scanning the crowd.

"Gentlemen," Everett called out, all jovial, his hand extended in the picture of confidence.

They offered thin smiles in return, wary around the eyes. Anyone could see the Denver crowd was in unison. That left the Cripple Creek faction on the back foot, or so it felt.

"Allow me to introduce Charles Montgomery, the owner of the plat." A slight thaw as a round of handshakes ensued. Every one of them shook hands except for Harper, who hung back along the periphery, grubby and hungover.

With a slight frown, Ev turned to the grizzled miner,

reached out, and propelled him forward into the group. "And this is Arthur Harper, the prospector of record."

The Denverites, if taken aback by his general scruffiness, hid it well. As there wasn't much in the way of chitchat, the men got into the hired carriage that waited —a carriage much finer than the blacksmith's wagon. Impressions, Everett knew for certain, counted for everything.

Which is why it was just as well that the prospector sat up with the driver this time.

The carriage drove straight down Bennett Avenue, conveniently skirting the more insalubrious district of Myers straight to the upper part, where the name and the atmosphere changed to Masonic. As directed, the hired carriage stopped in front of the namesake temple.

"Are you a Mason, Mr. Montgomery?" Mike Henderson, clearly the senior of the group, asked by way of making conversation.

Skiptown answered easy—a professional con to the last. "No, sir. But my father certainly was. He was always disappointed that I didn't join."

The Denver man's expression flickered. "Well, it's never too late to take the oath."

Everett and Skiptown let the Denver men alight first, furtive eyes locking behind the visitors' backs.

Inside the lodge they were greeted by an enthusiastic member. The Masons all shook hands, maybe even using one of those secret handshakes they went in for. Next, they were all ushered into a room located off to the side of the entrance. A formal wooden table presided, surrounded by high-backed chairs. Heavy blue velvet drapes covered one wall, giving the impression that a stage might lurk behind those curtains.

Which, in turn, meant anyone could have been listening in.

"What's the stage for?" Ev asked. "I'm guessing there's one behind those curtains."

"Well, if you were a Mason, you would know those things," Detweiler boasted, but his attention was claimed by Harper. "I didn't realize the prospector remained involved in this claim. Why is that?"

Harper, having caught the conversation shifting to him, hitched his pants skyward as was his habit and jumped in, unbidden. "Because I haven't signed the quit-claim, that's why."

"Well," intoned the third Denver man—the one called Mercer—"that's a bit unusual, isn't it?"

Everett interrupted, taking control of the direction the conversation was primed to flow. "Perhaps we should all take a seat and discuss the particulars."

With a few Denver twitches, they sat down, including Harper.

Mercer leaned back in his chair, eyes boring straight into Ev's. "You know, there was an interesting letter in the Cripple Creek *Morning Journal*. You wouldn't happen to have anything to do with that, would you?"

"I don't know anything about any particular letter. Why?"

"Well, it concerned an opportunity for investment. Somehow, it resembles this deal we're talking about today. Even more interesting was the return address."

The fancy man blanched. "The return address?"

"From Myers Avenue, would you believe it? Are you sure you don't have anything to do with this?"

"I do not," Everett replied in a ringing denial.

The Denverite cocked his head to the side. "The editor said the street number, whatever it was, belongs to the Mikado whorehouse. Now what would um...chippies... know about mining? It's a hell of a coincidence, wouldn't you say?"

Everett stuck his hands in his pockets and sprawled out a bit to illustrate his lack of concern. Why, he even lifted his eyes to the ceiling and laughed. "What the hell. It's still a free country, isn't it?"

At that moment, the door opened, and in walked the mining superintendent.

Unyielding, Detweiler explained. "We've asked Mr. Wilson here to check out the prospect."

Skiptown tried to smooth things over as best he could. "Of course. I take it we're going up to the mine."

"Yes," Henderson replied, with a pointed expression. "Ev, there's no need for you to accompany us...if you have someplace else you'd rather be."

Everett glared. "I'm coming along."

Mercer interrupted. "The matter of the letter to the newspaper is not yet settled. But it can wait. It *will* wait until after we have had a chance to let Jim inspect the prospect hole."

"It's a *mine*," Arthur Harper countered.

Of course, he was glared at for his trouble. By everyone.

The men climbed into two transports: the carriage and the mining wagon. The Denver men and Everett in the carriage, and the mining superintendent, Skiptown, and Harper in the wagon. From all outward appearances, the Denver carriage was silent as the grave, and about as welcoming. But in the mining wagon following behind, the men exchanged a few preliminaries.

"That prospect hole any good?" Wilson asked, with a long stare sideways at Harper.

"Yeah." Harper spat out a long stream of tobacco juice. "It's a *mine*."

"Well, it's been a pretty good-kept secret."

"Had to be," the prospector pronounced, folding his arms across his chest.

Skiptown, seated behind the two men, read them as best he could. "How do you suppose it's going in the carriage up there?"

Wilson half shrugged. "There's a few issues beyond the purchase of the mine," he replied. "But I don't want to get involved in all that malarkey."

"No reason any of us should." Skiptown smiled nice and practiced, leaning back and enjoying the view.

———

At the prospect hole, the carriage came to a stop, and the wagon pulled up behind it. Wilson tied off the horses and pulled out a rock hammer and a pickaxe from under a tarpaulin laying on the wagon bed. In a box was an assortment of lanterns. The sounds of mining rang out all around them.

"Give me a hand with those, would you, Harper?"

In no particular hurry, Arthur shouldered the box up to the carriage. Skiptown trailed behind, calculating odds.

"Let's see what we've got," the mining superintendent commented for the sake of filling the silent, empty spaces.

The lanterns and hard hats were passed around, the flint strikers sparked in the carbide lamps, and the men made ready to enter.

"Don't trip on anything," Harper cautioned in a flattened voice, leading the way without the slightest shred of deference or ceremony.

The men entered the darkened mouth of the adit, Harper going deeper into the mountain. Every so often Wilson stopped, whacked at some outcropping, and considered the dark vein running toward the pitch blackness of the back end of the mine.

Everett, not bothering to disguise his irritation, all but growled, "See that sparkle? Any of that grab your attention?"

For his part, Wilson wouldn't be goaded into a response. In fact, he ignored the lot of them. He picked up one sparkling rock, examined it, and, despite evident gold, he discarded it. Tossed it back down, in fact. He kept on with his tapping, poking, and surveying.

After a long twenty minutes stuffed into the cramped space, the Denver men risking their fine suits—but that was what happened when city-dwellers entered into mines—Wilson leveled his gaze at the businessmen.

"I do believe I'm satisfied," he pronounced without triumph or swagger. The same as he would offer any other unvarnished fact.

The Denver men all exhaled like they had been holding their collective breaths, and slight congratulatory smiles circulated. Slight smiles that certainly did not include one Everett Stevenson. And well the fancy man noticed.

———

There was no stopping for a celebratory drink on the way down into Cripple Creek. Everett shifted, uncomfortable.

That damned newspaper article put him in a bad light, and he knew it.

———

They all rattled up to the Masonic lodge.

Skiptown and Arthur were well within sight of the

finish line. But everyone knew for Everett, the match, contest, or general dustup hadn't yet begun.

Detweiler addressed the group. "I don't see a reason to delay these gentlemen further, do you?" Referring to Skiptown and Harper.

"No," Henderson replied. "Why don't you take them over to the Bi-Metallic and authorize their draft. Ask for Arnold Chamberlain explicitly. He made a point of telling me that—trying to make a good impression, I suppose. And so he might, seeing as how we'll likely be running more business and money through his bank in the near future."

"Yeah. Maybe we ought to see what kind of arrangements we can make," Detweiler added. "But that'll wait for another day."

Henderson's attention landed square on Ev. "Why don't you come inside with me," he commanded.

So, while Detweiler escorted Skiptown and Harper over to the bank, Ev paused on the steps to the Masonic lodge.

"This business is best conducted inside, unless you prefer your floggings in public," Henderson challenged, not breaking his stride as he climbed the steps into the temple.

Inhaling, Everett joined him. "And here I thought you would be pleased."

Wilson hesitated by the wagon, simply calling up to the two men. "You need me for anything else?"

"No. I'll expect to see you at dinner tonight. Say, seven o'clock?"

Wilson nodded, darkening in Ev's direction. "See you then."

The Denverite opened the door for Ev and a trailing Mercer. They passed through the foyer and strode directly into the room with the table. "Take a seat."

"Now if you're sore about that newspaper article, I don't..."

Mercer cut him off. "There's been unease attached to you for a while now. That advertisement put paid to such concerns once and for all. We'll pay you a finder's fee of one thousand dollars and your salary through the end of the month. Those are generous terms, and I'd suggest you take them."

Ev glared. "You never would have found that claim without me. Wilson knew about Harper, but he sure didn't know about that prospect hole."

Henderson's eyes were steely, and he didn't rush to answer. "Regardless. We're not about to continue a man's salary who does his best to undercut us. No reason to. Take the deal I've offered, or leave it. It doesn't matter much to me one way or the other."

Ev sat forward. "I could take you to court over it."

"How so?" Mercer snapped. "You got anything in writing from us? We never promised you a damn thing that I know of."

Of course he didn't, and they hadn't. What the hell; Cripple Creek was getting old anyhow. "I'll take it."

"Figured you would." Henderson withdrew a slip from his inside pocket. "Here's your final payment. Consider yourself terminated from all future dealings with the Amalgamated Mining Consortium of Denver."

Damn that fortune-teller. If she was worth her salt, she might have bothered to mention the outcome.

PART FOUR
A FRESH START

CHAPTER FORTY-SEVEN

MONEY ALL AROUND

S kiptown came swinging down the street. Spying him through the window, Maude hurried to the Emporium's door.

"Well?"

"You doubt?" He removed a black bag from under his arm. "I came straight over before the celebrations began."

"Come in," Maude instructed, wary. She should have been overjoyed, but history was holding her back. "No need to air our business out on the street."

Rose moved out from around the counter, rubbing her hands with glee. "Let's see the proceeds."

Skiptown grinned as he untied the cord and pulled out stacks of bills. "Five hundred dollars for Maude, and a trip to the courthouse to make me a free man."

Maude held out her hand, and he handed the money over.

"Have a feeling the cards are stacked against Stevenson, but that has nothing to do with us. One of the Denver men escorted me to the bank, and we marched right up to the head man. 'Pay him five thousand dollars,' he said.

Just like that. And, before you knew it, there were stacks of bills getting stuffed into this very bag."

Maude's back muscles relaxed ever so slightly. He could still pull something, and she wouldn't put it past him.

With a grin, he indicated the bills. "Five hundred dollars for you. I still have a debt to settle with Harper. Another damn four hundred and fifty. Well, if I pay it. He already signed over the quitclaim."

Clutching the bills, needles of worry poked all over Maude. "You're thinking of bilking him?"

"Oh, don't go all stiff. Let's assume my better nature will prevail. After all, who's to say I can't do it again." Skiptown had the air of a man who was actually on to something. How little he knew, Maude thought.

Not that he noticed a darn thing.

"I'm planning on a night on the town," he blustered.

Maude sniffed. "You'd best put your money someplace safe. To come so far and have it lifted, well...That wouldn't do. You'll need that money for your train fare out of town."

"Want me to hold it for you?" Rose asked with a smirk.

"Nope, and no offense, darlin'. And who said I was going anywhere?" He beamed.

Maude clenched, all over. "You did. Earlier."

"Well, that was before I knew how easy this was all going to be! Hell, Maude...why would anyone want to leave?"

Maude watched with a surreal detachment. Disbelief rippled across Rose's countenance, but, to her credit, she held her tongue. Rose didn't know the underbelly of Charles Montgomery firsthand, but Maude sure did.

"You'd be smart to take your windfall and try your luck elsewhere. Things aren't as easy here as they might seem."

"Maybe not for you, Maude, because you just don't have enough pluck. I'm staying put. If you don't like it, I guess that's too bad."

Rose's mouth twitched. "I'd say you got lucky, for what it's worth."

"Luck is for suckers," Skiptown replied.

"You said it," Rose countered. "And that's what happened for you. You got lucky."

The two ended up glaring at each other.

"Too bad making friends has never come easy to you, Maude. You might have a better stock to choose from."

It wasn't the time for an argument.

"I still want that divorce," was all Maude said on the matter.

———

It took all of six dollars, five minutes, two signatures, the clerk acting as a witness, Skiptown tapping with impatience, and Maude emerged a free woman. No one in her family had ever gotten a divorce before, but there she was. And it sure felt good.

Skiptown jogged down the courthouse steps. Having no hard feelings on the matter one way or the other, he was already over the dealings. "Catch you tomorrow. I'm going to go find Harper."

She felt, every inch of her, as if she were being discarded on the courthouse steps. "Don't give him his money now—he'll just drink it. Best give it to Millicent..."

"Nah. What fun would that be? Besides, I'm not about to go chasing down to Poverty Gulch. That's the Harpers' problem—not mine."

And, with that, he jogged off in the direction of the Palace.

Maude watched him until he passed from sight. Again. She hoped he tripped and fell on his face.

When he was good and gone, a hollow-stomached feeling started to creep in. She turned toward the Mikado, wondering if she would have to fight for her money down there.

————

Nearing four in the afternoon, Julia sat inside her office presumably going over the accounts but, more accurately, waiting. A ring came at the door.

"She's in her office," an indistinct female voice told the arrival. Julia figured the new girl must already be answering the door. And that was just dandy.

Maude gushed as she entered the office and saw Julia seated at her desk. "It worked!"

"So it did," Julia replied. "I've got the money, less my five hundred dollars."

Without any further prattle, the madam proceeded over to the safe, turning the dial until the door opened. "It's fireproof, you know. I've put the proceeds in here for safekeeping. I'd suggest you either leave the money here with me until you have a plan or go open up a bank account."

"Rose told Charley to do the same thing, but he won't." Maude eyed the madam. "What?"

Julia sniffed as she pulled out the money. "I have some news. Bad news. Maybe you had better go ahead and sit down."

Maude sat on the edge of the chair, and Julia abandoned the money in the middle of her desk.

"Now, I've never quite figured out your feelings toward her a hundred percent, but Lizzie died three nights ago. An overdose. Not exactly a surprise, but still not a happy event."

An uncomfortable swallow, the uncertainty how best to respond. "No. Not exactly a surprise." The niggling memory. "I worried about that...and saw it coming. I told her to quit the drugs..."

Julia stared out the window, voice distant. "She didn't come back down after a client. I went up to her room and couldn't rouse her. The doctor came—he probably gouged me on the price there but I paid it—then I sent her to the Sisters' Hospital." A glance cast over her shoulder at Maude. "All to no avail."

Numbed, Maude remembered the spark in the dolly's step and the initial kindness in her eyes on that very first day.

Julia didn't appear hampered by any such illusions or memories. "None of them quit once they get started on the dope. Pity, really, but there are worse ways to go in the end."

Maude brushed a strand of stray hair from her face, eyes welling. She blinked the tears away. "I got the feeling she just wanted someone to love her. Really love her."

Maybe that bothered the madam some, for it roused her. "Hell, don't we all! I didn't mean to ruin what ought to be a celebration of sorts—but I figured you would want to know." She thrust out the banded bills. "Care to count it?"

Maude shook her head. "Should I?"

"No need. I already did. You're still trusting. That's kind of sweet, in a spectacularly misguided and lame-ass way. Don't take it so hard...about Lizzie, I mean."

"I guess. It's hard not to."

"If I know anything, it's that you can't save people from themselves. Still, that doesn't mean we don't sometimes try. By way of thanks, it's best to plan on getting bitten in the ass, every time. How's that for futile?"

Maude thought about Everett and Red Florence. "More changes will be coming," she offered in a soft voice. "And I'm afraid those changes might be concerning you."

"I am not going to take to the bottle or the dope over Everett. And it doesn't take a message from the *other side* to know he will be leaving, one way or another."

Maude sighed. "That's about the interpretation I'd put on it."

Julia shrugged, hard in bearing. If she was disappointed, it was sure hard to see beneath her mask.

"Maybe I'll just leave the money with you—less twenty dollars. I haven't the gumption to open up a bank account this evening, but some new clothes wouldn't go amiss."

"Fine." Julia returned the money, less the twenty dollars, into the safe with a clang and spun the lock.

Maude offered a smile. "Thank you for the help, Julia."

The madam tossed her head. "You've grown on me," was all she said.

Maybe that was enough.

———

Everett didn't return to the Mikado that evening. In fact, he stayed out all that night.

He came barreling into the Mikado late the following morning, hungover and still hot under the collar. Spewing whiskey fumes an hour before noon.

"I'm out of here, and don't try to stop me," he yelled upon entering, to anyone within earshot who might have shown the least amount of interest.

Julia hurried down the stairs and accosted him in the

entryway. "Trying to wake up the entire house? Where were you last night?"

He sneered. "Hell, yeah. I was down the street having a good time in another...establishment."

"So, I take it they paid. That money burning a hole in your pocket? Because if it is, you've got some repayments to make here..."

"Repayment my ass. I've had it with Cripple Creek, I've had it with you, and I've had it with the Amalgamated Mining Consortium of Denver."

"But you got paid..."

"Not enough, that's for damn sure." He glared at Julia, then lifted his face toward the ceiling. *"Florence!"*

Julia's eyes narrowed as she rested one jeweled hand on her hip. "And what do you need her for? Sure as hell, I knew when you got money you'd leave."

He screwed up his face into something ugly. "What was your first clue? *Florence!"*

The girl leaned over the upper banister.

Julia eyed her before fixing back on Ev. "So—they didn't miss the advertisement you took out behind their backs. Fancy that..." She turned her face up toward the girl. "And, Florence? You turn right around and go back into your room."

Ev still bellowed so any and all could hear. "What do you know about any of that—and, Florence, she's right. Go back to your room and pack your things, because I'm leaving, and I want you to go with me!"

The dolly's eyes grew wide, but sure as hell she turned on her heel and rushed back to her room to pack.

Roused by all the commotion, the other girls gathered in clumps upstairs, watching the show unfold.

Julia stuck her tongue in her cheek, stepped up to Ev, and threw a punch that landed square on his jaw. Shocked and reeling, he raised his fist to pull a punch of his own, but Gretchen came up from behind and hung onto his arm with the bulk of her weight.

"Get off me," he snarled.

Gretchen didn't release her hold one bit, until she received a slight nod from a now out-of-reach Julia, whose nostrils flared and bosom heaved.

"I knew about the advertisement," the madam threw across the foyer, not that anyone had asked. "A little matter, but one brought to my attention on account of how I have people who are on my side, unlike you!"

Another sneer. "Yeah, like that clairvoyant. A fat lot of good she's done you!"

Julia's eyes narrowed. *"Florence,"* she shouted up the stairs. "If you go with him, I'm not going to take you back —not even if you come crawling."

Ev smirked.

Defeated silence hung heavy. Julia tried again, still shouting, but not as emphatic. "He's a bloodsucker. If you think he's going to support you, you have another think coming!" Voice trailing off. "It will be the other way 'round."

She latched back onto Everett. "Proud of yourself?"

"Want fifty bucks?" he replied, hands on hips.

"Sure." She held her hand out. "I'll take it."

And surprise of surprises, he actually took the cash out of his pocket and handed it over.

CHAPTER FORTY-EIGHT
THE TOWN AIN'T BIG ENOUGH

The next morning, all bright and shiny and in new clothes, Maude made her way to the Fortune Emporium. On time and willing, she took in her surroundings, well aware that time grew short.

Rose was already in the shop, perusing those damned old newspapers.

Maude entered, swallowing the lump in her throat.

"Well, my my my. Look what we have here!" The gypsy took in Maude's new clothing. "One good run, and see how fortunes change? It's the way of this place."

"I couldn't help myself." Maude opened her purse. "And here's your money as well."

Rose crowded close, eyes sparkling at the sight of so much cash. She rubbed her hands together with glee. "Oh ho, my girl! Shoot fire! I always had a feeling about you, that there was money to be made! And this just proves I wasn't wrong about that."

Maude glanced around at the contents of the shop, dusty and still downtrodden.

"Well. There was room for worry. I think we lucked out this time around."

Rose was fanning out the bills. "Lady Luck is a fickle bitch; I'll say that for her."

Maude sat down at the business end of the fortune-telling table, bittersweet. "Hear anything around town? I wonder what the ultimate verdict will be."

"Who the hell cares—we got paid!" Rose was still caressing the paper money. "It'll go something like, 'The Amalgamated Mining Consortium of Denver purchased a hitherto undetected claim for an undisclosed sum. Cripple Creek holds its collective breath as it waits to see if the venture pays out.'"

"That sounds like you read it out of a newspaper." Maude pretended to be put out. "Then what?"

Rose shrugged. "Who knows, and, better yet, who cares? Chances are that life goes on as usual. Let's see... Julia's man will leave if he hasn't already. The Harpers... well. Hard to say there. But you. What will you do now that you have a reputation to maintain? I'd say customers will pick up. Well, for a while at least."

Maude pursed her lips with a brief shake of the head. "This will be hard to live down, I'd say. This was a bolt out of the blue, although I was too stupid to know it at the time."

Rose's gleam died down. "That doesn't sound very optimistic. You ready to move on beyond the Fortune Emporium? You aren't setting up shop for yourself, are you..."

"No. And it never did pay all that well. Until now." Maude didn't waver. "The thing is, I don't think anyone will find another strike like this. Those days are gone. Besides, if Skiptown is staying, I'm leaving. I don't need to spend my days tripping over him."

Rose stuffed the money down the front of her dress and patted it. "No, you surely don't. As for me, I'm considering a change as well. Trying my hand at something else. Maybe writing a column for the newspaper. I've been practicing, even. *Avenue Flashes* or something of the sort."

"Well. I like the sound of that." Maude stuck out her hand. "Give me your hand, and let's see."

And, at the contact, Maude's spine warmed, and a smile bloomed. "It should work—you're a natural, as they say. But maybe start off a bit slow. Newspapers can probably only handle so much...vibrancy...all at once."

"Ha! This gypsy persona is just one of the many in my repertoire." The mirth died down a bit. "You know anything about that advertisement? The one about a new claim seeking investors?"

Maude shrugged. "Guess it was Julia's fancy man testing the waters."

"Still think that claim is good?" Rose cocked her head. "Not that it matters where we're concerned, I suppose."

A frustrated toss of Maude's head. "I don't know. In fact, the only thing I'm pretty certain of is that I want out of the mining business altogether."

"Good choice." Rose calculated at something beyond mere words. "It's best not to go back to the same well too often, if you catch my drift."

"Like Skiptown, you mean?"

"Like Skiptown, like the Harpers, like many others," she replied. "Greed is what gets a lot of people in the end."

Maude hesitated, knowing the truth those words held. "You know, Rose, I'm thinking of starting over. Up in Denver where no one knows me or my history. If word gets out down here about my involvement in all of this, people will be wanting assurances that I just can't give. Funny, that's what I thought I wanted all along. To advise on mining claims. Now I'm not so sure it was ever a good idea at all."

"You sound kind of weepy. Don't forget that this paid

out," Rose replied with that old damn spark. "Something else on your mind?"

The truth of it all landed with a stinger. Tears pricked. "Lizzie died of an overdose."

Rose's eyes narrowed, taking Maude's measure. "Well, that strikes me as a definite closing curtain. Yes indeed, it does have that feel."

There was no reason to argue. And the cold hard truth was that there was precious little to keep her in Cripple Creek.

"I guess I don't much feel like telling fortunes today." Maude picked up an old burlap sack much like the ones Millicent used.

But any nostalgia was completely missed by Rose. "And, with five hundred dollars, I don't even care," she beamed.

———

Afternoon now free, Maude thought to make one last visit to the Mikado. And collect her money. Not necessarily in the order of importance.

She stood outside the brothel for what she knew to be the final time. The furnishings and the trappings didn't draw her in like they once had. Enough, in this case, was enough.

Half reluctant, she approached the front door, rang the bell, and waited.

Strange enough, Julia herself answered.

"Sure you aren't looking for a job," she halfway teased as she opened the door. "You know, if your reputation is suffering, you could always come around to the back."

Maude snorted, but it gave her a jolt. *She could have been going around to the back this entire time.*

"I just came by to tell you goodbye. I've decided to try

my luck up in Denver. Maybe in stenography school, or something like that. I could learn a respectable trade. I guess I'll need to get my money."

Julia stood aside with a slight bow. The smell of the whorehouse was the same as it ever was, the sad disquiet in the shadows and corners.

Of course, Julia noted none of that. But she was studying Maude.

"You don't say. Well, all things considered, you fared pretty well here. Otherwise, you would have ended up in this place as one of the boarders." A long, strangling pause. "You know Everett and Red Florence took off? Leadville seems the most likely spot, but who's to say."

Julia went into her office and straight up to the safe.

"You could probably find out, if you wanted." Maude watched as she spun the combination. The door clicked open.

"Well, hell," Julia exhaled, pulling out a bag. "Maybe I don't give a rat's ass. I guess I can hardly do worse going forward. And a new girl is coming up from Denver. We'll see if she's got what it takes."

She handed Maude the bag. "See to it you don't get jumped."

"I'll miss you, you know." Maude slipped the smaller bag into the burlap sack.

Julia jutted out her chin. "Don't suppose you'll drop me a line to let me know how you get settled, will you? Or, if you get the chance to use a telephone, you might call." Her eyes glistened damp, and she coughed to cover it up. "Something must have got caught in my throat."

The two women stood there, words dying out. Then Julia ushered them from the room.

"Go on, and don't let the door hit you in the ass," the madam said, halfway to pushing Maude out onto the porch. The door shut behind her, firm and decisive.

Out on the street Maude turned to wave farewell but dropped her arm at the futility of it all.

She thought, for the briefest of moments, inside the shadows of the brothel she could see the faint outline of Julia offering a tentative, fading wave.

They never were on the exact same side of the battle. Deep down, both knew as much. Deep down, each knew their paths, although different, were hard and unforgiving.

CHAPTER FORTY-NINE

ALL THAT GLITTERS IS
NOT GOLD
(AND SILVER WILL WORK JUST FINE)

That goodbye at the Mikado proved strangely disturbing and difficult. Mind made up, there was no sense in dawdling. No sense in hoping the wind might change and blow Skiptown out of Cripple Creek. As a result, Maude trudged over to the depot, headed straight up to the ticket counter, and slammed her purse down upon it.

"A ticket on tomorrow's train to Denver. *Second* class." She owed herself at least that much, the way she saw it. "Wait! Make that the day after." She flushed at her indecisiveness. An indecisiveness that seemingly sprang up from nowhere, but she knew better.

"Two dollars even," the agent stated, bored.

On her part, there were no trembling fingers, no wondering what might happen should she not be able to afford suitable accommodation. She pulled out two shiny silver dollars and placed them on the counter, finding the snap of the coins on wood entirely satisfactory. Nothing less than a triumph, no matter if he didn't see it.

The man wrote out the ticket and slid it across the counter, no longer interested in the transaction. She tucked it away in her purse. With a nod in his direction for politeness' sake, she left through the station doors. Outside, Cripple Creek swept up and down and sprawled over the mountainsides, bustling and impatient. Her original assessment had been correct—it was one hell of a town.

She headed downhill; the saucy image of Lizzie pressed in with a pang. How glorious she had shone when she half challenged Maude over her shoulder before sashaying away on that very first day. Well. That swagger didn't last all that long.

Maude had best make sure her own swagger did.

Easy money turned out to be either a myth or a con. It didn't much matter which. Bennett Avenue still spoke of money—but not for the likes of her. She drifted over to the Fortune Emporium and pushed on in.

"Can't keep away, can you?" Rose deadpanned.

"Oh, I'm not in a big rush. I've got my ticket for the day *after* tomorrow. Seven twenty-three in the morning. Guess I came here out of habit. And to say goodbye. Again."

Rose came around from behind the counter and grasped both of her hands. "You sure seem to go for drawn-out goodbyes. Having second thoughts? Because if you are, don't."

"That's kind of unsympathetic, isn't it? You never once asked me to reconsider."

"Maybe it is unsympathetic, but maybe it's needed. You going to say goodbye to Clayton, or have you given up the ghost on that one?"

The skull started humming. Rose followed Maude's gaze.

"Go on. A deal is a deal. Take him with you. My fortune-telling days are hopefully done, once and for all. Thank goodness."

Maude picked up Charley. "I'm going to try to find a proper resting place for him when the time comes. Maybe he'll let me know where and when. I just know it's not here in Cripple."

Rose nodded and held her arms open wide for Maude.

As Maude hugged her, one notion still sparked. "Speaking of Clayton, let me ask you something. He said you stood up for me about the Mikado business. Why, knowing how you felt?"

"That," Rose huffed. "Someone had to. It wasn't looking good from his perspective. Besides, I knew you fancied him, and don't bother to lie to me on that count. *Maybe* you still do."

"It wouldn't work. You were right. He's too strait-laced for the likes of me."

And that was the end of that.

———

Skull in hand, Maude traversed through the streets of Cripple Creek, barely aware of the spectacle she created but not exactly caring. Sure, there were double takes aplenty, and more than a handful of strange expressions. She didn't have anything to carry Charley in—besides, she got the feeling he enjoyed the change of scenery. She was leaving anyhow...

Of course, she had to say goodbye to Clayton, if for no other reason than decent manners.

He was working at the forge when she angled her way up. Hammer blows ringing and sparks flying. Holding back at a respectable distance, she waited until he plunged whatever it was into the nearby water bucket— the hiss of steam releasing.

"Hello, Clayton."

"Maude!" A wide-eyed horror. "Is that how you go about town?"

For a second, shame flared up, and she didn't know what he was talking about. Then she remembered what she held in her hands. She laughed. "He was a part of the deal from Rose. I guess I'll figure out what to do with him when the time comes."

He froze. "Why are you carrying him around? If you were worried about your reputation before, that will certainly seal it, once and for all."

"Ah. That. Well, I'm leaving town and going to Denver. For a variety of reasons."

He turned his back to her, raking the coals, words coming out jagged. "I thought—you'd be happy. You got your divorce, didn't you?"

"And some money, for once." She shrugged, although she watched his reaction close. "Maybe I was chasing after the wrong things; maybe I wasn't. But, one thing's for certain: I don't want to do any more mineral dealings."

He nodded, back still toward her. Finally, he turned, wiping off his hands. "People are saying Stevenson has lit out of town. Not that he was well liked, mind you. It's a shadow hanging over the proceedings. Some are saying the deal might turn out a fraud. You know what salting is, don't you?"

Maude shrugged. "Is that what they're saying happened, or you? Either way, I'm out of it now. The assay results came back good—and the Scavenger's mining engineer checked it out and approved the sale. Are they saying he doesn't know what he's doing? I thought his reputation was good..."

"It's always been buyer beware. You running before the fallout?"

"I'm not running at all. Besides, Skiptown thinks

there's easy money to be made in the district, and I don't want to be around for *that*."

"Can't blame you there. What'll you do up in Denver?"

"Maybe go to stenography school." She shrugged. "I've got enough money to learn an honest trade, for once. Maybe I'll be a clerk in a shop. Maybe...tell run-of-the-mill fortunes and be grateful for the opportunity. I guess the future is wide open for me and Charley here."

A vein throbbed in Clayton's jaw. "When are you leaving?"

"Thursday's seven twenty-three morning train to Denver," she replied, heart hanging heavy and near her stomach.

And, to that, he nodded miserable and didn't say much of anything at all.

———

That night as Maude packed her things, the ghost girl rippled to the surface in a gray and green swirling miasma. Maude stopped all movement and waited for the wraith to form.

"Hello," she said when the girl materialized as far as she was going to. "I'm glad you've come. I was worried I wouldn't get the chance to say goodbye."

You are loved, the shade's silver-water voice rippled. *Watch out for fire.*

"I don't know about any of that," Maude whispered. "What do you mean?"

But the wraith said no more and faded from view.

CHAPTER FIFTY
LIGHTNING DOESN'T STRIKE TWICE, DOES IT?

APRIL 25, 1896

Six pistol shots in succession—one, two, three, four, five, six. *Fire!*

Maude's hand froze mid-air, her solitaire game to kill the time in Rose's company forgotten. Rose rushed to the door, then outside into the street. Others were doing the exact same: the previously quiet street transforming like ants rushing from a nest.

Maude dropped the cards and rushed out on her heels.

Sure enough, black smoke was billowing up into the air. "Looks like Myers burning. Wonder who the hell kicked that off."

Unease rippled through the street, and likely the entire town. Everyone knew what fire meant, and many wooden gold camps had burned to the ground in nothing flat. Fire was something to fear, but Cripple Creek and Victor had professional firemen.

"What do you think?" Rose asked.

"Wait and watch, I suppose," Maude replied, uneasy

and thinking of the ghost girl. The ghost girl had given her a warning. "She did say..."

"Who?" Rose's question came out sharp.

"The ghost in my room. She lodged there before and worries about fire..."

"*Hmph*. Well, we've got fire companies now." Rose stepped back inside. "All the same, we'll keep our eye on it."

Still, she sounded worried. Maude eyed the cards and decided she'd rather not know.

————

Thirty minutes later, it became obvious the fire was spreading along the clapboard structures of Myers Avenue and licking up against the backs of the fine buildings on Bennett.

"Go home and get your valuables—women and children are supposed to go over to the reservoir until the fire gets put out. Now, hurry!"

Maude rushed in the direction of the Morning Glory. It wasn't easy to get there. Everyone scattered, rushing into the streets and darting down alleyways in a panicked horror. Roiling, billowing black smoke shot up even further into the sky as more structures became engulfed. Dwarfing everything below, the smoke plumes were a dark menace that showed no signs of abating. Horses and wagons careened down the streets; pedestrians bolted at random lugging treasured possessions. Those professional fire crews they had all been so confident of struggled with pressureless hoses. The water ran at a trickle from the hose nozzles. Myers was burning, all right, and poised to take the rest of Cripple Creek along with it.

In the choking smoke Maude ran past Lampman's Undertaking Parlors, the Mush and Milk House, and landed on Myers Avenue. Eastward down the notorious street, her watering eyes calculating a long row of jerry-built structures ripe for the burning. The Topic and Red Onion dance halls, the Bucket of Blood, Crapper Jack's, and other establishments of ill repute emptied. Three soiled doves appeared trapped on a second floor of a dance hall and threw mattresses out the windows to soften their landings. The screams and shouts of the people were something horrible.

Dynamite exploded at random intervals in attempted firebreaks—or maybe sparks had ignited supplies stashed around town. No one knew. The constant sound of fire engulfing and consuming everything grew and crackled. Glass shattered. Horses screamed.

The southern wind picked up and blew harder.

The Victor fire brigade came tearing in like hell was a-popping. Which it was. The firemen took to dynamiting shacks on the east side of Third Street as Maude ran on toward the Morning Glory, smoke drying out her throat, nose and eyes streaming.

A drunk stepped in her path cawing with a stick of dynamite, fuse already lit. A firebug, he just stood there and cackled, delighted, before flinging the stick onto a perfectly sound roof.

It exploded and caught fire.

Maude picked up a rock and smacked him upside his head. He crumpled, and Maude went on.

At the Morning Glory, Eunice stood stoic on her porch, watching Cripple Creek burn.

Maude could only croak. "I just knocked out a firebug. And why are you just standing there?"

"I've got insurance," she claimed. "Besides, where would I take anything? Word is, the reservoir's run dry."

Maude placed her hand against the wall, panting and sensing. The house felt stable and solid. Nigh-on certain that the house would remain standing, Maude nodded. "People are going to need help," she said.

Eunice brushed her hair back from her forehead. "They can sleep on the lawn, if need be. I'll go check to see what I have by way of extra blankets. It's going to be a long, long night."

The wind died, and the fire burned itself out, almost where it had begun. Maude checked the contents of her room, Charley chattering away from the turmoil and ferment.

She ran a finger over the top of him, thinking. Her train ticket was for the morning. But she hated to leave the town when it smoldered, and her friends might be down.

In time, as the fire became contained, Maude traced back through the wreckage to discover the fate of the Fortune Emporium. Strangest of all, although hardly surprising given the nature of the town, the saloons were already setting up makeshift planks across barrels. These rustic bars were covered with oilcloth and doing a brisk trade in libations in front of their smoking, burned-out ruins. Cripple Creek was rising from the ashes. For once, Maude didn't know whether to laugh or cry.

A few streets later, although many buildings along the way were burnt, the Fortune Emporium stood solid and unharmed, the door locked and the sign turned to *Closed*. Maude breathed a heavy sigh of relief.

Something about that sure felt final as well.

Tempting fate, Maude butted shoulders as she fought against the stream of foot traffic heading back into Cripple Creek. She wanted to see if the forge had withstood the onslaught. There was more devastation the closer she got. As she rounded the last corner, she stopped, stock-still. Half the forge was burned away, but the barn was still standing. Stomach clenched, she ran the remaining way, pulling up short in the yard.

"Clayton! Fred?" she yelled, but no one answered.

Edging her way forward, she looked inside to where the actual forge had been. The bellows were burned away, but some of the tools looked serviceable. But where was everyone?

She glanced around and tried again. "Hello?"

There was no answer. No one was in the forge, no one had collapsed and was lying in a heap, so the next place to try was the barn out back. She pulled open the barn door and looked inside. The horse was missing, but everything appeared as it should. "Anyone here?"

She would have felt a whole lot better if someone had answered. But, as it was, it wasn't great, but it wasn't tragic either.

She returned back over to Myers, where the conflagration had started, and the booze flowed regardless. She stood catty-corner from the Mikado, and it looked the same as always. Unremarkably, customers were off. Of all things, Julia stepped out onto the porch. It only took her a moment to clock Maude.

The madam's hand went up in a tentative salute. Maude did the same, and no word was spoken.

———

On the morning of her departure, she wrapped Charley in her nightgown and put him in the valise, thinking it was better starting off on her new chapter without too much controversy. She sought out Eunice before she left.

"I know collections for rebuilding will be going around." She handed the landlady some folded-over bills. Five hundred dollars, in fact. "Could you see to it that this goes toward that and is well spent."

Eunice smiled and took the bills. "I'm partial to hospitals, schools, and libraries."

"That is just fine," Maude replied. She gave the landlady a brief hug and walked out the door.

She was never much of one for goodbyes.

———

The train was waiting at the platform. She boarded the second-class compartment.

"Do you need help stowing your bag?" a man asked, in marked contrast to her arrival.

She smiled. "Thank you. That's very kind." It was hard to ignore the difference.

She settled in a seat next to the window, feeling a bit down. The walk through town had been depressing enough with all the burned-out shells. But work was already underway. Cripple Creek seemed to shake off the fire much like it did everything else.

No one had come to see her off, but that wasn't surprising, considering the state of affairs. The conductor's warning whistle sounded, and she waited.

The opening of the door at the rear of the compartment half registered, but she didn't think anything of it.

A male voice. "Is this seat taken?"

She looked up with a start. "Clayton! What are you doing?"

He fished around in his pocket and came up with a silver dollar. He held it out for her.

Puzzled, she took it.

"Isn't that what good fortunes cost—one silver dollar?"

Through the welling tears, she laughed. "Maybe I should be giving you that dollar."

He laughed, too, as he sat down beside her. "Have you heard about that claim you sold? Turned out the miners busted through a wall and found a very good vein of gold. It's going to be hailed as quite the discovery. Probably be in all the newspapers today."

"I'm done with that. So, everything came to pass all right after all."

"I think it did," he agreed. And smiled before giving her a kiss.

A LOOK AT: BRAND CHASER
DARK RANGE BOOK ONE

"...couldn't put this page-turner down...that ending left me with a knot in my throat that's still there... –Peter Brandvold, bestselling author of the *Rogue Lawman* series

Randi Samuelson-Brown, known for her award nominated and compelling historical fiction of the Old West, engages her passion for storytelling to paint an unflinching portrait of the seedy underbelly of the modern-day West.

Emory Cross is a young and tough, no nonsense brand inspector in Colorado cattle country. She's intent on preserving her family ranch's traditional way of life in Colorado at all costs...even if it means crossing some lines.

Prior to becoming a brand inspector, she finds a pair of calves that have strayed onto the Lost Daughter Ranch and decides to brand them as her own, even though she's technically operating in a grey area of cattle rustling...something she'll soon be meant to be ferreting out rather than participating in. That decision leads her down a road fraught with danger, and exposes an uneasy past leading to an uncertain future for both Emory and her family's legacy.

AVAILABLE NOW

ABOUT THE AUTHOR

Randi Samuelson-Brown is from Golden, Colorado, now living in Denver. *On the Fringes* is her second full-length novel. She is also the author of *The Beaten Territory* and *The Bad Old Days of Colorado: Untold Stories of the Wild West*—a finalist in the Colorado Book Awards for History. She specializes in Colorado stories, whether fiction or true. When not writing (or working at her day job), she loves exploring the wide-open spaces of the West and listening to stories the inhabitants tell.

www.ingramcontent.com/pod-product-compliance
Lightning Source LLC
Chambersburg PA
CBHW011421010726
47494CB00011B/2436